gen

HOLLY CAVE

G000152078

Copyright © Holly Cave 2015

The right of Holly Cave to be identified as the author of this
work has been asserted by her in accordance with the Copyright,
Designs and Patents Act 1988.

All rights reserved. No part of this book may be reproduced,
stored in a retrieval system, or transmitted, in any form, or by any
means (electronic, mechanical, photocopying, recording or
otherwise) without the prior written permission of the author,
except in cases of brief quotations embodied in reviews or articles.
It may not be edited, amended, lent, resold, hired out, distributed
or otherwise circulated without the author's written permission.

Permission can be obtained from holly.cave@gmail.com.

All characters in this book are fictitious and any resemblance to
real persons, living or dead, is purely coincidental.

Published by Holly Cave in 2015
Cover design by Kit Foster
Edited by Sarah Kolb-Williams

ISBN: 978-0-9931506-1-6

For my father.

Genes helped. So did Blinky's Planet.

That which we do not bring to consciousness appears in our lives as fate.

Carl Jung

ROGET'S DICTIONARY, 34TH EDITION, PUBLISHED 2021

Background, *noun* : concise summary of findings from an individual's birth diagnosis

birth diagnosis, *noun* : genetic blood test conducted on newborns to derive extensive medical and psychological information

executor, *noun* : an individual whose professional occupation it is to carry out birth diagnoses and formulate Backgrounds

Tag, *noun* : a graphene-based identification chip which contains personal information including criminal records and Background data, usually inserted in the neck above the submandibular lymph node

PROLOGUE

Despite the date, spring had not yet arrived in London. The pale petals tucked neatly inside the buds of the cherry trees had refused to show their faces, and the people in the streets were similarly shrouded in layers of disguise. Strange eyes did not meet; they were too focused on the perilously icy paving, and for this, Dr Elin Nagayama was thankful, because the skin around her own eyes was marbled with the aftermath of hot tears. The ongoing fallout from the Takeover two years earlier and the preceding years of chaos and poverty made the atmosphere frostier than it was in her youth. Her delicate, yet-to-wrinkle skin stung in the frozen air, and every so often she would stop and hold the tips of her gloved fingers up to her face, trying to press warmth into her cheekbones.

Even at this pivotal time in her life, in the very depths of despair, Elin was irrevocably self-conscious. In the hospital just an hour before, she had been calm and polite so as not to make a scene. She now walked with equal care back along the road to her apartment, cursing herself for not saying the things that had battered against her skull like ravaged demons trying to escape. She took some small pleasure in imagining her alter ego giving the speech of her life to the counter signatory on the form—the senior medic she had never even met before—who had strolled in, glanced perfunctorily through the text and scribbled his signature before vaguely nodding in her direction and leaving again. Elin had lay there tensely on the bed, hoping that perhaps he would question her own doctor's judgement, that he might consider raising hers as a case for further discussion. But no; just a signature and a rapid departure, knowingly leaving Elin to her fate, her half-naked body cursorily covered in a white paper sheet from the waist down.

In the eyes of the medical profession she was damaged, unfit; there was something about her unable to create an adequate new human, a problem as yet ironically indefinable by the science she had devoted her own life to. The apathetic nod from the senior medic and Elin's evolving interpretation of it were things she already feared might stay with her for the rest of her life. She thought about it now as her running shoes negotiated the contours of ice and paving stones, as her brain subconsciously filed the number of steps remaining until she reached her apartment. The nod had been a gesture she might have asked him to repeat had it been a spoken phrase, but no such subtlety can be replicated in quite the same way as a murmur might make clear. So she had simply watched him go, closing the door gently behind him. But now she wished she had said something. Anything.

I'm so sorry, Elin, her own doctor had whispered after the door had closed, touching her arm. Like all great crimes, the person authorising it had the easiest deal; they got to tick a box and walk away. They did not have to see the visceral outcome of their signature on a form. Elin had looked her doctor in the eyes by way of a response. Perhaps only another woman could appreciate it fully, could manage not to put it in the same mental filing cabinet as a broken limb or failing eyesight. Elin had smiled, or at least she thought she had; the smile may not have made it to the surface. *But it's for the best.* Her doctor had moved her cool fingers down Elin's bare arm and squeezed her hand. If there had been a smile, it had faded.

For the best. Elin had wondered, had never stopped wondering, whether this statement could be proven true, for her baby could never be born. It was not a fair test; there was no way to tell if her child would have lived a happy, if short, life—or even, in the minuscule margin of error that she continued to drape her misery upon, whether the tests themselves might have been incorrect.

As she traced the lines of cracks criss-crossing the pavement, her mind trailed over the glass vessels sitting a mile or so away on the shelves of her lab, the clones of mice, zebra fish and *C.elegans* that crawled, swam and slid over each other: genetically identical, visually similar. They had been spliced from the same egg by her own hands. Simple organisms, certainly, but she knew she could make them whatever she wanted them to be; her nurture, whether on a whim or in a pre-planned experiment, could alter them for better or for worse, for life or death. She knew of chemicals that would change an animal's sex, but she could not yet truly see inside their brains, the final frontier of biology. That ongoing battle between the psychological and the physical: who knew what secrets her mice contained?

Ahead of her on the street, two children, perhaps a brother and sister, close enough in age to be twins, were slipping and sliding behind their father. They grabbed onto the hemline of his overcoat but he seemed not to slow down, not to accommodate for them. How desirable they might be to him one day, Elin mused. Along with everything else—the genetic tests at birth, the new social policies—the State was talking of introducing a one-child policy to Europe. One child would have been enough.

A taxi pulled up alongside her to let a passenger out, and an irrational spirit in her suggested grabbing one of the children under an arm and climbing in through the open door. The little boy caught her eye as he turned to pick up a fallen glove and she grinned, winking at him, wincing at the cold air against her teeth. She again surprised herself that she could smile at all. The boy stared back sternly, as if he could read her thoughts of abduction, and pointedly took hold of his father's hand, pushing her away with his eyes. Elin bit her lip and turned the corner into her road.

It had been the fifth, and the last, time. She did have some options left, but none she would pursue now. She doubted whether she could even afford them. Funding for her latest research project had dried up, and next week she would have to fire one of her lab assistants. It would be Archie—last in, first out, but she would hate to do it. *If we do get the funding,* she could hear herself saying, *and I'm sure we will eventually* ...

Her half-Japanese frame was slight but her bones were strong, well-structured enough beneath her skin that she had always looked athletic. Every morning, before heading to the lab, she would run the streets of west London, circling the garden squares and the Edwardian paving until her thighs begged for mercy. The result of her ancestry and her exercise regime meant that even at thirty-seven, she could easily pass for a woman fifteen years younger. It was a perpetual source of astonishment, even to her, that she could not find a man. Often, they were too young; doe-eyed graduates or arrogant bankers who chatted her up in bars and online. She dismissed them out of hand. They did not want her as she really was; they could not see.

But a man had not been necessary; or rather the lack of one had not been the problem. She had selected the healthiest, most fertile sperm from the best banks; her doctor had taken that short list and matched them to her genetic profile to give her the very best chance of conceiving. But every single time, on five separate occasions over four exhausting, drawn-out years, something had gone wrong. As Elin, running the story through her head once more, came back to the unavoidable blame she held somewhere in her body, the tears spilled over her eyelids again. One early miscarriage, one car crash (she only suffered whiplash), and now three forced terminations in just over a year. Three. Three children which only a few years before would have been born, faults and all. But the Takeover had happened, and certain things were unacceptable to the State. They wanted no dependents if they could avoid them. Perhaps Elin should have tried to leave the country—but there was always her work. Anyway, it was too late now.

Reaching the door to her building, she struggled to get her key into the lock and forced it with one hand, wiping her face with the other. She jogged as fast as she could up the flight of stairs as if she was running for the toilet and fumbled her way into her apartment, slamming the door behind her and letting the agony, held in for an hour, finally burst out in a scream that deteriorated within seconds to an anguished moan.

As she knelt miserably on the rug in her lounge, around her were the signs of optimism. The flat was neater than usual, designed to welcome her home with good tidings. The ingredients for a vegetable stir-fry were laid out; all those nutrients, so good for the baby. Elin remembered the bottle of non-alcoholic champagne she had bought and placed in the fridge this morning. She had been reluctant to allow the possibility that there might be cause for celebration to enter her thoughts, but it would be drunk regardless. Elin clasped at her hair with her fingers, pulling on her scalp until it felt like it might tear from her head completely. She rocked herself backwards and forwards, pulling her head down onto her thighs and letting the tears splash onto her jeans.

On the calendar above her head, the notes for today were as clear as the day she had written them. *Three months.* She stared at the two words and remembered adding them to the calendar eight weeks before, together with a reminder of her appointment at the doctor's. It had been a clear winter's day and she had stared out at the crisp blue sky, toying with the idea of allowing herself to add an exclamation mark. She was glad now that she had resisted.

She felt her phone vibrate in her pocket, and she took a few moments to compose herself before answering the call.

'Elin?' Her friend's voice was calming, soft like butter.

'Hello,' Elin managed weakly. Even in two syllables, her voice audibly wavered.

'Oh Elin, no ...'

'It's gone. They took it from me again.' Elin descended into wracking sobs, covering her face with her spare hand.

'I'm coming round, just stay where you are,' the woman on the phone said, then paused as if trying to phrase her words correctly. 'This world, Elin, it's gone crazy. It doesn't mean there's something wrong with you—you know that? It doesn't even mean there's something wrong with them, with the babies.'

'They said it would definitely have lived this time, that it was a difficult decision.'

'Fuck them. I'll bring some food. Just sit tight.'

The call ended abruptly, and Elin found she had momentarily stopped crying. From her vantage point on the floor, she gazed out of the small window over her dining table. Birds flew in a line through the grey sky, so far away that they looked like threads being woven through a canvas. She wished, for a brief moment, that she believed in heaven, in God. The birds flew on to wherever they were going, and their freedom, combined with the clarity of her friend's words, mixed together like quick-setting concrete inside her stomach.

None of this should have happened, she thought. *Not to me, not to anybody.*

After five anguished years, the anger had finally arrived.

1

Thirty years later: London, 2052

London's acid rain had almost stopped falling and it lay black and satin, eating into the pavement. The full moon was pierced upon the corner of the Centre Point tower block, a chunk cut from its perimeter by the concrete.

There was a tension to the air that could not be fully explained by the passing storm. Gaggles of young girls cut through the traffic, screeching and shouting, clutching their sequins close. Packs of men followed those in the shortest dresses, each striding along the straightest line to his goal of waking up with a hangover and at least one naked woman sprawled, glittering, across their bed.

Beneath the labyrinthine streets, the quieter Saturdayers were seeking out a sombre drink. Most people missed the small stone in place of a brick by the door. It spoke in a few simple words of the hundreds of plague victims buried beneath, the ground so thick with bones that the tube line had to curve around it.

Raith's was a stylish spot; a legal bar designed to look like an illegal one. Modern jazz drizzled through the speakers, the melody warm and the notes sticky. The basement windows were largely obscured by a wall at their base, the lower limbs of smokers visible only at the top, creating a dynamic collage of cloudy calves.

Freya's fingers traced the maze of wood grain threading through the mahogany bar. Her dark brown hair lay down her back slickly, flicking out at her shoulder blades. She still had the softly rounded face of a teenager, yet today was her twenty-ninth birthday. Freya was alone. She did not want to celebrate; she felt nothing to rejoice in. She sucked on her last olive like a cough sweet, the salty tang sliding down her throat.

'You want another?' the man behind the bar asked. She nodded, smiling sweetly. He deftly leant across and swiped his tracker against her neck. He placed the device on the bar and assessed it with one eye as he casually started to pour the vodka.

'Yep, you're good for a few more, you lucky girl!' He winked.

Freya's affection for alcohol and her ability to drink it in large quantities was unmatched by most women of her age but so common now for those few who, like her, were virtually resilient to its effects.

She smiled acidly to herself. *Ah, the power of modern genetics.*

Two men muscled in next to her at the bar and propped themselves up on some stools. Freya's stomach felt suddenly hollow with anxiety, and she stared down at her fingernails, tapping them against the base of her glass. The last thing she wanted was to be drawn into a conversation. She had always avoided small talk with strangers.

'One house whisky and a White Russian, please,' one of them shouted at the bartender, lacking Freya's manicured delicacy. They were young, one much taller than the other. She wished they had sat a little further away. One of them cracked a joke and the other, taller one backed into her, laughing, jabbing his elbow into her shoulder forcefully. He immediately spun around and placed his hand on her shoulder as she fought the urge to wince.

'Oh, I'm so sorry, darling.'

'No problem,' she said, crossing her legs and shifting her weight in the opposite direction.

He ignored her body language and squeezed her shoulder, circling her collarbone with his thumb. It was an intimate gesture, but she could tell immediately—something that could not be clarified eloquently, little more than a *feeling*— that she was not the one he was interested in. Perhaps it was the way he was behaving towards the other man. Her intuition manifested in a small smile. The man's shorter companion summoned the bartender and directed him toward Freya.

'What would you like?' he called from behind his companion, leaning across the bar to reach her gaze.

'Really, no, I already have a drink.' She subtly leant back from the grip and waved her hands to reject the offer.

'Kane,' he said, pressing his hand over his heart. 'Go on, have one!' His face was unusual; he looked almost Asian but for the sprinkling of sandstone freckles across the broad bridge of his nose and the watery green of his irises. His hair was dead straight, black and shiny. His eyes were almond-shaped and they smiled back at her.

'Well, okay. Yes, another martini then, please.' She spoke directly to the bartender and he nodded.

'Thank you,' she said to the men, and she inclined her head toward them slightly, shyly. They exchanged a certain look and she felt that they were judging her. Did they think she was one of those girls who sit in bars waiting for a well-dressed man to buy her a drink?

'I was just telling my friend here a little bit about my Background—it's a funny story,' said Kane, as if in explanation for their rowdiness. Freya nodded politely.

The taller man seemed to like physical contact. He put his arm around her, squeezing her close to him, and with his spare hand he drew a frame in the air around her face with his index finger. She saw the glint of a heavy silver ring.

'So, what's yours? Let me guess—artistic streak, tendency to depression, early onset biological clock?' He tick-tocked with his tongue and wagged his finger like a metronome in front of her eyes.

Kane moved closer and splayed his hands apologetically. 'I'm sorry about him. We've actually only just met.'

'Don't you want to tell us?' The other man pressed her, his voice hardening into a challenge.

Freya felt sleepiness settle around her temples. She had had too much to drink, she thought, as she swallowed back the martini in two deep gulps. Tag scanners did not account for tiresome conversations. The alcohol stung her throat as she stood and made her apologies.

'I'm sorry; I've got to be going. It's getting late and I'm tired,' she said. 'But thank you very much for the drink. I'll buy you one … next time.' She shrugged, smiled, and threw her coat over her shoulders, placing the splintered cocktail stick she had been fiddling with onto the bar. She walked up the steps as quickly as her skirt would allow, fabric dancing over the backs of her knees.

As Kane watched the woman leave, he realised he, too, wanted to go home, to be alone. Tonight had been another failure.

'You know, I've really got to go too, Nathan.' Kane flinched at his own rudeness, for the first time noticing a weakness in his companion, as if this big man could be crushed with his words.

'Oh, okay,' Nathan replied meekly as Kane turned and walked away.

Kane pulled at the hand rail as he jogged up the steps, his eyes on the exit. As he swung the door open, the cold made his breath catch in his throat. He stood, momentarily, on the pavement outside, looking up and down the street for the woman. He finally spotted her as she swerved to avoid a man stumbling into her path.

It took just a few moments for Kane to catch up with her, although she was walking quickly, her hair swinging across her back as she strode. He waited for her to notice him walking beside her before he spoke.

'Hi again,' he said. 'I'm going home now, too. Mind if I walk with you?'

'No, of course not.' Her tone was cautious. They walked together in silence down the street towards the tube station. The metal from the woman's worn-down heels clicked off the concrete and set his teeth on edge. They should have exchanged Backgrounds by now, but somehow Kane felt reticent to ask the question first, and so they continued in silence a little longer, wordlessly acknowledging their mutual, temporary disregard of the law. Their breath hung weightlessly in the air, intermingling. They passed a group of girls and boys, running past with bottles of beer in their hands, screaming with infectious delight. Kane and the woman exchanged a grin.

'Ah, teenage rebellion,' she murmured. 'Did you ever have one?'

'Of sorts,' Kane replied. 'School was okay. I did pretty well, really, but when I was eighteen I decided I'd had enough. I'd saved up loads of cash from working on all the neighbours' allotments over the years—I was quite a geeky kid, I never liked to spend it—but I blew it all on a three-year trip around the world.'

'Really? Wow—I've always wanted to do that.'

'Yeah, so I just holidayed at first and then I did a bit of work here and there—painting, drawing portraits. I only really came back because my mum missed me so much.' He laughed, shrugging as he dodged a puddle in the road, and recognised within his own mind that his joke was rather close to the truth.

'So, what have you been doing since then?' she asked, pulling the lapels of her coat in closer around her neck.

'I pay the bills by working in a pub. But I'm an artist, really—whenever I sell a painting or a drawing, that's my spending money. I don't sell as much as I'd like, but it's alright.'

'Alright?'

'I get to keep myself to myself.'

'Funny—you don't strike me as the shy, retiring type.'

Kane laughed again. 'Everyone needs time to themselves, I guess.'

They fell back into silence as a rickshaw screeched past, splashing their ankles with storm water. Kane fought the urge to stop and wipe the polluted grey droplets from his polished shoes.

'And what do you do?' Kane eventually asked, drawing himself back to the thread of their conversation.

'I'm a teacher,' she said, smiling. She paused and leant to the side slightly to level the flat of her hand a few feet from the ground. 'Little ones like this.'

Kane stopped too, turning to face her under the street

light, hands in his pockets. The woman's smile seemed to have warmed her cheeks, turning them pink against the chill. 'What's it like?' he asked.

'I love it, actually. It's really rewarding. I like making them feel good about themselves, watching them grow, and my weekends are my own.' Her eyes twinkled as she spoke. Kane pursed his lips and grinned. He looked again at the glossy, blow-dried tendrils of hair swirling over the smart leather edging of her trench coat. He could not quite imagine her looking anything less than glamorous.

'What?' she asked, tilting her head and widening her eyes. Kane wondered momentarily if this feigning of childlike innocence was something she did deliberately.

'I just can't imagine you as a teacher, that's all!'

'A lot of people say that to me, but I tie back my hair into a bun, I put on a brown suit and—really—it's a complete transformation.'

Freya pulled a serious face, sucking in her cheeks and winding back her hair in demonstration, only managing to hold her expression straight for a few seconds before giggling. Kane felt the tension around her disperse into the evening.

'I'm sorry,' she said. 'I've never introduced myself. I'm Freya. Miss Passingham to you.' She offered her hand and he grasped it with both of his as they both took a deep breath to clear their mirth. Kane noticed a diamond glint on her finger.

'Wow—you're engaged?'

Freya shook her head. 'No.' She pushed her hands back into her pockets and there was silence; for a few seconds she was gone again. They began to walk onwards again, towards the tube.

'Guess what?' Freya asked quietly, her arms folded tightly against her chest. 'It's my birthday.' Her eyes sparkled, wet from the cold breeze coursing towards them down the street. Her cheeks were flushed with its bite, her long hair catching in her mouth and clinging to her lipstick as she spoke. Kane thought she looked less polished than in the bar; more beautiful.

'Why on earth didn't you say so earlier?' Kane stopped in

his tracks and shook his head, laughing. 'Well, you can't possibly walk on your birthday!' He scooped her up in a fireman's lift and ran for a few steps with her over his shoulder as she shouted and shrieked with laughter. She kicked her legs violently in protest and he put her back down.

'Fine—you can carry me if you like,' she agreed, allowed herself to be gathered up in his arms, giggling. They staggered for a bit along the street and crossed, attracting a few laughs and whistles from a passing crowd of girls. Kane put her down on the pavement, teasingly feigning exhaustion by wiping his brow. Freya grinned and they both leant back against the wall for a moment, either side of a narrow passage. They looked across at each other and laughed. The alleyway continued the other side of the road, leading away into the darkness.

Kane glanced across the street at the neon sign hanging above Kenny G's. At the front of the queue, one of the open-shirted security staff was swiping his tracker against the necks of the eager partygoers. Kane wondered whether his companion from earlier had cut ahead of them and was inside already. He imagined his strong body up against another man, sweating slightly in the heat, a drink in hand. Although he had stood cautiously in the queue a few times, including tonight, Kane had never actually stepped inside the door. Yet he knew that Kenny G's was not the kind of place for silent types. Everyone had their place these days and Tags ensured that this was a strictly gay club. He should be in there, too. It was where he belonged.

'So, if you don't mind me asking, how old are you today, Miss Passingham?' Kane asked, turning his attention away from the club.

'Twenty-nine.' Freya sighed heavily.

Glancing sideways at her, he could see that she was looking away from him, down at the drain in the road and the swirling water inside it.

'I'm twenty-nine too, actually. It's been a good year so far.'

'I'm sure it is,' Freya replied quietly. 'For some people.'

Freya and Kane could never be sure, but days later they each came to wonder which of them had spotted the tiny female figure running up the alley first, and what might have happened if neither of them had seen her at all. At first, it was hard to tell which direction she was moving in, but then she appeared on the street, tripping and falling onto the pavement.

Exchanging a quick glance with Kane, Freya ran straight across the road to her, Kane at her heels. They narrowly missed a bicycle rickshaw, the driver shouting abuse at them as he swerved. The girl knelt, staring at her hands, which were marbled with bloody scrapes and strands of torn skin. Her dark brown eyes were wide with adrenaline and endorphins, free of tears.

'Are you alright?' Kane said from behind Freya.

His voice seemed to rouse the girl slightly from her shock. She nodded and looked at them both as they knelt on either side of her.

Freya scrabbled through her bag and pulled out some tissues and a small bottle of water. 'Here, that looks painful,' said Freya, pressing the tissues onto the girl's bleeding hands and setting the bottle on the street in front of her. 'What's your name?'

The girl mutely dabbed at her palms, watching spidery red spots seep through and merge. 'Marie,' she said, still panting.

'Where were you going? Do you need some help?' Kane half stood, crouching over her protectively.

The girl gazed up at him, gulping the air. 'There's a man inside that club.' She gestured toward Kenny G's. 'He's going to blow it up.'

'What?' Freya stared over to the entrance, wide-eyed, and then looked back to the girl. She did not seem crazy.

'He's got a bomb.'

They all stood at the same time, looking around them; at each other, at the people smiling at the bouncers as they slipped behind the red velvet rope, at the dancing shadows flung against the windows by the refracted light of disco balls. Time hung still for a long moment, as if it had become caught in syrup, struggling to pull the seconds along.

'We need to stop him. I think I can talk him out of it. I'm sure I can.' The girl spoke urgently, a sudden passion in her voice.

'How long have we got?' Kane asked.

'He—his name is Sal—he was in the back, in the basement of the club.'

'But how long, Marie?' Freya begged urgently, her hands spread, fingers drawn taut, her handbag lying forgotten at her feet.

Kane shook his head. 'It doesn't matter—we just need to get them out. Freya: stay here and call the police.' Kane left them, running over to the entrance to speak to the bouncers.

Numbly, Freya held her finger against her Tag, mumbled a request for emergency services and waited for the connection to be made.

'Police, please.'

She looked up at the multiplying bouncers, some shouting to those in the queue, forcing them away, and others with their fingers to their necks, making calls, searching for help. Kane had disappeared. Her words did not seem real to her.

'And maybe ambulances, too. There's a bomb.'

2

Sal was in the bathroom of Kenny G's. He breathed shallowly, shakily, walking in small circles as he shook his head wildly, hitting his ears to his shoulders as if to loosen more adrenaline from its bodily hiding places.

Sal would not normally have even been out at this time, and as that thought returned to him, he surreptitiously reached beneath his scarf and fingered the barely healed skin on the side of his throat, where his Tag had been lodged until the previous week. In the darkened backstreet room, he had held the bloodied flake of graphene and gold in the palm of his hand, had scrutinized it in wonder, morbidly fascinated by how it could have caused him so much pain. Until tonight, it had been years since he had been out of doors after nine o'clock. If his Tag had still been in place, the searing pain that emanated from it to mark his broken curfew would have hit the top of his spinal column hours ago, rendering him temporarily paraplegic, to be carried home by the forces of the State. That had only happened once, in the early days. After that, he had no wish to repeat the experience. The agony had been unbearable.

A man walked out of the only occupied cubicle and left without washing his hands. Sal wrinkled his nose in distaste and then almost laughed at himself. *What a time to be thinking of hygiene.* The bathroom was empty. This was it.

He took a wooden wedge from his pocket and pushed it tightly under the main door so it could not be easily opened. He pulled a brand-new razor blade from a leather pouch in his other pocket and laid it in the sink, neatly, below the plughole. As Sal tried to swallow back the rising vomit, his ears tuned in to the noises outside the toilets. A popular tune had just reached its chorus and people were singing along at the tops of their voices, whooping and laughing. Kenny G's was full of people, bursting with life.

He glanced at his watch, looked back down at the blade and felt suddenly, violently, sick. He threw up into the sink, the mixture of stomach acid, rum and coffee burning his throat. He heard a knock on the door and he jammed the wedge in further with his foot. There was nothing else left to do now. He tipped out the leather pouch and a shower of tranquilliser pills fell into the sink, pinging against the ceramic. He caught most of them before they spiralled down the plughole, scooping them up and tossing them to the back of his throat. He had added this bit into the plan himself, but now he felt as if he was somehow cheating, abdicating the role of martyr.

He leant over the sink and took a deep breath. He looked at his watch again: only twenty seconds had passed. He studied himself carefully in the mirror and picked up the blade between his finger and thumb. He saw a strong nose and a weak chin, bad skin and heavily set brows. He looked unbalanced. He felt unbalanced. Either way, he was dying by his own hand. It was just that perhaps this version of death he had more control over. He had bought the blade, packed the tranquilisers. The bomb had come from goodness knows where. Sal was aware that his thoughts were becoming increasingly jumbled, and it was as if he could feel his sanity ebbing away. This was not how he imagined it would feel.

Angie stood at the window, shrouded in darkness. She nibbled at the side of her thumb and blood entered her mouth little by little, easing the tense expectation that held her prisoner in this unlit room. Running her hand down over the cold skin of her neck, she watched the figures on the street many floors below for a few broken moments, letting her attention be drawn to individuals before tearing her gaze away again in schizophrenic distress. Nothing but people; people everywhere. She fixed her gaze on the blacked-out windows of the club across the street. From here, each pane of glass was smaller than a fingernail.

Crushed between her folded arms and her breasts, Angie's Index leaked a muted blue glow into the darkness. Minutes earlier, she had finished composing the first of many statements that she would send out, perhaps tomorrow, perhaps the next day.

It will be hard, she thought, *despite all of this.* Hard to send out the message securely; hard to get anyone to discuss it openly; hard for it not to be swept under the thick, woolly carpet of the State. *But,* she thought, as a fresh smile crept back over her face and flickered in her crow's feet, crackling against the tiredness there, *this has the capacity to shock.*

Over years of secretive planning, campaigning, and slow, steady recruiting, they had built a vision of how the world could be, what it would have become without the Takeover. Angie snorted in revulsion and curled her lips. The hypocrisy alone was worth dying for. *How could the State insist there was no more segregation, no more inequality?* In these new times, honesty was supposedly the best policy, and now two generations of people had nothing to hide behind. Birth diagnosis had ensured that they knew exactly what to expect from life and the State knew what to expect from them. There would be no more surprises, the Head of State had announced eagerly. Money and resources would all be allocated to the right people. *But what meaning did the word 'right' have these days?* It was all there: racism, ageism, sexism, still bubbling under the surface, not daring to be spoken of.

Angie listened to the time and fought the nausea rising up in her belly as she began her silent countdown. She slipped on her sunglasses, and now only the glitter of the distant street lights reached her. For once in her life, she was untouchable. It was a pleasant feeling, such a turn of events. The club, buried far below her, looked small and insignificant.

She lifted her glasses briefly and squinted, searching the streets below for a glimpse of Sal. She was not yet aware— none of them were—that not just one but four of the people below were soon to become key players in her game.

Sal sank down from the sink to the floor and slumped with his back against the wall, staring down at his sliced wrists. He felt a foggy sense of relief. When a man finally forced the door and walked in, swearing upon seeing him, he could barely lift his eyes to look. The man stared at what he surely thought was an already dead body, an animal that had fought for territory or food or its offspring and lost. And that was true. It was all of those things and more, so much more. The man ran out again and Sal's half-open eyes flickered feebly to his watch. There were mere seconds to go. He tried to count down through his stupor, willing the blood from his veins.

In the wrong frame of mind, thought Sal, there is no limit on disillusionment. He had found more and more things to be disillusioned with and to greater depths. And that was of course the real curse upon him, the one he was leaving—indelibly—behind him as he positioned himself beneath the sink and let the numbness swarm. *My blood is a permanent marker.* Beyond the shock and the trauma for those closest to him, he was still cognizant enough to realise that he was forcing disillusion upon those who had loved him. He was taking away a chunk of their hope and forcing them to become complicit in his descent; he was bringing them that little step closer to the animal he had become.

Except that Sal was not loved. He had no one, not any longer. He had no one to disillusion but the whole world.

'They're coming—and we need to get out of the fucking way.' Freya pulled at Marie roughly, but she could tell the girl was still fixed upon the crowd, her eyes flickering, neurons firing at their fastest, piercing the throngs of people now emerging from the nightclub. In the distance, Freya heard the low-pitched moan of sirens.

A man tapped her on the shoulder. 'Do you know what's going on?' he asked as they gazed across at the gathering crowds.

'I think it's a bomb.' Freya spoke without looking at him. As she spotted the crisp whiteness of Kane's T-shirt emerge from the crowd, Marie wrenched away from her grip and ran toward the building. Within seconds, Freya had already lost her in the crowd.

She felt, more than anything, a disarming sense of irritation at this girl who seemed so intent on her own destruction, on the bizarre idea that she might somehow save a potential mass murderer from his chosen fate. It seemed so strange that she and this stranger were simply standing there, looking almost calmly across the street, as if they were watching something terrible unfold on television; something that might upset them, shock them, but never hurt them. She almost smiled, but around them, people suddenly started to catch glimpses of the fear and confusion in each other's faces.

Like a match being struck, the street transformed from an untapped power into an outpouring of energy. The man left immediately without a backward glance, his stride quickly turning to a run, as though he finally had proof that Freya knew what she was talking about. From walking to sprinting, from laughing to frowning and screaming—the street had changed within moments from a playground to a zoo, with all the animals in one enclosure. The first fire engine swung around the corner, its sirens blaring, and stopped at the end of the street. The firefighters jumped out and started to wave people up the street, away from Kenny G's.

Freya stood frozen to the spot, unable to decide what to do.

She looked frantically for Marie and Kane amongst the scrambling crowds before spotting them in the middle of the street outside the panic-stricken nightclub. Kane grabbed Marie as they collided in the middle of the street. He held her like a doll, his hands huge around her shoulders. She was shouting, shaking her head like a madwoman. Freya winced slightly as she saw Marie kick him sharply with a practised shot to the middle of his shin before skirting around him, weaving away into the people that were now streaming from the building.

Kane looked back at Freya. It seemed he had known where she was all along. Their eyes locked for a second or two before he gave her an apologetic shrug and ran after Marie, pushing through the crowds streaming from the nightclub.

'No!' Freya shouted, an urgent fear smashing through her chest, but as she ran after Kane, one of the firefighters caught her in his arms. She screamed into his chest as he forcibly held her, dragging her off the road. Freya's head was buried in his suit, her ears protected as the blast ripped through Kenny G's and exploded onto the street.

Even suffocated in the thick folds of the fabric, Freya heard every sound that had ever existed collide with each other at once. The deadly concerto was birdsong and a high-speed train. It was the tinkle of glasses in a bar and the steady drone of the heart rate monitor at her brother's bedside. It was the sharp, tinny shake of every tambourine's cymbals and the flat slam of a thousand angry doors.

Freya never knew if it was the force of the blast or the firefighter himself who threw them both to the floor, but afterwards she remembered the glass showering onto the pavement, like sequinned confetti being sprinkled above her head as the weight of his body forced the breath out of her. She squeezed her eyes shut and passed out.

It was in this instant that lives were ended and changed forever, exactly as Angie had intended.

3

The men and women employed on Frith Street laboured throughout the night, floodlights casting them in workable twilight. Now they continued in the light of day on shorter shifts, working for four hours at a time and sleeping for two. They combed through every centimetre of the club, running scanners and DNA brushes through the dirt, squashing the lumps of ash into dust, extracting and placing into evidence bags anything larger than a grain of sand.

In the men's bathroom they found a razor blade, the remnants of an Index and some small change where a man had once lain. A specialist spent hours searching for the remnants of a Tag, but to no avail. The items underwent on-site DNA analysis at five a.m. and within two minutes the profile was linked to the fragments of a rucksack where the bomb had originated. Within another two, a match had been found in the database.

Salman Winstan, born in Euston in 2025, became the main culprit for the bombing of Kenny G's. The detectives folded their arms and crossed their brows. As they stood, coughing amidst the ash of vaporised bodies, their immediate shared thought was that it must have been a homophobic attack. It was an old-fashioned theory but a solid one nonetheless. But it would go no further than their own thoughts.

These were days of equality, of sympathy and understanding. *We Are One,* insisted the screens placed strategically in every public space around the country, gold-tipped lettering edged on either side by the Gothic burgundy shields of the State. There was a status quo to maintain, an ideology to protect. In the same way that falling trees do not make a sound if no one is there to hear them, then if homophobia was ignored, it could not exist. For the detectives on Frith Street that morning, the case was closed. They would have to say it was the random act of a rogue individual. It would be a compromise for the State to admit that a mentally ill person had managed to avoid medication, but this was damage limitation.

But Angie had guarded against this. Her victories would not be swept to one side, left to idle, misinformed rumour.

No, the State might not discuss it. No, the State-run media corporations might not allow it to make the news. No, the survivors and those present might not be told the truth. But there were people out there, people who had lived before the Takeover, people who understood the meaning of free will and who still held a vestige of their former influence and power. And at this moment, some of those people were waking up to her anonymous message on their Indexes. They would know of a quiet revolution, one that was serious enough not to let human lives get in the way.

She had lain awake all night talking herself through the strategy, staring at the ceiling as the adrenaline and oxytocin faded from her bloodstream, and fighting the irrational terror that a Sentry would walk right into the room and arrest her as she lay numbly in her bed. If she was traced, if her name was even vaguely connected with the bombing, then it was game over, and she knew it. It would be back to prison, no soft-touch place this time but into darkness and damp and shackles, if the stories were to be believed.

It simply could not happen; she could not allow that to happen. She had to be here to see it through. But she had also expected that interest in something so revolutionary would not just fade away. She was sure of one thing though: her revolution was beginning.

4

Freya held Marie's hand with the lightest of touches and tried to imagine how she must feel. She looked weak and extremely helpless, like a slowly braking train. Was the morphine, coursing like rocket fuel through her body, bringing her to a standstill rather than pushing her upwards?

Marie opened her eyes a little. Lines etched her pretty face. Her jaw was clenched tight and she looked pained.

'Where am I?' Marie asked. The whites of her eyes glowed and she struggled, as if to try and sit up.

'Oh, oh, you're awake!' Freya smiled and leant over her, brown hair falling in curtains around their faces.

'Are you okay?' Marie whispered. She looked disoriented.

'Shh, be quiet. Just lie back,' Freya whispered.

Marie seemed to suddenly calm and her body softened again against the sheets. Haltingly, she turned her head towards Freya. 'How long have I been here? Where am I?' she asked.

'You're in hospital. You've been here for several hours, I think.' Freya double-tapped at her neck and listened for the time, gazing out of the window at the dawn light. 'Yes, a good few hours. You've slept well.'

'It went off, didn't it?' Marie asked.

Freya heard Marie's control over her voice temporarily return. Looking into her eyes, she could almost see the fogginess clearing. Freya nodded slowly, watching Marie wince as if in pain. 'Yes, it went off,' Freya said and paused, wondering what the girl might be thinking. 'But you couldn't have stopped it, you know.'

Marie hummed vaguely in response, closing her eyes

again. Every syllable must be an almost insurmountable effort for her, thought Freya. *They always say to keep people in pain talking, to stay alert, or that's it—they're done for.* But Freya found herself wanting to let Marie lie quietly, in peace.

Marie opened her eyes again and looked at Freya.

'Don't you like hospitals?' Marie asked.

'No. No, not really,' Freya said as she absorbed the scene, the space continuing to fill with beds and patients. She tried not to look too closely. 'My brother died when I was young. I think it shocked me a bit,' she said. A lump rose in her throat, as it always did.

'I'm sure it was nice for him to know you were there.' Marie said, slowly, seemingly to need more time to form each word clearly, painstakingly through her lips. Freya nodded with each one.

'It's nice to know *you're* here,' Marie whispered, solemnly, and closed her eyes again. 'What's your name?'

'Freya.'

'That's a pretty name. You're beautiful, you know. Like an angel.'

'Oh, hardly!' Freya laughed and tucked her hair self-consciously behind her ears, thinking how terrible she must look with her worn-through make-up and tangled hair, and then immediately cursing herself, as this girl with a plastic burns mask fitted to half her face gazed at her in wonder. Marie did not seem to mind, she simply smiled. Her eyes sparkled; they had some life back in them yet.

'I think about the stars,' whispered Marie, and Freya found herself wondering whether the girl was concealing a complexity that Freya could not have comprehended or losing her grip on reality. The talk of the stars—so quixotic, so closely linked to heaven. She looked at Marie tenderly.

At that moment, Kane appeared on the other side of the bed. His arm was wrapped in a rigid, metallic gauze supported by a sling.

'I had to wait for absolutely ages,' he said. 'There are so many people here, just so many.' His voice trailed off as he cast his eyes around the room at all the people less fortunate than himself, his gaze eventually falling upon Marie.

'Hello,' he said. 'I'm Kane. I saved your life.' He smiled wickedly, and Freya could see that he was one of those people who used humour as a crutch.

Marie smiled back at him, her teeth dazzling through her battered lips. She reached for Freya's hand and then went to reach out to Kane, but gave up, merely looking him in the eyes. Her voice was still barely audible.

'I think we were all meant to meet each other, you know,' she sighed. 'There's something, some sort of magic that brought us all here.'

Freya listened. Marie was probably feverish, she thought, not thinking straight.

'You didn't know Kane before last night, did you?' Marie asked.

Freya shook her head. 'No.'

'No,' Marie echoed, smiling mysteriously, as if she had already known the answer. Her eyes closed, and it seemed within that same moment, she was already fast asleep again.

Freya and Kane's eyes met across the hospital bed. Their expressions were grave, and they individually recognised in that moment the great sadness that each of them held within themselves—that their lives could never be their own—and how difficult that was, even in a world where atrocities happened every day. Each of them knew they should count themselves lucky, but it was so difficult sometimes, so hard.

'I'm tired too,' Freya said, looking at Marie and collapsing back into the chair.

'Tell me about it,' Kane replied, rubbing his temple with his good hand. He moved his finger to his Tag and listened. 'It's only six. Freya, you ought to try and get some more sleep if you're going to stay.' His voice was suddenly cooler, more distant. He looked around the ward as he spoke to her.

'Of course I'm going to stay,' Freya said indignantly, remembering in parallel that only a few hours before she was not going to come to the hospital. She had not wanted to get inside that ambulance. Too many terrible memories. Yet she had followed Kane as if he was some kind of light and she was the moth.

27

Kane's eyes stung with tiredness and confusion. His brain crackled uselessly like the remnants of a fire. As the full light of day broke through the clouds and spilled into the ward, the horrors of the previous night could be seen more clearly than ever. The hospital had slowly filled throughout the night and was now buzzing with people. Many patients were only walking wounded like Kane, leaning on crutches, with bandaged faces or arms in slings. Others, like Marie, were lying in beds or in emergency zones or simply on the floors on top of coats and blankets, waiting. The ward should have been closed, but people were wandering through, calling out for loved ones. Their voices were strained, desperate, and it hurt to hear them.

Doctors and nurses, who looked as if they had been on duty for many hours, skirted through groups of people; Indexes and scanners were tucked under arms, hands free in case something else was flung at them.

Kane had replaced Freya at Marie's bedside while she had gone to find a coffee. He tried to distract himself and looked around, feeling the need to help but lacking the ability to see what he might be able to do that would not just get in the way. He wanted to read the notes in the panel at the end of the bed but he knew the screen had a password on it, and besides, he was not sure he wanted to know.

He focused on Marie. He was simply to watch her and call someone if she stopped responding. The nurse had told him earlier that she was moving in and out of consciousness, and her green-shadowed eyelids were still flickering open and then closing again like butterflies drying their wings in the sun. He reached to touch the side of her forehead, one of the only parts of her body that looked untouched by the explosion. She was hot, and tiny beads of sweat he had not noticed before clung to her skin. She looked terrible. Kane looked down at himself, at his broken arm, and felt another surge of guilt that he had not been able to protect her. He looked around the ward again, seeking out Freya's face. A doctor came to the foot of the bed and introduced himself as Marie's anaesthetist.

'Is it bad?' Kane asked in a voice little more than an

undertone.

The anaesthetist folded his lips and logged into the patient notes at the bottom of the bed. 'She has a long way to go, sir,' he replied quietly. 'To be honest, she was lucky to reach us alive, but we'll have her into surgery as soon as possible to remove the dead tissue now that the skin grafts are ready. Then we just have to hope the infection doesn't take over.'

'Okay,' Kane replied, nodding.

The anaesthetist stopped and spoke very quietly into his ear so that his breath tickled. 'The surgeons are both very experienced with this kind of trauma,' he explained. 'They'll be trying to excise the skin and tissue that have been damaged beyond repair and then insert the grafts. Her stem cells grew well, but she *is* in a delicate state. The infection already seems to have set well in—I'm afraid we really have no way of telling at this point how it will go.'

Before leaving, the anaesthetist crossed his fingers in a gesture that Kane considered dismissive. Kane was left nodding to himself beside Marie's fevered body. He tried, desperately, to remember what had happened in those last few seconds. He tried to recall how much she had struggled, how hard it had been to restrain her from running inside the club.

He looked down at the metallic gauze on his arm and ran his fingers over the sterile strips that decorated the side of his face. *Would he swap his place for hers?* It was a question that could not be answered. He should not have asked it. The challenges of his life, the seemingly colossal inconsistencies that made each day so difficult, were suddenly swamped by the effervescent closeness of mortality. He was, as he was every day of his life, lucky to be alive. He swept his hand in big circles around his head. This day was one for feeling thankful for what he did have, and yet the doubts, the tinkling cries from the pit of his stomach seemed more alive than ever.

'Pass me my coat,' Marie whispered. The words were barely audible above the din of the ward but the sound of her voice made Kane jump.

'Sure.' He picked up her singed, ripped coat from the end of the bed and laid it gingerly over her stomach. She smiled at him with all the strength she had left. She slipped her tiny, bandaged hand out from under the sheet and crept her fingers into the pocket. Marie grimaced as if every movement hurt in new ways, pushing tears into her eyes, forcing the breath out of her chest. Gripping it awkwardly between her middle and index finger, she drew out Sal's little black notebook and held it out towards Kane, nodding for him to take it.

He smiled politely, opened the cover and read the first line of its hasty, swirling scrawl.

Salman Winstan, b. 2025, Euston, London. Anti-Genetics Movement?

That was all there was on the first page. The question mark was big, and it had been traced over several times. He flicked through the other pages, all written in a churning, barely legible hand. He looked at her questioningly, confused.

'That's him,' Marie mouthed, although the sound she made was vanishingly thin, like a distant tide. Tears slid over her cheeks, and Kane tenderly caught those on the side of her face nearest him with his fingertips, like a lover might.

'Look after it,' she said.

'Don't cry, Marie. It'll be okay.' Kane smiled at her as widely as he could manage, trying to make it sparkle.

He once again thought back to the moments before the bomb went off. He remembered screaming at her, grabbing hold of her and then them rolling, over and over each other until it was down to no one but a higher power who stopped where. *I tried so hard to save her.*

Kane felt he had reassured her. He solemnly placed the notebook inside the pocket of his own coat and then laid his hand on hers, a silent promise. He squeezed just a little bit. A female nurse appeared beside Kane, laying her own hand across Marie's forehead.

'We're ready for you now in theatre, darling.' The nurse

was smiling broadly at Marie as she held the scanner to the side of her neck, waiting for the gentle vibration. She began to pull the bed away from the wall, taking Marie's hand from under Kane's and gently folding it back under the sheet.

'Does she have to go now?' Kane asked, then immediately realised how selfish he sounded as he looked around for Freya. 'Can we come with her?'

'Are you her next of kin?' the nurse asked without even looking at him.

Kane shook his head. The nurse was so businesslike all of a sudden. Perhaps that detachment had kicked in, the kind all these health professionals seemed to have, the ability to switch off their emotions to protect themselves from the endless tragedies they must see day in and day out. They would see more than most today. Kane wondered again why Marie did not have a next of kin logged against her name: he had not known that was even possible. It made him sad and his thoughts spun to the sound of his mother, crying in relief when he had called her hours earlier as he waited for his arm to be scanned.

'Okay, well sit tight and we'll let you know when she's out,' the nurse said. Her face was apologetic, as if she already knew the outcome but was not willing to let the patient know the truth, the severity of the situation.

Marie looked very alone as the nurse pulled the sheets up to her chin. She was an angel in white clouds. Kane felt an overwhelming sense that Freya should be here but he stood, dumbly, in the middle of the ward as the nurse wheeled the bed away. He felt himself shut down, switching off each emotional circuit with every metre that the bed moved. He watched until it reached the far end of the corridor, turned left and was gone.

5

Eyes closed against the brightness of day, Kane smelt the coffee Freya was holding before he saw her. He turned to see her staring open-mouthed at the space where Marie's bed had been. He took the cup of coffee from Freya and placed his hand flat between her shoulder blades, silently guiding her out of the ward. As they walked down the corridor to the waiting area with its cold, hard seats, he dared to glance across at Freya's pale face. Her eyes were full with tears. They sat down next to each other.

'I can't believe they took her while I was gone,' said Freya. 'I was five minutes. You said it would be alright.'

'I looked for you,' he said. 'You didn't even want to get into the ambulance, Freya.'

Freya only nodded, her eyes fixed on the floor, lips pursed as if she was biting her tongue.

'So, we haven't told each other our Backgrounds,' he continued. 'Now it seems I'm not just gallantly escorting you to the tube station, how about you tell me?'

Freya was exhausted and angry, but she actually liked to tell this story, despite the train wreck of it all, the shockwaves of which continued to reverberate. She remembered learning to do it correctly, with passion, at primary school, despite the fact that its entire contents had been uploaded onto the graphene bundle in her neck at six months of age. They had all been expertly taught to explain their Backgrounds clearly and honestly, with humour and deference where it was needed. It was essential, and quite a skill, to offer just the right amount of detail without giving too much away. Storytelling had become an art again, and explaining Backgrounds was a skill that her generation was the first to learn.

Freya thought it was probable that everyone, at least once in their lives, considered lying about their Background. Yet this was, apparently, a rarity. Not only was it a serious offence punishable by law, but there was a pervading sense that it would be a pointless endeavour: Everyone you had grown up with, your family, your school friends, your doctors, your bank, your insurance company—they all knew the reality. Any Sentry with a scanner could check it, and before you knew it, you would be caught in an exhaustible web of lies; a fate worse than dealing with the truth. Honesty was indoctrinated. Without the bare facts, you were nothing.

'Yes, okay,' she said, and she began to talk.

Freya was six or seven when she began to notice things that must have completely bypassed her before. At school, she realised that everyone had very different lunchboxes, some filled with fruit and others with candy. A little girl called Jemima ate hardly anything apart from chocolate but the teachers never told her off, they just laughed and told her she was lucky, that they wished they were like her. It was strange. Freya began to wonder for the first time why a few of her classmates did so much more exercise than her. They were already taller and stronger, and she would watch them from the window of her Mandarin class, running around the field over and over. Her little legs ached just looking at them.

At her weekly ballet class, she became aware for the first time that she was the plumpest, shortest one. All the other girls and boys looked like models from the catalogues. *They are graceful,* she thought as she gripped the bar, trying to lift her leg as high as the girl in front of her. Mrs Myrtle walked down the line, meeting her own eyes every so often in the mirrored wall. As her teacher looked back at her, Freya saw that her eyes were wide, liquid, and that there was a temporary, deep, vertical line at the top of her nose between her eyebrows. It was the same, familiar line that appeared on her mother's face every time Freya fell off a chair or dropped a spoon. It was the same face her older brother made when she missed kicking a ball back at him.

And right there and then, Freya made a sophisticated realisation. It was not concealed annoyance or frustration etched upon her ballet teacher's face, hidden within her mother's expressions and in the voices of her brothers; it was pity.

Mrs Myrtle continued on to the end of the line and clapped three times. The music stopped and the girls and boys scattered across the room towards their bags. Freya walked slowly to hers, neatly placed on one of the chairs. She unfolded a sweater from inside and pulled it on over her ballet dress. Looking down at her collar, she realised that it was the wrong way round and tried to pull out her arms and twist it around without taking it off. She was still struggling, the last one left in the room, when her mother walked in. And as Freya looked up, there it was; the same face.

'Oh, sweetie! You've got all tangled! Let me help you.' Her lovely round face smiled down on Freya, lines and all, as she reached for her arms.

Enraged, Freya tore herself away from her grip with a strength she could not achieve in her ballet steps.

'Stop it! I can do it!' she shouted. Defeating her own point, she pulled the sweater over her head and threw it angrily on the floor. Tears were trickling down her hot cheeks as she ran out of the hall into the busy street. She stopped on the pavement as she heard the thuds of her mother's feet catching up with her.

'Do *not* do that again, Freya. Never run away from me again!'

The flesh of her mother's cheeks burnt crimson through her olive skin. Her eyes were watery and the force of her breath made steam in the cold air, condensing on Freya's face. Standing perfectly still, Freya stared at the lobe of one of her mother's ears, at the aquamarine stone that sparkled there, trying not to cry again. She became slowly aware of the vice-like grip around her arm, her mother's pale knuckles.

'Tell me you won't do that again, Freya!' she demanded once more, and Freya shook her head gently from side to side, overwhelmed.

When they reached the bottom of their street, Freya's

mother put her hands around her shoulders, turned her gently around and knelt in front of her so that they were face to face. 'I know there are things you don't understand, Freya,' she said, her voice uneven. 'And you're a big girl now, so if there's anything you want to ask me, you can.'

'What do the doctors know about me?'

'You learn about genes in school, don't you, Freya?'

Freya nodded.

'Well, when you were born, the doctor did the tests they do on all babies. They took a little bit of blood out of your foot'—she paused to tickle Freya's heel playfully through her pumps—'and looked at your genes. And they told me that you would be beautiful, and clever and kind.' She was crying now, crying without sobbing, the tears just slipping down her cheeks. 'They said you could be a teacher or an artist, but they also told me that you had some funny genes.'

'Funny weird or funny ha-ha?'

'Funny weird.'

'Oh.'

'Yes. And they said that you wouldn't live as long as your brothers, that you would get ill when you got older.'

'Like when I had the flu?'

'Not really.' Her mother's voice shook a little bit. 'Different from that kind of ill. They say that you won't be as strong, that you might fall over a lot. Things like that.'

'Like when I wobble at ballet?'

'Maybe.' Freya's mother hugged her close. 'If you ever don't understand something, just ask me.'

At school, she did not have to ask, she was taught. But every now and again, Freya asked her mother another question. And so it turned out, over the years, that she was going to have a disease named after somebody called Huntington. It would make her shake, make it hard to walk, tire her out. Following her birth diagnosis, the doctors had looked at the telomeres in her cells as if they were a clock into the future and figured out that symptoms would manifest when she was thirty or thirty-one.

At the age of eight, that seemed a very, very long time away. A lifetime, no less.

'Wow.' Kane breathed out heavily and raised his eyebrows at her. 'And you said it's your twenty-ninth birthday today?'

She nodded. 'Well, yesterday, now.'

Kane hesitated, slowly understanding why she seemed so reticent to celebrate.

'That's right,' she said before he could interrupt. 'Sometime in the next two years.'

Kane knew what she meant.

'They say I should really start to see the symptoms appear in the next year or so. I won't just be clumsy, the drugs won't be enough anymore, and they won't be able to hide it. I'm actually having another brain scan next week. I'm bloody terrified.' A lopsided smile, hiding emotions too afraid to come out, rounded her face again, taking away the years.

'Look, I'm sure it'll be alright.' Kane knew his words were meaningless but struggled for anything else to say.

Silence lingered for a few moments. 'Your turn,' she said eventually, raising her eyebrows.

Kane leant back and folded his arms, cocking his head to the side. 'For a start,' he said, pausing to glance at her briefly, catching her eye for a split second. 'I'm gay.'

Freya looked surprised. 'But I'm not very good at it,' he continued, feeling embarrassment weave roughly through the hairs on the back of his neck.

'What on earth do you mean? You don't have a boyfriend?'

'No, no boyfriends. Nothing.'

'Nothing?'

He shook his head meekly.

'Never?'

Kane sensed that she was still prickling from his accusation that she didn't want to come to the hospital. He nibbled the inside of his lip but held his head up, looking straight at her. Freya rested her head on her fist, her eyebrows raised. She looked emboldened by his insecurity.

'But you're gorgeous! You've really never ...?'

He shook his head, letting an earnest, toothy smile spread across his face. Already, he had been sloppy. He was already diverging from the official version of his Background, treading a trickier path than he ought, certainly with a stranger. She was leaning in closely to hear his whispers.

'Really?' she asked, incredulous.

He met her eyes again and smiled a little. She touched his arm and he realised that he must look upset. His fifteen-year-old self was suddenly everywhere: on his skin, in his head, deep inside his chest. He took a few shallow breaths. For some reason, he wanted to tell her.

'So, Kane, I understand that you are here today because you are having trouble accepting your sexuality profile?' The psychiatrist focused on him, piercingly.

He nodded.

'Can you tell me in your own words what the stumbling block seems to be?' *Stumbling block?* She was so casual.

'My Background is quite clear on the fact that I'm gay, but ...' He had to be careful here, not to give away his cynicism too soon. He fought for the right words. Dr Seymour did not once lift her eyes from his face, which made it all the more difficult.

'You don't *want* to be gay?' she asked.

He shook his head. 'No—I don't *feel* gay.'

'Ri-ight.' She drew the word out slowly so that it seemed to be mocking him, and then she paused, her eyebrows knotted. 'And what is your sexual history?'

Kane shrank back into the chair. He was coy like this, his friends would joke. He hated to discuss sex. His fellow teenagers found it fascinating that he shied away from unabridged honesty.

'Well, I'm only fifteen and I haven't really ... I don't really have a sexual history as such.' He had thought she would take notes, but she simply sat there in her chair, unmoving, nodding.

'So, no boyfriends yet?'

'Well, that's sort of why I'm here. I have been having, um, feelings for someone.'

She nodded, encouragingly.

'A girl,' he clarified.

The look of relief on the psychiatrist's face faded as quickly as it had appeared. She opened and closed her mouth a few times before she finally spoke.

'That's, um, *unusual*, Kane.' The wrinkles across her forehead burrowed into the groove above her nose. The way she spoke made her words feel like a schoolyard reprimand.

'Mmm. I know.' He paused and looked out of the window, away from the intense disbelief of her stare.

'Your Background is very clear, Kane. This really is quite worrying.' As if it was his fault.

She came and sat on the matching leather chair next to him and ran her finger along the edge of the glass coffee table. The glass fell into digital darkness and Dr Seymour flicked through documents until she found the file she was looking for. Opening it up, she pushed the sharpening pixels of once-handwritten notes towards him, annotated in places with flowing feminine loops and asterisks.

'These are all case studies of boys who suffered similar problems in early life.' Her voice softened. 'Please, have a look.'

She laid her hand gingerly on Kane's arm as he scanned the pages. *Abuse. Distrust. Trauma. Damage. Assault.* He was speechless.

'If anything like this ever happened to you, you can tell me.' She paused. 'Any of these things can affect, possibly permanently alter, your birth diagnosis. Anything you say to me here is confidential, of course.'

'No, nothing! There's nothing wrong.'

She dragged the file back to her side of the table and with one sweep of her hand it was clear glass again.

'Well, Kane, I believe there *is* something wrong.' She stood and dragged her chair back behind her desk, perching in front of the screen in her desk. 'But I don't think this is anything psychological, and you seem in perfectly good health.' She tapped on the screen. 'So I'm just going to prescribe you some hormone balancing treatment—we'll see if taking that for a few months does the trick.' She shot a broad smile across the room at him.

This is not why he came; this is not what he wanted. But

what did he want? As Kane sat there in the mundane little office, family photographs on the walls, birth diagnosis profiles and Backgrounds piled high within the glass table, the trappings of his world seemed stronger than ever. Silently, he panicked. But what choice did he have? The system was against him, he was the odd one out and nobody would ever be able to accept him.

Dr Seymour handed him a small cartridge. 'This is the best I can do for now. It's done the trick for a few other young men like you. Spit in it, shake a few times and take it to the pharmacy as soon as the purple numbers appear on the outside. They'll give you a few packets of personalised tablets. One a day. Come back in three months and we'll see how it's going for you. Feel free to make an appointment on the way out.'

She looked happy and rubbed the back of his shoulders maternally as he stood. They caught each other's eyes.

'It's for the best, Kane. Believe me.'

They shook hands at the door and he found himself smiling, however limply, back at her. *Perhaps this is the best option, the easiest choice,* he thought. *And what was so wrong with that?*

Later that day, Kane sat on his bed, staring at the packet of pills in his hand. He had collected them earlier from the pharmacy. He had gone on his own. That small rite of passage in itself had given him a good feeling, one that eased the frustration that had been building up in his mind to the point of exhaustion. The pharmacist, disinterested, had simply taken the cartridge from its packet, fed it through the medicine printer behind his desk and handed over a small box in return. He had read aloud, in a rapid monotone, the instructions printed along the side: *One a day with a glass of water.* Kane had wanted to ask how many he would need to take in all, but before he could, the pharmacist had told him that a new packet would automatically arrive in the post. And Kane had realised that it was forever. These little pills sitting in his hand—candyfloss pink as it happened, like some sort of crass in-joke from the pharmaceutical company—were to be part of his life now.

The half-digested remainder of his lunch sat heavy in his stomach as he read through the possible side effects: Nausea, weight gain, migraine, depression, lack of sociability, reduction in libido. He was not even sure he knew what all of it meant. The list ran on and on, in several different languages. Kane roughly folded it back up and shoved it back into the packet. He pressed one of the tablets out of the blister pack, pushed it onto the back of his tongue and swallowed it with clenched teeth. His throat was dry and he could feel it slowly slip down to the top of his stomach, catching in every fleshy crevice.

A few weeks later, Kane lay in bed, his Index on the pillow next to him. He was flicking through his favourite websites, ones he had deliberately not visited since going to the clinic. This was his test to himself. The moving images did not look as alive as they usually were, the brightness of the skin no longer burst from the screen. Today they looked like dolls, these women; beautiful dolls lying there, barely needing oxygen. Kane felt nothing and he did not try to feel otherwise.

And now the second part of the test, the bit he was dreading. He switched to another site, the name of which always made him squirm a little. A video appeared, something that Kane would normally find monstrous in its detail. But these men too were lifeless mannequins to him, and Kane sighed shakily. He had been so worried that he *would* feel something, that desire would rise unwanted from his groin. The relief came as a rush in itself, an intense burst of pleasure.

He switched off the screen and laid the Index down by the side of his bed. It had proven to him what he had already felt developing over the last few days; the sensation that a switch had been completely flicked in his head, a light that had been extinguished. It was turned off and would forever be turned off if he kept taking his hormones.

In a way, it came as a sudden freedom, a sense that his feelings could no longer hold him back. Nothingness, numbness was preferable. Dr Seymour had been right after all.

Kane felt calm, purged, as he finished his story. Freya was staring down at her nails, picking at them. A frown was engraved between her brows. After a moment or two, she looked up at him, her head tilted questioningly to one side.

'That's quite a strange story,' she said quietly.

'Is it?' he asked. He rarely thought about it now and her comment interested him.

She nodded slightly, still looking at her fingers. 'Don't you ever wonder what things were like for our parents?'

'Sometimes, I guess.'

'It's just that sometimes I think it would be better not to know the things we know, to have to find things out our own way.'

Kane shrugged impassively. 'I think everyone feels like that sometimes.'

'Do they? I think it a lot. I look at my brother now and I just think he's so lucky. He missed out on compulsory birth diagnosis by a few years. He could have paid for a private one but always said it was too expensive. Life's not been perfect for them. He's had cancer, and he and his wife had trouble conceiving, but they've been more or less okay at the end of the day. They didn't really need to be told anything; they made it through. But we were forced to hand over knowledge about ourselves that we had no say in, as little babies. How can that be right?'

'Because it's supposed to help us, to help society, isn't it? The State can allocate resources to the right people ahead of time. *You* must benefit from that, with your illness.'

Freya nodded weakly. Her mood had switched from one of irritation to sadness.

'Yeah, I would do if they'd just hurry the fuck up and find a cure,' she whispered, blinking back tears. 'Sometimes, I just wish I didn't know.' She shook her hair back over her shoulders and Kane watched her compose herself as she pursed her lips and refocused her gaze. Her pupils bore into him. She was quite stunning now, stern; the little outer strength she possessed was clearly transient. She looked so womanly but in a moment her girlishness could return.

They talked for a while longer before falling asleep, Kane cross-legged on the floor, Freya in a chair.

Hours later, Freya opened one eye and peeked down at him, at his ribcage moving slowly up and down. Looking around her, Freya could see that the ward was still busy but people were moving quietly and considerately, as if through a graveyard. A cleaner tried to sweep and disinfect the crevices between sleeping bodies being tended to along the walls. Nurses and doctors came and went solemnly, exhausted expressions upon their faces; most had probably been up for the whole night.

It was a different scene to the one she remembered on the day that Jim had died. He had been in a private room, and Freya could not remember seeing anyone else's faces apart from those of Jim, Matt and her mother—not even a doctor, although there had been one, she remembered; a woman with soft hands who took her to the toilet.

Lost in a sleepy, thoughtless haze, she crawled from the chair onto her hands and knees and burrowed into Kane's warm body. She traced her fingertips across the shiny gauze around his arm, hard and warm to the touch. Their noses almost met. He roused a little, murmuring something unintelligible, and pulled her legs closer with his foot, snaking his lower leg between hers. With the tips of his fingers sticking out of his sling, he stroked her forearm. They kissed softly, briefly, and fell asleep.

They drifted in and out of sleep, until the surgeon came in to tell them that she was very sorry, that she had done everything she could have done, but that they would not see Marie again. Sepsis had killed her, an infection of the blood. *There was very little we could have done,* she repeated.

After the surgeon left, they sat in shock for several minutes.

'I can't believe she's gone,' Freya said.

She watched as Kane pulled a blister pack of tablets from his pocket and pushed one out. He placed it on his tongue and tipped his head back. Freya realised that she was envious of such a simple solution. She tried to imagine that one pill a day could make everything alright. As he squeezed her hand, it felt like a taunt.

Kane suddenly stood up, stretching out his stiff legs and neck, rolling it from shoulder to shoulder as if warming up for a race. He looked every inch the athlete, apart from the sling, Freya thought as she ran her eyes over the muscles of his bare upper arm. She watched, confused, as Kane bent to pick up his jacket.

'Well, I should be going. I need to go check in with my family. My mum will be freaking out about this.' Kane gestured to his broken arm and pulled a silly grin.

'Oh, right.' Freya stood to face him, arms folded, eyebrows knotted.

'So, take care of yourself.' He jabbed her in the shoulder with his index finger, playfully, and turned away.

'Do you even have my contact?' Freya said to his back. A note of indignation was strung through her words. Kane stopped and turned.

'Sorry, yes, of course.' He held his unfurled Index to her neck, avoiding her eyes.

Hers filled with tears and she swallowed back the things she wanted to say, the remonstrations. She scolded herself; what else had she expected?

Kane squeezed her briefly, half-heartedly, around the shoulders with his good arm and then walked away. He got a little further before she summoned enough courage to speak again.

'Stop taking them, Kane. Stop taking the pills.' Freya's sorrow choked her voice and it clattered in his ears. Yet he did not turn around. Rubbing the back of his neck as if to soothe an ache, he carried on walking. Freya watched until he disappeared through the revolving doors and out into the afternoon, tears slipping down her cheeks.

Freya found herself wandering the corridors of the hospital before she left that day. She looked down, placing one foot after the other, watching the jewels adorning the toes of her high heels glitter back at her. Eventually she found herself in a lift, and upon looking at the list of departments, followed the directions to the Backgrounds Wing.

She followed a young nurse through the door. Compared to the rest of the hospital, it was brand new and glistening white. Flecks of silver in the flooring sparkled like a migraine, rousing her from her daze.

She looked up. A white wall to her left was lined with office doors, and to her right, newborn babies gurgled, cried and slept in rows of cots. She stopped, leaning against the glass. Some of them already had small circular plasters over their heels; others were still waiting for the clairvoyant blood test that would tell them their future. They all looked tiny, all dressed in the same white hospital suit, in matching white plastic cots. They would be back in six months to have their first Tag planted in their necks. Freya poked at hers now with the tip of her finger, a tiny knot of solidity that rose and fell with each pump of her heart. These two procedures would be the first and last thing they would get for free. Everyone had a Tag now, but anyone much older than Freya had only identification and public records stored upon theirs. Only she, these babies, and everyone in between had Backgrounds on there as well. She had been part of the first generation, the first citizens blessed to have so much knowledge quite literally at their fingertips.

A small baby nearby had seemingly fixed its gaze upon her. She raised her hand and waggled her fingers at it, smiling widely. Open-mouthed, it stared beyond her. Freya thought about her fertility reading on her birth diagnosis, which said she would be infertile by thirty-six. *Not really a problem* was essentially the gist of the executor's dry comment, seeing as in all likelihood she would be dead, or at least incapacitated, by then. A couple were walking down the corridor towards her, talking animatedly, the man cradling what must be their newborn child. It was already out of its white hospital vest and dressed in a pink cotton playsuit and matching hat dotted with fabric flowers.

'It's fantastic. I'm so relieved, honey,' he said.

'I know. I was so nervous,' the woman agreed.

They were about Freya's own age, and she noticed immediately that no wedding bands circled their fingers. Most people had children before getting married these days;

too many parents failed to cope with negative Backgrounds and the associated stresses.

They continued past her and Freya's eyes settled on their shoulders, gently inclined towards each other. She tried to imagine the conversation her parents would have had after her own Background was revealed. There were probably some tears; they would have already known from the pre-birth test that she carried Huntington's, a condition luckily not on the forced termination list, but only the post-birth blood test would have revealed its early onset.

As Freya continued to watch the couple, leaning with her back against the glass, the baby's outstretched arm emerged from in front of the man. Her fat little fingers were so perfect, her fingernails so soft. The relief flowed from the couple in tangible waves, as if they knew their baby's future was one of happiness. They thought they knew when she would die, whether she was susceptible to any major diseases, what her personality would be like, her sexuality, her ability to love. The list would run over ten pages.

But, Freya thought, *a broadly positive Background does not make you immortal.*

That couple did not know whether their little girl would die in a bomb blast; they could not tell whether she would travel abroad and pick up one of the new strains of malaria; they could not even know if she would decide to take up a dangerous hobby and die jumping out of a plane. Although a tendency toward thrill-seeking behaviour was probably covered in there somewhere, it would be framed to sound positive, exciting. *How lucky we are,* they would think, *to have a child who makes the most of her life.* They would be so shocked when they got the phone call.

Before Freya left the wing, she looked back over her shoulder, a thought tugging at her. Marie had come into her life and left again very briefly, a tiny Tinkerbell flitting between worlds. Somehow, despite Freya knowing so little about her—not even her Background—Marie had reached into the small, tightly closed corner of Freya's chest set aside for love, and nestled inside.

6

After spending Sunday evening and Monday at his mother's house, Kane went home on Monday evening to his own apartment. His youthful, working-class ghetto in Shepherd's Bush was an area inhabited by people similar to him: people who were genetically and medically decent, if morally variable. Everyone lived within the collection of modest apartment blocks with shared allotments and a little park in the middle. Lots of singletons lived here. Although well furnished, the apartments were too small for most families or even a couple.

Kane walked into his bedroom and sat on the edge of the bed, laying his coat beside him. For a little while, he stayed there, his feet planted firmly on the ground. All was quiet but for the shouts of kids outside his window. He wondered why they were not at home yet; they had just five minutes until curfew. Living here was all about knowing your place in life, accepting that you were not cut out for anything amazing and just sitting quietly and getting on with it, not causing too much trouble. Those kids would learn that eventually … some with more resentment than others, perhaps.

Sighing, Kane dropped back onto the bed and laid his palms across his forehead, staring at the ceiling. He tried to empty his mind, but he found himself trying to decide which, of the thousands of thoughts in his mind, was the most important *not* to think about. Was it the recoiling shock that a matter of hours ago he had been inches from death? Was it that he tried to save a girl's life, and failed? Was it that he had kissed a woman, and that it had made his insides shiver? His stomach churned.

He listened carefully to the noises outside, convinced that

he'd been followed. Anyone who'd been at the club on Saturday night might be questioned, in whatever manner a Sentry felt like questioning them. Some enjoyed roughing up innocent citizens a little too much. The playing children seemed to have quietened. Footsteps passed and were gone.

In that magnificent way that our brains work, in the manner that makes the philosophically minded wonder if there is really such a thing as free will, the neurons that held Kane's visual memory of Marie's black notebook fired without a palpable trigger. As he remembered, he wondered why he had not even thought of it since he had slipped the thing into his pocket. He pulled his coat closer and withdrew the notebook from within.

Having this changes things. If anyone knew, or found out that I had it … It was unsanctioned information, which, despite outward appearances, was the very thing the State did not want its citizens to have. Kane held it on his stomach for a moment, the shiny cover cold against the line of exposed flesh where his T-shirt had ridden up. Yes, Marie's notebook was definitely a dangerous thing to have. Anything handwritten was considered immediately suspicious. Writing by hand, pen on paper, was no longer taught in schools. It was too hard to trace, too transient a form of communication.

Reflecting on this, Kane was surprised that Marie could write so fluidly; while he could just about form sentences, his were full of errors and misspellings. Gingerly holding the notebook up, he could see that it was thin, yet well put together, the pages sewn neatly into the spine. It reminded him of its owner, her slight frame, and her old head on young shoulders. He thought of her lying in the operating theatre, imagined the surgeon calling the time of death and felt weak inside.

I should burn it now, Kane thought, but instead he opened the cover and reread the only line he had seen when she first handed it to him. The name of a man, the same age as him, from a place he had never visited, coupled with a phrase that meant very little. *That's him,* Marie had mouthed. Less than two days ago, she had fallen at his feet, scraped and panting.

He tried to remember her words, wholly unexpected words that had hit him from left side. She had known that there was a man inside with a bomb, and she had called him Sal. She had been desperate to stop him, so desperate that her battered body was now lying in a hospital morgue.

Kane stared at the paper. So this was him; this was the man who had set off the bomb and, seemingly, the organisation he was linked to—one Kane had never heard of. *Why would anyone do such a thing?*

He flicked through the other pages, filled with swirling ink that was apparently all that was left of Marie. It read as a dialogue and it felt rushed in places, written quickly, letters slipping and words dropped, punctuation forgotten. The first few pages covered some basic things about Sal that even a distant acquaintance would have known: his Background, his appearance, the quirks of his character. It was clear that Marie had never met him before. She had learnt as she had written.

Sal was seventeen when he finally fell in with the wrong crowd. Cynics had said it was only a matter of time in the current system. He was already tired of his life by this point. He was tired of curfews, of the lack of trust placed in him by his parents and society at large. He was tired of trying so hard to impress, to be good, with no reward. It was exhausting.

Mo and Darren were partners, and after befriending him through the school gates one day, they took Sal under their wing. Together they stole small things at first, and then jewellery and designer bags. Sal finally felt he was where he belonged with these older men. They cared about him; they were fair with him, sharing profits and buying him beers afterwards. Together, they smiled a lot, laughed together. They became more of a family to Sal than his real one, and he spent little time at home.

One evening, at one of the all-night bars they frequented, Mo introduced Sal to his younger sister, Ciara. It was the early hours and Sal was hazy with whisky and the cannabis they had smoked outside the back door. He was sitting with

Darren, watching the women on the dance floor, when they all fell away to reveal her, like she was the sun shining through the panes of a stained glass window, casting the colours onto his skin. Sal liked to think that he fell in love the moment he first heard her name. She was undeniably beautiful, her long, lustrous hair falling around her shoulders, her dark brown eyes twinkling shyly at him. They talked all night, and by the end she was sitting on his lap like a gangster's moll and he had her number.

He called the next day and they met up, walking around for hours. He took her to his father's secret church, where they crept in at the back to watch him preach. His parents' belief had been undiluted by the new rules of the State, despite the physical destruction of their church and the threats to their freedom. In the years following the Takeover, the riches of cathedrals had been dismantled, melted down, the profits given to charities. But congregations still met, still soundlessly distributed sermons and services on pieces of paper that would be dropped into the fire on the way out. Faith could not be so easily erased by the State.

They slipped out again, going back to his house for a safely private half-hour. They made love in his bedroom, quickly and awkwardly. Lying together afterwards, the afternoon sun directing its glow over them, Sal felt the happiest he had ever felt and stared down in awe at this beauty in his arms, asking himself why on Earth she had chosen him.

For a summer and an autumn, they were inseparable, save for the times when Sal was with Barney or out on a job with Mo and Darren. He had started to see them less, and although they teased and pressured him to continue living their life, Sal no longer felt the need to do what they did. He had decided he wanted to get a proper job, or to go to university and study. His father was pleased to often find Sal reading in his bedroom late at night, and he even started to wonder if his son would prove a success after all. The anger that Sal had always felt was dwindling, and ironically the effect of its shrinking in his stomach made Sal consciously aware of it for the first time. Squaring up to his past, he felt himself become happier; he felt redemption, and it had come from Ciara.

It became winter, and the coldness, combined with Sal's tiredness, made his tangle of anger shrink more slowly than it had in those heady summer months. His time became more stretched than ever between Ciara and his studies, although he now spent hardly any time with Mo and Darren. One bitter evening, Ciara had been round for tea. She had chatted with Sal's sister about her favourite pop groups, politely discussed community issues with his parents and eaten every scrap of shepherd's pie before leaving, a lingering scent of frangipani trailing behind her.

'Ciara really is lovely,' beamed Sal's mother, Cherry, as she washed up at the sink. 'Won't you miss her if you go to university?'

'I don't have to go far, Mum. We can still see each other.'

The two of them washed and dried the dishes quietly, Sal rubbing each dish conscientiously until it gleamed. It was a practised arrangement, and he cherished these moments standing next to his mother while his father watched a film next door. They both knew that all that was required of them was to work together in silence. It was rarely a time for talking or reprimands. This was their shared time into which they would both retreat, a sanctum for their relationship.

But that particular evening, Sal's sister Tiane strolled into the room, her lips pursed, holding Ciara's silver Index in her hand. She perched on a chair and unrolled it on the table, sighing loudly and flattening the device with her palm. She irritated Sal immensely and he found it hard to ignore her, especially now, bursting into his moment of peace.

'What?' he snapped.

She merely shook her head and sighed again, smiling to herself.

'Why've you got that?' he said and slipped the Index from beneath her fingers.

'She left it here.'

Sal slipped it into his back pocket. 'I'd better take it back,' he said to Cherry, dropping the dishcloth over a chair. She nodded.

As he walked out of the kitchen door, he heard Tiane speak, deliberately slowly and loudly to Cherry. 'I hope he doesn't read anything in it. He won't like what he finds.'

A veil of shock fell over Sal and the hairs stood up on his arms. He walked out of the house before he could hear Cherry rebuke his younger sister, before her whining began. He strode fiercely, the Index weightless in his pocket, towards Ciara's house.

His mind was electric under his shroud of disbelief, his thoughts bouncing against each other. It felt like a migraine; glitter began to fall around the edges of his vision as he finally pulled the Index from his pocket and read as he walked. His lip quivered and curled up, his brow thickened as his eyes skipped through the words. He changed direction onto a smaller road at the next junction and forcefully threw the device to the ground in front of him, stamping on it as he strode on. It felt like the string snapping on a guitar, a sudden release of tension.

Sal found himself at the doorway of the bar, a place he had not been to for months. He walked in, barely restraining himself, breathing deeply. He was the rim of the crystal wine glass his father would run his fingertip around after dinner, humming with tightly packed energy. As he looked around, a voice inside him prayed that Darren was not there. But this was Sal's fate, and so of course there he was, leaning against the bar in his usual corner.

Sal was upon him before anyone could pull him off. No words came at first as his fists multiplied and rained upon Darren, his jaw, his ear, his neck, his chest. As the older man fell to the floor, Sal screamed at him manically.

'You fucking bastard! How could you touch her? She's mine. She's fucking mine!'

For a moment, Sal felt sick at himself as he watched his boot repeatedly sinking into Darren's stomach and head as if he was an inflatable toy. He saw Darren's front teeth crumble like cottage cheese onto his tongue, the blood pouring from his nose. He felt the arms pulling him back but he could not stop. Rage boiled through him, the desperation of feeling he had nothing left to lose set in and his feet began to stamp, cruelly and effectively upon Darren's upper body. He might never have stopped until someone else—an unknown man who, in retrospect, probably saved both his and Darren's lives—knocked Sal into a week-long coma with a single well-aimed punch to the head.

As Kane read on, the words became more spaced, more precisely written. Marie must have taken longer to write them. Perhaps Sal had spoken slowly, erringly at this point. The strength at which the ink ate into the paper increased as each page went by, possibly as Marie realised the significance of the words.

Prison had been hell for Sal. He had spent most of his time keeping himself to himself, trying to avoid fights and drugs and awaiting precious visits from his parents. He knew his father would never come. At first, his mother brought Tiane along, but his sister's visits became fewer and further between until eventually she stopped coming altogether. On whose part this decision lay never became clear to Sal, and he thought about it more than he would have done if he had other things to do with his life than sit in a cell. Whether Tiane had found better things to do with her Saturday mornings, whether she became gradually more disturbed by her brother's apparent derangement, or whether Cherry finally sensitised to her son's contempt for his sister, the jury was still out.

Sal's jury, on the other hand, was not out for long at all. He was swiftly convicted after pleading guilty. The hardest thing for Sal was seeing Barney shake his head sadly at the verdict and waving tearfully at him as he was led away, another failure of the system. He worried his old psychologist would forget him, but he still came, once a fortnight, to talk things through, to "keep him company," as he put it. He no longer played the role of counsellor or therapist but became his friend, perhaps the friend Sal had needed all along.

Sal often wondered whether Barney had felt he had failed; there often seemed an undercurrent to his visits and his words that silently spoke apologies for missed signals, self-retributions for not being there at the right time, in the right way. Barney talked of his family, trips he had taken, interesting conversations he had had. It comforted Sal to watch his long, hairy eyebrows bounce as he spoke, to listen to stories of a life he might never know.

One particular morning, as Barney joyfully discussed his retirement and the forthcoming end of his professional career, he suddenly paused and leaned in closely to the circular holes cut through the plastic divider. He pulled a pen from his pocket and a torn-off piece of paper, scribbled quickly and held it, covered by his palm, against the glass.

I don't believe in any of it any more, Sal. Not in the system, not in birth diagnosis, not in Backgrounds. Not in any of it.

'Yeah,' Sal snorted a laugh. 'But why would you? Look at me—I really bucked the trend, didn't I?' His sarcasm was spiked, cutting like a knife down the row of inmates. He twisted, flicking his eyes at the woman sitting behind him, waiting her turn. Sal had felt her gaze over his shoulder, he could tell she had read Barney's note. She appeared to be listening intently but then she looked away again, down into her lap.

He had seen her before, on occasion, exercising in the yard or reading in the library. She looked a decent sort of person, he had thought, too decent to be in here. Her brown hair was cut into a stylish bob below her jaw line, sharpening her features. She always wore make-up, not a lot, but enough that she looked as if she had made an effort each morning, as if she was off to work rather than to slop out the previous night's food in the kitchen. It was admirable, if a little odd.

A guard called her and she moved to sit at the screen a few seats down from Sal. She pressed the palm of her hand up against that of a tiny girl on the other side, the plastic sandwiched between them. The child was dressed in a pink flowery dress, tight blonde curls across her head. She was giggling, delight sparkled on her face and the woman's intense frown had become a broad smile. Sal turned back to face Barney, casting him a warning look. Barney was shaking his head, a weary smile upon his face.

'Well, I don't believe it—and neither should you. You are better than this, Sal.'

'No, I'm not.'

'But the point is that you just did what everyone thought you would eventually do. You only did what was expected of you. Psychologically, Sal, on a deeper level, you just followed the rules.'

After Barney left that day, Sal spent a long time in his cell thinking about what the old man had said. *You just followed the rules.* It was still circling his thoughts as he ate dinner that night, silently and without humour as he so often tried to do, blending into the background.

What he felt was guilt. Barney was the only person who had ever really made him feel like he could be somebody, convinced him that he could achieve something for himself beyond the limits of his Background. He owed Barney more than this, having to come and visit him behind bars. On the other hand, the old man had only been doing his job all these years; he was paid to make Sal feel better about himself. But Sal loved Barney and he scolded himself for having such thoughts. *Being in here must be making me bitter,* he thought.

Within minutes of sitting down, the woman he had seen during visiting time appeared beside him, sliding her tray up the bench to sit next to him. Up close, she was slim, almost wiry, her short, dark hair pushed back with clips. Her sleeves were rolled up and he noticed for the first time that the skin of her arm was withered and scarred, as if from a burn. Her dark blue eyes flashed at him briefly. She sat uncomfortably close to him, and although she looked so feminine, so harmless, Sal felt nervous, a familiar feeling in this place. Their elbows rubbed as they ate.

'Hello,' she said, quietly. Sal nodded in response.

With the tip of a toothpick, she scratched words across the back of her hand and showed him: *Anti-Genetics Movement.*

'Have you heard of this?' she said, this time under her breath, not making eye contact but looking around, her eyes rapidly scanning the faces of the men and women around them. Her voice was level, light-hearted, as if she were starting small talk at a cocktail party. She licked and rubbed the skin, obliterating them completely.

Sal paused to look at her and shook his head, then spooned another mouthful of stew into his mouth.

'You were talking to that older gentleman today?' she asked.

Sal nodded again, frowning. She sounded quite upper class, each consonant was pronounced crisply.

'Well, whoever he was, I thought he summed it up pretty well.'

'He was my psychologist when I was growing up,' Sal said, pausing for a few moments before he continued. 'And my friend.'

The woman nodded and smiled, holding out her hand: 'I'm Angie. And you are?'

'Why are you talking to me?' Sal spoke more loudly, warningly, and dropped his spoon into the bowl, aiming to draw attention so that this woman would fade away again. But she continued, unperturbed, with an intriguing urgency in her soft voice.

'I'm talking to you because he is right. And not only that, but things need to change. It can't carry on like this. You and I—we simply do not deserve to be written off like we have been. And neither do our children, or our children's children.'

Sal looked her in the eyes for the first time and held her gaze. Her pupils were wide and the whites shone as if lit from within. He wondered whether she had been thinking of the tiny little blonde child in the flowery dress, who he imagined was her daughter, and his own thoughts turned to wondering what rules she would be forced to follow in her life, what fate was written into her genetic code.

Sal was only in prison for three years, in the end. He was released on his twenty-second birthday following good behaviour, overcrowding and a series of brutal rapes inside the prison walls that helped his lawyer's case. Too old to be overseen by a psychologist and living for the first time outside of the family home (his father would not allow him in the door), he was placed by the State into what was deemed appropriate employment for someone like him: daily cleaning of three floors of an office block in central London.

He would arrive and have his iris scanned each morning at five, before the important, wealthy people who worked there were even in their showers. He would start at the top of the building and work down, finishing at ten. He did his job well and took a certain pride in it, conscientiously cleaning each desk, emptying the bins, washing up the discarded coffee cups in the sink, polishing the chrome door handles and glass room dividers. It was a thankless job with terrible pay, but he got to work alone, and it allowed him to live in a small flat of his own, which he loved.

Once he got used to the early starts and dressing in the dark, he liked the quiet of the mornings, with only the soft hum of the air conditioning to disturb him. It was after nine a.m., when the people started to arrive, that his peace was ruined. They would often pass him on the stairs, some ignoring him completely, a few regulars stopping to joke or give a cheery 'good morning.' Others unconsciously cast him pitiful looks, which burned into him and sent him home in a terrible mood.

Sometimes, if no one had arrived early and the office lay empty, he would take a short break at one of the desks. His favourite one had a view of the park below. There was a stool tucked underneath the desk that he rested his feet on as he sat, admiring the natural light falling on the toes of his shoes, freshly polished to a sheen by the imprecise sweep of his mop over the bathroom floor. On either side of the computer dock were photographs in frames, one of a woman and the others of the same two children at different ages. It seemed they were now young teenagers, spotty and awkward-looking. Sal would sit there and wonder about the desk owner's seemingly perfect life. He tried to imagine what it was like to be old enough not to have a birth diagnosis; he visualised the man telling jokes to his colleagues over a beer after work, laughing uproariously and then returning home and slipping into bed with his beautiful wife.

But in the last few months, in the afternoons, Sal had developed a new routine. He would leave the office and walk home for lunch. Then he would shower off the cleaning chemicals and dress in new clothes—nothing eye-catching, usually just jeans and a dark T-shirt. Leaving his apartment, he would walk down the same network of streets until he reached a house twenty minutes away. Checking around him first, he would ring the doorbell and someone would answer, quickly ushering him in. Many different people answered the door; he thought perhaps around ten people might live inside. He had been offered a room there once but preferred the seclusion of his own place.

The last time he had been to the house, just a week ago, a little girl had answered the door and giggled piercingly at him by way of a greeting. She was wearing shorts and a T-shirt, but he recognised her blonde curls as she ran out past him and down onto the street. She had grown since he had last seen her, that day in the visiting room in prison. He followed her with his eyes as she ran to a car and kissed the man in the driver's seat before climbing into the back.

The man inspected Sal, then looked up at the windows of the house before pulling away. Catching his eyes for a second, Sal saw that he was blinking back tears.

Kane realised he was holding a confession and a last testament. It was as if the pages were resonating in his hand, shivering like a prima donna's last spine-tingling note. Somehow, he knew Marie had wanted him to do something with these words, but he was entering murky waters for merely being in possession of it.

Why did she give it to me? Why not to Freya?

He held the notebook flat against the nervous rumbling in his stomach and cursed himself for letting something so important slip from his mind. He really did not need this burden, but Kane sensed he was at the beginning of something; he had somehow got locked into something that was far, far bigger than him.

Feeling tense, he walked through to his bedroom, opened the drawer and slipped into his mouth one of the pink pills he had taken every day for the past fourteen years. He did not need water to swallow it down anymore; it was as if a channel had formed in his throat, etched to the exact size and shape of these small, daily sacrifices. As he swallowed, Kane's mind slipped momentarily to Freya again, but with a toss of his head he shook her away, her image scattering like ripples across a reflection. Walking into the bathroom, he awkwardly stripped off his clothes, untied his sling and threw everything down in a pile. The instantly hot shower water coursed over him, opening his pores and pulling out the dirt, the exhaustion, the misplaced guilt. The water ran over and off the metallic gauze of his bandage.

Minutes later, the buzzer rang out, its crisp sing-song tones extending for much longer than a casual visitor would allow. Kane tightened and let the shampoo suds flow through his eyelashes as he stared at the door of the bathroom. It was unlocked. His flexed his toes, making them grip the plastic beneath him and turning the joints white. He moved his hand to turn off the shower.

Or would they have already heard it?

He decided to risk not answering the door. He could always say he hadn't heard the buzzer. He hung there, hand beside the shower sensor. It felt like minutes passed until the buzzer rang again, immediately followed by a clatter of bangs on the door. Kane cast his eyes over the pile of clothing on the bathroom floor and tried to remember where he had left the notebook.

And then it began. The thumping on the door ceased and Kane heard the release on the door open. He or she knew his code, meaning that it was probably a Sentry. In a way, he was surprised that it had taken them so long. They must have been waiting for him to be alone.

Tightening his jaw, he turned up the rate of the water flow, wiping out the noise of the stranger making their way through his apartment. He would have to try to play it cool. He started singing to himself as loudly as he could: Frank Sinatra's 'High Hopes.' The notes threw themselves back at him from the glass; he was cocooned in his own voice, dampened with heat, moisture and panic.

Kane had convinced himself so fully, it took several moments for him to realise that a man was standing in the doorway of the bathroom. Only the cool, dry breeze alerted him. He made himself jump and feigned shock through the misted-up glass, peering cautiously around the shower door.

'What the hell?' Kane tried to tread the fine line between surprise and disgruntlement as he reached for a towel to wrap around his waist.

'You didn't hear the buzzer?' the man asked, smirking as the doorbell rang out again, loud and clear in the bathroom.

So there were two of them at least.

'The door was shut. I was singing.' Kane smiled winningly despite the thudding of his heart. 'Loudly. I'm sorry.' He gestured to the man to back out of the bathroom and the man did, moving into the lounge. His companion walked into the room at the same time, returning from the front door.

They were Sentries, sure enough. They turned up at work a lot, sticking their noses in and asking questions, and by now he could tell them straight off: brash ties and smart three-piece suits, old-fashioned haircuts and narrowed eyes. They all wore the same outfits they had spent a month's earnings on in the days when Canary Wharf was still buzzing with profit, before the Europe-wide tumble, before the Takeover. These were the men and women who would still do anything for money, and the State loved them for it.

Their expressions were weary, impatient. They clearly didn't have time to waste; the one who had not spoken yet was already holding Marie's notebook in his hand. Kane just had to hope they had already expended their energy on another fight today.

'What's this, Mr Ong?' the second Sentry asked, waving the notebook. His face was small, with sharp features. His nose was a classic piece of old-fashioned cosmetic surgery; poker straight and oddly narrow across the bridge. His nostrils flared slightly as he spoke. Kane would have to be careful, but if pushed, a well-timed fist towards the nose might put this one off.

'Would you mind ever so much if I just put some clothes on first?' Kane asked in his most camp voice. There were times when stereotypes could work in his favour.

The one with the narrow nose curled his lip slightly,

almost imperceptibly. 'Please sit down,' they uttered in perfect unison. Kane sometimes wondered whether they were human at all, but for the ravages of their faces, features so lined and worn by tough times that they couldn't possibly have been replicated.

Kane sighed and sat on the arm of the sofa, tucking the towel more tightly about his waist. He waited for them to sit opposite him, but they continued to stand.

The Sentry who had found him in the bathroom raised his eyebrows. 'I'm waiting. And I don't like waiting. You are a survivor of the bombing on Frith Street on Saturday night, correct?'

Kane nodded. 'I guess you could say that.' He knew it was best just to tell the truth straight away, as much as he hated to give in to the Sentries. 'I tried to save this girl—the girl whose notebook that is—was. I took her to the hospital but she died in surgery on Sunday morning. She gave me that,' he said, pointing at the notebook, which was already being slipped into a pocket.

'And you've read it?'

'Oh no, not properly, I just flicked through.' Kane did not even believe himself. He had always been such a terrible actor.

The Sentry asking the questions, clearly sensing the lie, narrowed his eyes and his eyebrows crept upwards. He stood and walked towards Kane, who reflexively sat straighter, like an animal trying to increase its bulk in the face of a predator. After all, he could not run.

'You've read it.' It was not a question this time.

Before Kane could answer, the Sentry plunged at his neck, pressing a metal-like piece of string against it and pulling it tightly up against his jawbone. The Sentry's knee came up onto the sofa, pinning Kane by his groin and grasping his head with fists. Kane choked and his vision swam as the blood pooled in his cheeks and throbbed behind his eyeballs. The pressure of the Sentry's body was painful against his broken arm. But he tried not to struggle, flexing his good hand and fighting the urgency to claw at the man's face. He was sure they would let him go if he acquiesced.

While the Sentry exerted his force, the other one spoke in a chillingly collected tone. 'This was not yours to see. You don't know anything about the bombing. You don't know who did it or why. Understand?'

Kane tried to nod, the blackness creeping around him.

'You will not mention this to anyone, and if you already have, you will say that you were wrong. We don't want to have to come back here.'

The rope released and Kane slipped from the sofa to his knees on the floor, tenderly feeling the skin around his neck with his good hand. They had already turned away and were letting themselves out.

He had got off lightly.

7

Freya had struggled sightlessly through Sunday and Monday and was now walking home after leaving work promptly. As she wandered south across Tower Bridge, she ran her fingertips along the blood-red handrail, casting her eyes over the cavities from which ancient emblems of lions and coats of arms had been torn decades before. She should not have even gone into work, her head teacher had said to her as she left, suggesting that she had the following day off. Yet there had been moments during the last few hours in which she had started to feel at peace, blurry and rested as if warmed by a few glasses of vintage brandy, before her mind had pulled her back to the events of Saturday night.

She remembered watching the nurse lift each of Marie's blistered arms in turn, carefully wrapping them with a clear, gel-like material. Her eyes had lingered on the charred white tissue and the gaps, grey holes where flesh used to be, filled by the gleaming, milky white of bone. She had laid her shaking hands on top of Marie's fingers. *Try not to touch her anywhere else,* the nurse had said. Freya had felt the shock and fever palpably oozing, clammy, from Marie's palm as she whispered her dying thoughts.

Yes, the events of Saturday seemed so inconceivable, already so distant. Yet her heart, which had seemed fragile but resolutely solid before, now felt as if it had been torn in half and handed abruptly to two people she had known for what was really no time whatsoever. It was a feeling that bore some resemblance to aspects of her past, to things she had long since given up on and tried to forget.

Freya had always been a sensible girl; she never worried

her mother by having boyfriends years older than her, possessing motorbikes or drug habits. At school, she had been seen as stand-offish and, because she was pretty, somewhat above herself for not socialising with the opposite sex, but it had simply not been something that had interested her to any great extent. At least, not until the second week into her teaching degree, when, as the cliché would have it, she bumped into Dylan and spilt the contents of her bag all over the canteen floor.

As her feet fell over each other in their rush to get home, Freya remembered the moment with absolute clarity. Through the dark autumnal evening, his dappled amber eyes glowed in her memory as if she had just beheld them for the first time. The exchange that evening, all those years ago, had been brief; the awkward moment filled with the embarrassed giggles of a girl who had no idea how to flirt with a man and the silence of a boy who had no idea what to say. Later, he told her that he had been dumbstruck by the sight of her long hair falling from its loose ponytail as she leant over, falling in waves over her shoulders. She would never admit to him that it had been love at first sight, or love as she thought it might be, appearing from nowhere, unwanted and unexpected: an event horizon.

Weeks later, they spotted each other in the student bar during an amateur comedy routine and rolled their eyes at each other at precisely the same time. In that little shared gesture, as such things so often do when someone already enraptures you, it seemed that their fate was sealed. Later that night, after a shy kiss in the corner of the room, they shared their Backgrounds for the first time, albeit somewhat adjusted and personalised to the person opposite them; a potential future partner, and the vanishingly small but ever-present chance that this could be the person they would share a vast proportion of their lives with. They went into it with their hearts pushed open as wide as they would go.

Dylan's Background, it appeared, was fairly standard. Little stood out to shock or to inspire awe—a relatively high risk of heart disease and a few other minor ailments, a few personality traits that needed to be kept in check, but nothing more. Freya did tell him the full extent of her Background in that first conversation; she knew that. Those were the old days, and she had drunk a couple of glasses of wine and nothing else. Dylan, however, had drunk a significant amount more than that. Several months later, they were sitting in an empty lecture theatre chatting when it suddenly came up again.

'Freya—I have an admission to make,' Dylan said. He pulled his head back into his shoulders and looked coyly through his lashes at her.

'What?'

Her nervousness, always just lapping at the edges of her consciousness, shot to the fore. She found herself gripping her hands together in her lap, bracing herself.

'When we first met—I was really drunk.'

'Were you?'

'Yeah, I'd been there all afternoon.' He shrugged and laid his hands on the table. 'So, to be honest, I don't remember anything you said to me. I only knew to call you the next day because Jay told me to, and you'd put your contact details in my Index. So, although none of that should matter now'—he paused to place his hands on hers, lowering his voice apologetically—'I still don't know your Background.'

Freya felt suddenly cold as she looked back at him, shifting her gaze to stare through him. All this time she had thought he'd accepted her for who she was, but he had no idea. He must have completely missed or written off all the references she had made to 'making the most of their time together' to her natural sentimentalism. As they sat there, Dylan awaiting her reply with an increasingly confused look upon his face, she had a strange sense that this might become a turning point in her life.

'Why haven't you mentioned this before?'

'I felt so bad that I couldn't remember, and I thought it would eventually all come up in conversation anyway, but you're quite a private person. And ...' He trailed off and wrapped his arms about himself, looking around the empty room. 'And now this feels, well, serious.'

'Serious?' Freya was baffled.

'I know we've only known each other a few months, but don't you think it feels like this is really going somewhere? You know I'm crazy about you,' he murmured shyly in his usual manner, with the characteristic half-formed smile and gentleness that she found so handsome.

She could only bring herself to nod as she began to ask herself how he would take the information. She could feel her face hardening as she closed herself off. She wondered whether she could excuse herself, if it would be better if they could have this conversation another time, but he carried on talking.

'I mean, it hardly matters—I feel like I know everything about you, about who you are—but it's just the medical stuff I've been wondering about lately. I mean, if we were to have kids or anything …'

'Kids?' Freya exclaimed. She barely knew where to begin.

'So is there anything?' Dylan's face was starting to show signs that he understood he might not like the answer to his question.

Freya stared back at him, trying to remember how she had told him the first time, how she had built up to it, how she had made it seem fleetingly important in the grand scheme of things. She had thought at the time that she had pulled it off rather well. He had dismissed it out of hand in a manner that she thought was just polite but now, for the first time, realised might have been in blurry misunderstanding.

'Dylan, I'm not well,' she found herself saying as time slowed down, curving awkwardly around her. 'I have an early-onset form of Huntington's disease. The exhaustion, the aches and pains …?' she asked him, her brow furrowed. He shrugged and shook his head slowly, his mouth fallen open. Freya started to cry before she could summon the energy to begin speaking again.

'I only have until I'm thirty, maybe thirty-one,' she managed through her sobs. She wanted to get away from here, to be distanced from the unbelieving gaze in front of her.

'You'll what? Die?' The words were crisp, shot forcefully through horrified lips. The tone that bore them made Freya stand up and gather her belongings quickly, shakily, into her bag, adrift in her emotions.

'No, but the disease will start and I won't be the person I am now. I won't be *me* anymore. So forget it, forget all of this.' Shuddering, she threw her bag over her shoulder and started to walk away. 'Find somebody else.'

The last words were almost a scream, both it and the tears inside her head loud enough to drown out the effort Dylan was making to call her back to him. She did not, could not hear him; she was overwhelmed. She walked back to her flat in the rain, relieved that it hid her tears to the passers-by.

She heard nothing for a week. Then, a package appeared in her locker with her name written in impersonal capital letters on the front. She sat down on her bed that night to unwrap it. Inside there was a small box and a note, which she read first. It was brief and bewildering: *Freya, I bought this for you and I still want you to have it—you deserve it a million times over. I'm so, so sorry and always will be. Dylan*

Inside the box, despite its red velvet exterior indicating quite clearly what was inside, Freya was stunned to find a slim, shining golden band set with a single, square diamond.

Freya's memories of that time were blurry; she had changed too much since then to expect them to be as crisp as they once were. She glanced down at the ring on her hand, which shone less brightly than it had done all those years ago, before slipping her hand under her coat and rubbing the skin over her collarbone. Already early evening was drawing in around her; clouds played against the sun caught between the soaring towers of London's skyline. She closed her eyes momentarily against the biting breeze and thought of Marie's odd manner and her intriguing words about magic and fate. She tried to run through in her mind everything she knew about Marie, but there was very little to summon.

She reached for her Index in her pocket. *Surely by now,* she thought, *surely he would have been in touch.* The screen blinked at her blankly and she slid it back into her pocket. Kane had taken her contact details, but she knew nothing about him, not even where he lived. Freya knew it was silly, really, for her to even hope.

She thought about how Kane had walked out of the hospital yesterday morning without even looking back. She closed her eyes and watched him leave again, one hand in his pocket, the other rubbing the back of his neck. It was as if he had switched something off inside, and she suddenly panicked that perhaps that really was it; perhaps she would never hear from him again. *Why do I repeatedly seek out men that I know will reject me?*

As a passing thought, it was jarringly close to the truth, and for a moment, it paralysed her. She stopped in the middle of the bridge and turned to lean out over the rail, gazing down at the icy, churning water. Freya folded her hands into her armpits, burying her chin into the nook they created. Anguished sobs, heated by time, bubbled out of her violently, like a volcanic spring.

The buzzer sang out again as Kane was pulling on the last of his clean clothes. He ruffled his hands through his hair and reluctantly opened the door.

'Hello, Kane,' the police officer said. First name terms were their new thing. He imagined she had been watching from somewhere nearby, waiting for the Sentries to leave. Her eyes flickered across the welts on his neck as she showed her badge. A hologram wavered in front of his eyes and he nodded her inside, gesturing for her to take a seat in the living area. He sat down opposite her.

'As you might've guessed, I'm following up on the people who were at the bombing on Saturday night. Our system tells us you were in the immediate vicinity.'

Kane nodded.

'I'm sorry you were injured,' she offered.

Kane shrugged; the faked formality of the situation irritated him, as glad as he was not to have a rope against his neck this time.

The officer rolled out an Index on the coffee table and nodded to Kane to indicate that she was recording their conversation. 'Would you mind telling me a bit about your experience of the incident?'

'Sure. I got there around ten, I'd guess, and started queuing for Kenny G's. Then I got chatting to this guy and we decided to go for a drink first up the road at that basement bar, the one with no sign outside.'

'Raith's?' the policewoman interjected.

'Probably, that sounds familiar,' Kane paused, reclaiming his train of thought and in parallel wondering why they even needed these details. *Why were they even pretending?* 'So we were there for a bit—I'd say about an hour or so, maybe more. I got talking to a woman in the bar and then we left together to walk back to the tube. As we were walking back in the direction of Kenny G's, towards the tube station, a girl appeared out of one of the side alleys and literally fell at our feet. She had scraped her knees and hands and we helped her clean up. Minutes later, the bomb went off.'

And she told us there was a bomb. And I didn't save her life. And she gave me something.

'And you broke your arm in the event?'

'Yes.'

'Is there anything else you can tell me?' The woman barely attempted to contain the ennui in her voice. It was all a front, a thinly-veiled attempt to make people believe nothing had changed. There are still police. They still investigate things. They are here to look after you. Honestly.

'I'm sorry, that's pretty much it. I really don't remember much else.'

'I see.' The officer paused before nodding and placing her Index back into her jacket. Her eyes narrowed and she scanned his face intently, morosely. Kane thought she might ask to look through his Index, but she seemed satisfied and limply reached out to shake his hand.

'Thank you, Kane.'

8

'Hello?' Despite being half-asleep, Inspector Kim Cheung instinctively swiped at her Index to trace the call. These days, she was rarely off duty. In the shadowy darkness of her bedroom, she pressed her hands against her cheeks and pushed her fingertips into her closed eye sockets as she listened. The line clicked for a while as sleep swirled around her, trying to pull her back in.

Eventually, a gruff, strange-sounding voice spoke six words before ending the call, not quite giving her Index enough time to identify the caller's location.

'It was the Anti-Genetics Movement.'

She had not heard the sound designating a video link, which in many ways Kim was thankful for. At this time of night, more often than not, the videos were in some way obscene. Men must find it a turn-on to call a female police officer, she had decided. They reacted oddly to her uniform and her position at times, in a way that never failed to fascinate her. Perhaps it was the image of fallen glory that turned them on, the desire to have a woman who had once been powerful, who now could be handled as they wished. It was always older men, ones who still held, or at least pretended to hold, the naive belief that she might have some vestige of real authority. Normally, she would manage to identify the caller and send one of her heavyweight male colleagues over to question them or bring them in. That was always fun.

Kim rolled onto her back, let her Index curl up on top of her stomach and sighed out through the tiny gap between her lips. For a few minutes she practised her yogic breathing, counting the seconds as she filled and emptied her lungs, pushing out her abdomen, blowing the air out steadily through her nose. Calls in the middle of the night were not unusual in her line of work, but they did not cease to irritate her. There was nothing that could not be said in normal working hours.

She glanced at the time with one half-open eye and groaned as she switched on the lamp. So it was morning then. *Why at five a.m.?*

Out of a habit bred from recognising her inability to recall things hours after the event—a lack of key detective skills which had embarrassed her more than once—Kim repeated the caller's message aloud and watched the words appear on screen. *Save.* So, perhaps it was not as straightforward as the random attack of a lunatic which had been reported. Of course not, that would have been far too obvious. Perhaps it was not even rooted in homophobia, as she herself had suspected.

She placed the Index back on the bedside table and turned off the light. The room slipped back into darkness and the sharp light of the bulb repeated like a ghost across her vision when she closed her eyes. She slipped quickly back to sleep whilst mulling over in her head the possible significance of the unfamiliar phrase.

Two hours later, Kim strode into her office, a mug of steaming water and sliced lemon in her hand. She was in her casual clothes, no uniform. Today was going to be a desk day; several solid hours of reading, research and phone calls. Her three members of staff were already there, hunched over their desks and archaic computers. They suspected that they had been told to wrap up the case, and they knew, if so, that Kim would be ignoring that order for as long as possible.

'What's new, lads?' she hollered as she slammed the door behind her.

They grumbled, one lifting a hand in acknowledgement. They were, in her opinion, useless, although one of them had a bit of character, something about him that suggested he could go a long way.

'Nothing new's turned up then?' she asked.

'Nah,' replied one of the men, barely turning his chair to face her. 'I was hoping we'd have traced his Tag by today, but no luck. He must've had it cut out. I've been through all the standard stuff—birth diagnosis, family and friends and so on—but it's nothing we didn't already know.'

'Msembe?' she asked, directing her attention to the man at the other end of the office, sitting alertly with his legs crossed out in front of him.

'Yes, ma'am?'

She did like how he always called her that, and she smiled graciously at him.

'I want to task you with something in particular. I got one of my phone calls early this morning. Not a dirty one this time, but it was at five a.m.—*so* bloody unnecessary. It was definitely organic, sounded like a man but could have been a woman. The call was brief and I didn't have time to trace it, but it seems to be a lead of some kind. Maybe towards a dead end, but you never know. Have you ever heard of something called the Anti-Genetics Movement?'

Ivan Msembe shook his head, sticking out his bottom lip.

'No, me neither. But I want to know everything you can dig up on it, unconfirmed or whatever, sources or not. Anything. Get what you can to me by the end of tomorrow. If you can, see if you can find any links between them and this Winstan guy. I don't think he's a random psycho after all.'

Msembe left it ten minutes until everyone had settled back into the rhythm of their working day and then left the office, letting the others know he had to make a call to his doctor. He walked down the corridor and slipped into the lift as the door began to close. The pretty brunette from the floor above pressed for the exit level and smiled at him. That was unusual; he had been grinning at her for weeks with no payback. Pleased, he smiled back and winked.

Leaving through the revolving doors, he stepped out onto the square. It had started to cloud over, but the cover was still wispy and cotton boll white, no sign of rain yet.

There had been only a few days of rainfall over the past few months. It was a bit early in the year still for regular rain; when October hit then they might get some. It was certainly needed. Msembe suddenly remembered he had not watered his tomatoes the previous day and he pictured them now, yellow and shrivelled. The allotment manager would tell him off again for neglecting his duties. He ran a hand over the stubble of his shaved scalp.

He crossed the street carefully and walked straight into the park, casually checking over his shoulder to see if anyone was behind him. He found his usual bench, looking out at the island in the middle of the lake where the birds nested, and sat down. He checked around him. It was still early and most people were walking quickly along the path, late for work or rushing their children to school. No one was sitting nearby. He held his fingertip against the Tag in his neck.

'Angie,' he commanded, and it automatically dialled in. She picked up halfway through the first ring and a little video link appeared in Msembe's vision.

She looked different from the last time they had spoken; her hair was now a very dark, chocolate brown and a little longer than usual, falling halfway between her jaw and shoulders. It looked like it might be her natural colour, and he thought it set off her features well. He liked to admire her; he thought that there might be something between them, despite the age gap. *One day, perhaps,* he thought.

'Ivan—this is a surprise. How are you, my dear?' She smiled sweetly.

'I'm very good, Angie. How are things?'

'Well, I'm sure you can imagine. We're all very nervous. I've got them triple-checking the security this morning.'

'That's a good idea, given the nature of the situation.'

'So, what's happening? Are we out there yet?'

'My senior got the phone call early this morning. She couldn't trace it. It's worked out quite well so far, and luckily enough, I'm the one with the job of finding out more about you!'

'Ha! Really? Isn't it nice when things work out like that? Well, I think I can leave you to it. You can put out as much as you need, barring names and locations, obviously. If you're pushed for sources, we'll figure something out. It's a fine line we're treading here.'

Msembe let her words fade into white noise and paused for a minute, looking away from the screen and out across the lake. He pressed his lips together and squeezed his eyes shut. A woman wrapped in a pink coat was walking her dog, and a group of men were out jogging together. All these people; all just trying to get on with their lives.

'Did you know that many people would ...?' The words fell out of his mouth quickly and awkwardly. The last word was left unspoken; it might have triggered an alert on the line despite their precautions. Angie was silent for a few seconds. Msembe closed his eyes temporarily, fighting the urge to look at her expression.

'Ivan, we need to focus on the next steps.' Her voice was calm and level. 'You *know* that.'

The emphasis was clear: *We went through the options. You knew exactly what we were planning to do. You know what is important. You know what is at stake.* She did not have to say any of that for Msembe to understand every one of her multiple meanings. He averted his eyes from her frozen oval face and nodded.

'There's something else,' she continued. 'I've heard that some Sentries have got hold of a vital piece of the puzzle. They've virtually got Sal's testimony—a funny thing. Apparently it's the record of a conversation a woman had with Sal shortly before the bombing. Who knows what they'll do with it? It's probably already destroyed.'

'Really? Who would he have talked to, and why? Have you got it?'

'No, but I'd be curious to see it.'

'Do you know who they got it from?'

'Yeah, a guy called Kane Ong, living at 3F Warwick Crescent Block.' Angie paused, her attention diverted by something beyond Msembe's vision. 'We'll meet in person next time—I'm not convinced the fortress on this link is good enough.'

The video link disappeared down to a point, and then to

nothing. Msembe sat alone for a little while before walking back to the office, picking up a freshly roasted coffee on the way.

9

Barney and his wife had been visiting their grandchildren in Devon for the past two weeks. As they walked up the stairs of their apartment block in leafy north London, he could still smell the salt and sun cream seeping out from the curls of his beard. He felt relaxed, clear-headed. And for once, he felt truly retired, years after he had actually stopped work. As he followed his wife into their first-floor flat, he stopped on the doormat she had trampled across, looked down and chuckled aloud.

'Ha! Leila—look at this.' He bent to pick up the oblong of crisp white paper and held it up to her proudly, in the same way his grandson had presented them with shells at the beach that morning. She was already unpacking their bags on the kitchen table. 'An envelope—a letter!' he exclaimed, waving it in the air.

Leila watched him closely as childish delight played across his face, smoothing the wrinkles.

'Oh, honey, simple things do please you, don't they?' She mocked him playfully but showed interest in the letter, walking around the kitchen counter to him and taking it. Her eyes scanned the jagged, capitalised writing across the front but she could not immediately find a place for it in the contact book of her memory. It had been awkwardly, carefully written. She shrugged and handed it back to her husband, wandering away to the bedroom with their smallest suitcase. She would leave the larger one for him. She was old-fashioned like that; they both were.

When she returned ten minutes later to get a glass of water, Barney was reclined in his armchair with one hand over his slackened mouth, his thumb pressing into the hollow between his teeth. The letter lay on the floor beside his slippered feet.

'Barn?' She perched beside him on the arm of the chair, slid her arm across his back and rubbed gently as if he were a baby she was trying to burp. She searched his face for clues. His eyes were clamped shut, juxtaposed against his loose jaw. She kissed the top of his head, deliberately on the patch the size of a five-pound coin where no hair grew now, and rested her cheek there, staring at a mark on the wall. 'What's wrong, honey?' she asked.

He still did not answer her, only shaking his head. Leila slowly leant down and picked up the crumpled letter, and he did not try to stop her.

Unlike the envelope, the letter was printed, typed in a simple, typewriter font. It was brief and she skipped to the end at once. It was signed in pen with a single letter S, curling boldly, angrily across the bottom quarter of the page. She turned back to the beginning and read. It was dated over a week beforehand.

Barney,

I hope you and your family are well. Give my love to Leila, and to Lotty and Andrew. I'm sorry it's been so long since we last caught up but I've thought about you all a lot.

By the time you read this, you will have heard about a bombing on a nightclub in London. That was me, on behalf of an organisation called the Anti-Genetics Movement. I agree now with what you said that time when you visited me, and I'm sorry for what I've done, Barney, but I just 'followed the rules.' I hope that by doing this, I will make more people think about birth diagnosis and those it victimises. I'm writing to you not only to say goodbye but also to ask for help, because I can't be sure that my actions will be enough. You must do something. If anyone can find a way to change things for the better, it's you.

I don't mean to burden you. You have always been there for me, you've been my father, and I thank you for that.

S

Leila read the letter once more in silence and then looked at her husband curiously. He had opened his eyes now and his hands were resting on his knees. He was pale.

'Sal,' he said, answering her unspoken question.

She nodded once, slowly, recognising the name and remembering the story—one of many, but distinctive in its own way. *You've been my father.* She recalled the particular fondness Barney had for this boy and tears pricked at her eyes. She tried to sit quietly, letting the questions bubble up and out without being asked.

'I didn't know there had been a bombing,' she said quietly. He shook his head.

'Well, we haven't really been in touch with the news for the last couple of weeks, have we?' He stood and walked to the kitchen. To make a cup of tea, she imagined. She settled into the warm hollow he had left in the chair, hugging her knees into her chest and then clicking her fingers. Their little old-fashioned television sprang into life.

'Local news,' she called to it.

Barney came back to sit on the other chair and they watched for a little while in silence before they realised that the report they were waiting for would never begin. Barney scanned through his Index instead, searching for any blogs and maverick reports online that might have survived the State's blockades. He eventually found one and read it aloud to Leila.

'The police investigation into the apparent suicide bombing of the gay club Kenny G's has been formally closed by the State as of today. The bomber, Salman Winstan, is confirmed to have been a twenty-eight-year-old man, working in London as a cleaner. Winstan was known to be at risk of violent behaviour and had previously served time in prison for grievous bodily harm.

'This reporter has discovered that a week after the incident, one hundred and thirty-two people have been confirmed dead and seven people remain in a critical condition in hospital. Is this tragic event likely to reignite the underground debate surrounding genetically indicted people? I'd like to think so. While you won't see pictures of it on the

State news channels, there are already protesters on the scene bearing banners, demanding why Mr Winstan—a young man with a high risk of violence and evidence of such—had been released back into society. An insider at Scotland Yard has told me they were fully aware of the Background of this individual. His behaviour had been judged as stable by a number of psychiatrists, and on this basis he was released from prison at the end of his sentence for bodily harm. It seems possible that on this occasion there simply wasn't close enough psychological monitoring of this individual, but why isn't this being investigated? The State has labelled the bombing as the random action of a mentally unwell individual and has reiterated that there appears to be no further immediate risk to the public.'

Barney wondered to himself how Sal could have thought that an anti-genetics organisation would have ever received credit for the bombing. Everybody knew that the State and those that funded it were keener than ever to promote their genetics programme. There was no way that an organisation like this would be given airtime through any public channels. It would be hushed up, like every other anti-establishment opinion. Yes, it might cause a small buzz online and by word of mouth, but despite the tragedy of the situation, it was not enough of a scandal to keep tongues wagging.

'One hundred and thirty-two people,' Leila murmured under her breath, disbelieving. 'Did you ever have any idea that he would be capable of something like that?'

Barney shook his head and shrugged sadly, but his mind freewheeled. They both sat quietly for a little while longer: Leila wondering what Barney was thinking, Barney struggling to consolidate what it was that he himself was thinking. As the television tinkered to itself and Leila sat staring at her hands in her lap, he thought back to his little office, set within the red brick courtyard that held the local library. He had liked to slip out at lunchtimes to the second floor of the library, leafing through the books on zoology and evolution on its shelves, his extracurricular interest. He had found animals and plants—he had loved gardening, too, back when it had been legal to do it creatively—a distraction from the emotional traumas of his human clients. Nature always offered a perfect balance, a simplicity that the children he counselled had never known.

He had been sat in his old wooden chair with the worn velvet cushion against his back when Sal and his mother first appeared. He had listened pleasurably to the whispering outside the door as Cherry coaxed Sal into knocking. The two little raps rang out from so far below the door handle that Barney knew before they entered that Sal was small for his age, a wiry stoat of a seven-year-old. Barney remembered how they had all ended up sitting on the floor near the window, cuddling cushions to their stomachs, mirroring each other in their growing trust. Sal had been glum and unwilling at first, but Barney's kindness and patience—his forte, he knew—had won him over in a few short hours. He recalled fondly the first time he had made Sal break out in that starburst of a smile with the offer of a trip to the zoo for their meeting the following month. Sal had been grateful, much more so than any of the other children he worked with during his career.

Barney's stomach scrunched up as he proposed to himself now, for the first time consciously, whether it was Sal's appreciation he had loved so much: an ego boost to the old man he had been even then. Perhaps. But still, Sal had been a journey, like they all had been in different ways. Lacking in love, it was no wonder that he could not cope when he found it in that girlfriend of his.

When Barney saw him those times in prison several years ago, Sal's emaciated form had been a shock. A certain shine had left his eyes that Barney recognised very well indeed. It was when the light went out that the real trouble began. Barney had sat there opposite Sal across the thick plastic divide and thought of the children he had seen, already with no light left. They had often lost it at too young an age to get it back. Many geneticists would say they had been born without it, but he knew differently. It could be retrieved, it could be conjured from somewhere, sometimes only from a single trip to the zoo, sometimes from years of conversations. Barney had looked across at Sal one of those days in prison and had a strange sense that the young man had already decided to extinguish himself. His tone was one of hopelessness. A theory that Barney had hardly consciously formed into words before had appeared in the space between them at that moment, scribbled thoughtlessly on a piece of paper, hanging in their minds for longer and more loudly than they should have done.

I don't believe in any of it any more, Sal.

What a bombshell it had been for Barney, that life-changing admission. And how odd that he had made such a statement to one of his patients who had done exactly what his Background had instructed him to. Why had he not voiced this conspiracy theory to someone who had ended up living a decent life, to someone who had learned to curb their supposed tendencies, from someone who *hadn't* followed the rules? But from that moment, his own words had emboldened him and taken hold around his heart. In his late fifties, he had acknowledged to himself that he wanted to fight. But he had been about to retire; his grandchildren had arrived and tugged at his sleeve before he had figured out what he could actively do about this personal revelation. And now he was sat here, helpless and confused, with a call for help from beyond the grave he could not possibly imagine putting into action.

'Are you okay?' Leila asked.

Barney came round from his thoughts and felt she might have asked him that more than once in the past few minutes. They looked at each other at the same moment and then both stood to hug, without the need for words. Barney laid his head on his wife's shoulder and squeezed her as tightly as he had on their wedding day, albeit with an entirely different emotion. That day had been about saying how they felt, explaining why. Now he hoped to distract her from the ramping up of his emotions, from the thoughts and actions ordering themselves in his brain. They were so close to the surface and she knew him so well that he felt they must be evident to her; they rippled across him. He hid in her embrace, wondering what to do next.

The next day, Barney was reading the news on his Index as Leila rubbed on the wall in vain to try and remove a mark he could not see. A mug of tea steamed in front of him and he picked absent-mindedly at the remnants of scrambled eggs around the edges of his plate. Outside, it was the best of late autumnal days, sunny and still. The leaves on the trees were brown and amber, curled but intact. The sky was clear but for some thin, stationary strands of clouds.

'It won't come off, Barn. I think I might have to paint over it. Do you think that'll look odd? I'm worried it will look worse. I don't want to have to do the whole wall.'

'Um, I'm not sure.' He did not look up, and at that moment, his Index beeped and over the news screen appeared a private message. He accepted it and it opened in full.

Hello Barney, I need to speak to you about our mutual friend. He told me to get in touch—Angie.

As unexpected as the letter, the message instilled a very different emotion in Barney. He felt a sense of excitement, of intrigue, although deadened inside his chest, muffled beneath flesh and bone. He glanced at Leila but she had not noticed; her inquisitive eyes were not fixed upon him this time.

He tapped in a reply:

Where and when?

She responded immediately. Her reply must have already been written.

Here's a link to a map. Ring the doorbell when you get here. Come as soon as you can, but make sure you're not followed.

Barney thought about replying affirmatively but decided it was unnecessary. He slipped his Index into his pocket and walked to the bedroom. He had already dressed, but looking in the mirror, he decided he looked too scruffy in his loose jersey trousers and long-sleeved T-shirt. He changed quickly, unfolding his Index and laying it on the bed, watching it closely for further updates. He put on a dark pair of trousers and a shirt, tucking it into the waistband. He needed an excuse to get out of the house; he did not want to discuss this with Leila, although he felt bad for lying to her.

In her usual, perfectly-timed manner, she appeared in the doorway, one hand on her hip.

'Why are you getting changed?'

'I've got to go out, honey. I already told you, didn't I? I'm meeting Joe for lunch today in town.' Barney winced at his own lie, but he knew it was convincing because Leila smiled and winked, turning around and returning to her task without further questions. He tightened his belt and looked around for anything else he may need. Thinking of nothing beyond the essentials, he slipped his wallet and Index into his pocket and strolled out, kissing Leila on the way.

10

Kim Cheung had followed at a safe distance and she now sat in a café, watching them bid each other farewell from her concealed vantage point. Msembe was easy to spot in a crowd. He was tall, pushing two metres, and his shaved head revealed dark skin that always glowed with an attention-grabbing energy. She noted the seriousness of their profiles as Msembe and his female companion nodded firmly to each other and walked away in opposite directions. It was not the exchange of two lovers. Neither did it seem gentle enough to make them friends, nor business partners: there was no handshake.

Msembe walked out of sight into the trees of the park opposite and Kim dropped her gaze to the dregs of her coffee, letting her sunglasses slip lazily down to the tip of her nose. She sighed heavily and pulled the skin of her cheeks taut with her fingers. It seemed she could strike another member of staff from her trusted circle.

Kim was just about old enough to remember the early, riotous days of the Takeover, old enough to know that the police force had always had its problems, old enough to admit that things had not really changed. She and now just one remaining member of her team were among the few she could count as incorrupt. As she tried to count them now, swirling her cup in the palm of her hand like a rare whisky, not many names sprang to mind. Most were representatives of the State or had some other dark benefactor: they could be bought for a pay rise, for a promotion, for hard cash or as the result of a threat. Kim was not in the game for those kinds of deals.

She had captured a few photographs on her Index and she flicked back through them now. Zoomed in, the images were razor sharp, crisp enough to see the few strands of grey hairs on the woman's head. Kim knocked back the rest of her cappuccino and opened the facial recognition software. It brought up a name, and an accompanying ream of information filled the screen. This woman, despite her age, had a genetic diagnosis. That was still fairly unusual for someone of her generation. Kim herself was nearly a decade younger and she did not have one. *Although if the constant harassment continues, it won't be long,* she acknowledged to herself.

Angie Harker, female, 48. Genetic diagnosis filed at age 26. Key points include tendency to severe depression, high suicide risk, arthritis. Single. Unemployed. Spent conviction for smuggling and fraud.

Kim found the amount of information as overwhelming as always. She still found repulsion in it; a life lay bare, stripped before her eyes. Kim lifted her gaze out through the window and up to the trees edging the park. The woman she had seen had been well dressed, elegant even. She was made up, slicked with red lipstick and rouge, clothed in a wool and silk jacket. *She must be a serious operator,* Kim thought. She left quickly, jogging a different route back to the office, and was sitting in her chair when she heard Msembe return.

'Early lunch break?' she asked as she wandered back into the main office. It was eleven a.m. and he was sitting himself back down at his desk.

'No, I had an appointment with my doctor. I was last in the queue for the video link,' he said, shaking his head in an accurate mask of mild annoyance.

She watched him from the corner of her narrowed eyes, a familiar exhaustion creeping into her heart, before she stormed out of the office. She always got the scraps these days. The only reason they bothered to appease her at all was because her father was a high court judge with influence and fingers in political pies. This latest investigation had proved difficult. Leads were handed to her that to her experienced eyes had seemed too clean, too convenient. *Probably the action of a nutcase, or a homophobic attack, perhaps,* they had said, *but keep it on the low—we don't want people to be disturbed by it.* The case was now closed, but there was more to it, she knew there was. And there had been the phone call.

She walked out of the double doors and crossed the road to the park. She held her index finger to her Tag and called out a name. He would know what to do. Employed by the State news corporation or not, his network was growing in notoriety in underground liberal circles and amongst influencers. In the unrecorded world where non-electronic news content ruled, the spoken or written word exchanged in person was becoming the only way of spreading the truth.

This would spread like wildfire, surely. There was hope.

'Connor?'

'Kim?'

'Yes. Listen, I have come across something called the Anti-Genetics Movement. They did this bombing on Frith Street, I think to garner attention for their cause. I don't want to give them what they want, but ...'

'Look, I'm sorry, but you know if it's not on the news agenda then I just can't deal with this,' he said, pausing to allow her time to continue. It was a stock reply for anyone listening in. He was charmingly convincing, but she knew he meant exactly the opposite.

'But I have a name, maybe—Angie Harper. We need to find someone to hold accountable. Over one hundred and thirty people lost their lives, Connor.'

'Sorry. I'm really not interested, sweetheart.' He hung up and Kim smiled. *Sweetheart*—his key word. *Message received*, he was saying, *loud and clear*.

That evening, as Kim walked down the alley which was her shortcut to the bus station, she heard footsteps echoing behind her. She quickened her pace slightly without looking around and slipped the tips of her fingers over the tiny stunner inside her waistband. She took a deep breath and turned around, clasping it tightly in her hand.

'I'm armed,' she said clearly as she spun around, holding her hand open, just the thumb clasping the stunner to her palm.

'So am I.' Ivan Msembe smiled at her and angled his knife so that the moonlight ran down its serrated edge. He strode confidently towards her. She knew she could not stun him; a random stranger, yes, but not him. She would lose her job. The balance of power had shifted. Kim stood still as he slipped his spare hand around her throat and clasped it firmly.

'You know as well as I do that it wasn't an arbitrary attack, don't you?'

Kim struggled to nod, trying hard to keep the fear out of her eyes.

'But you don't need to worry about me, okay?' he whispered, aggression dancing through his tight grin. 'And you don't need to worry about Angie. Talk about the Anti-Genetics Movement all you want. *All* you want. But don't concern yourself with her.'

He drew away slowly and had turned to retreat when he seemed to remember one last point. He drew out the knife again and placed its point atop the skin covering Kim's Tag. He tapped once, twice, and Kim felt the inflexible edge of her Tag press sharply against her windpipe.

'We are listening to *every single fucking word you say*,' he said, punctuating each word, a vicious curl to his lip. He spun around and quickly walked away.

Kim watched until he reached the end of the alley and disappeared to the left. She trembled as she tried to compose herself and take the remaining, faltering steps to the bus station. So it was not the side of the State he was on. It was something else—perhaps this Anti-Genetics Movement. Whoever it was he knew, whatever it was he was mixed up in, she believed that he could have killed her there and then without causing any ripples. She should be thankful. Tomorrow, she would have to walk into that office as normal and smile at him and pretend to tell him what she wanted him to do that day.

Eventually, she thought, *this job will kill me.* It was just that she did not yet know whether it would be by the slice of a knife or by the desperation that comes with abject hopelessness.

11

Freya knocked three times, which was standard, she thought, not overly demanding but enough to be sure she was heard clearly. She noticed during the last knock, too late, a small bell at waist height on the edge of the door frame, and she wondered whether to press it as well. In fact, she wondered whether to turn and run.

Just then, through the translucent glass panels, she saw a large man lumber up the corridor, his sheer girth making him roll from left to right. The door opened and she was met with a stern glare. His eyes were gunmetal, boring into her with an intensity that took her aback. She was surprised to see that he was Caucasian, and pale at that: freckles on his arms and snowy white flecks through his dark grey hair. He was clean-shaven, and hairs sprouted from his nose and from patches on his folded neck. She watched his face as his eyes flickered across her chest and Freya felt as though she was stroking Marie's fingertips again in the ambulance. Her fading voice echoed in Freya's head.

'Hello. I'm looking for Marie's father?'

She paused. The man remained looking displeased.

'I was a close friend of hers,' she continued.

'Really?' He sounded genuinely surprised and regarded her suspiciously. He looked her up and down, more fully this time, from her hair to her feet, letting his eyes linger on the bare skin below her collarbone. Freya awkwardly looked away, aware that by doing so she was submitting in some way, already succumbing. She returned her eyes to his, fixing on him firmly, tensing her abdomen and holding up her chin.

'Might I come in?' she asked, hopefully.

Marie's father nodded cautiously and gestured her inside

down the dark narrow corridor. She wished she could have asked someone to come with her, but she walked into the house behind the man. A thick worm of dust lay where the carpet met the wall. The air smelt stale and she tried not to wrinkle her nose in distaste. They sat down opposite each other at the dining table. He did not offer her a drink.

Freya looked around the room as boldly as she dared. It was largely empty, entirely masculine in its decoration. There were a few cans on a shelf, a broom laced in cobwebs propped up in one corner. Her gaze caught on a bottle of vodka on a kitchen shelf, half-empty. She felt an immediate craving and looked away, down to the backs of her hands. She shivered a little as the relevant neurons in her brain fired and she imagined the cold sting of the vodka running down her throat and warming the pit of her stomach. There were other signs. Towards the back door, she noticed a neat line of bottles, all with the same red neck, and the same size. At first glance, she took him to be a litre-a-day man. Even at her lowest, she had never been that bad.

Out of the French windows that stood half-open, Freya could see that he took very little care of his allotment; it was weed-ridden and unkempt. He would be in serious trouble if a Sentry was to see it. It had been years since the State had added food cultivation to the Citizen's Pledge. Imports were expensive now, and the Head of State wanted Europe to be entirely self-sufficient. She searched amongst the weeds for the yellow flowers of courgettes or the tiny curling tendrils of peas but found nothing recognisable.

Along the right-hand side, though, against the fence, there was a neat strip of flowers. Cyan forget-me-nots and large orange blooms weaved around the base of three rose bushes. The marigolds, wallflowers and snapdragons of the English country garden were something people of Freya's age had only ever seen in picture books. The roses were magnificent, pink and full, tinged on the tips of the outer petals with a sunny yellow. She drew her breath in sharply, surprised. On the corner of the plot lay a little pile of deadheads and a trowel. Although it was just a small area, Freya knew that this indulgent display was virtually illegal at the moment, especially with the current food shortage and drought. The night of the bomb had been the first time it had rained for weeks, and Freya realised now that she had not noticed it rain since. On the way to the house, she had walked past two council workers digging up a grass verge for replanting.

'I'm so very sorry about your daughter,' Freya said, breaking the silence as she turned back towards him.

He shrugged, which could be interpreted as her death being nothing more than a minor inconvenience. Perhaps she had sounded too offhand. Or he was protecting himself, avoiding exposing himself to her, a stranger. She was intrigued enough to keep going.

'Were you close?' she asked.

'No, not for many years,' he said. She noted the slightest hint of sadness in his voice. Or had she herself placed it there? Had it slipped out through her tear ducts and found itself in his voice? He rubbed his bloodshot eyes with a thumb and forefinger and pinched the bridge of his nose. It seemed a familiar gesture, a habit, as if he was always a little bit sad. Freya wondered if she had a similar gesture of her own.

'I don't wish to be rude, but might I have a drink?' Freya asked. The words fell out before she could think about them. Like the automatic movement of a cockroach's legs, the question bypassed her brain. She inclined her head towards the shelf and its bottle.

He turned his head to follow her gesture and looked back at her with a wry smile across his face. She smiled back. As he poured generous shots into tall glasses they both sighed, at the same time, and then laughed. His was a deep chuckle, hers a light giggle, harmonising melodiously.

'Tonic or straight?' he asked.

'I'll have a little tonic, please. Half and half.'

'Ice?'

'Yes, thanks.'

He returned the glasses to the table and they both took a deep gulp. Freya savoured the moment of peace that followed.

'I paid for Marie's treatment in hospital,' Freya said, awkwardly. 'They couldn't find a next of kin on her Tag.'

'Oh,' he paused, staring at her face and then down at the table. 'Of course, thank you. I'll—I can cover that, obviously.'

'Thank you,' Freya smiled thinly. 'So when was the last time you saw Marie before …'

'She was my only child, but we fell out when she was a teenager. You know what teenagers are like. And we never really spoke since.' He scratched his nose and chewed at his lip and Freya saw the hairline fractures in his outwardly robust structure. He was cracked around the edges; irreparable damage that a few more years' wear and tear would shatter. 'She was a pretty girl, as you'll have found, and so clever. I tried to call her, quite often you know, every few weeks or so, but she kept changing the details on her Tag—must've got it done on the black market or something. She was always a streetwise kid. She wouldn't keep me updated on the new numbers. A few months would pass and I'd have to go for a walk around where I thought she was living at the time, asking people about her, trying to track her down. Sometimes I'd find her, more often than not I wouldn't. And then I'd wonder why I bothered at all. She didn't seem interested in me, really.' He paused for a few seconds, visibly concentrating, trying to remember. His defences had fallen.

'The last time I saw her was probably about a year ago. It might be longer—I can't remember, to be honest. Time just passes, doesn't it? It passes us all by so quickly.' He gazed out the window before continuing. 'I'd been looking for her around those tower blocks a little south of here—I'd heard she was back there with that boyfriend of hers. It was her birthday and I thought I'd better say hello. As I walked, I tried to call her and she picked up straight away. It was odd, because at that same moment I saw her, sat on a bench further down the path. It had never been so easy to find her before. Something in her voice made me hesitate, and I hid. Sounds stupid, doesn't it? And so I spoke to her, pretending I wasn't anywhere near her at all. When we finished talking I watched her stand up and walk away. She had a slight limp and I could see that she had a black eye, a huge bruise across her face. I wanted to go up to her but I'd just told her I was somewhere else. So I couldn't, could I?'

His last words invoked helplessness, invited her forgiveness. Freya had imagined this scene with absolute clarity as he spoke and she did not feel he deserved to be forgiven. Although she remembered so little of him, she knew that her own father would have run to her, held her in his arms and not said a word but taken her home, stroking her hair all the way, drowning her in his love.

'I'm sorry, I don't have much time,' he said, knocking back the last of his vodka and tonic, crunching on an ice cube. 'What else do you want?'

He had not asked for her Background. Clearly this was to be a brief meeting.

'Well,' she said. 'I know that Marie was interested in studying the stars … and I wanted to maybe have a look at her work. I never saw anything she had written and she spoke about it a lot.'

He was already standing up, his chair scraping back against the floor.

'It would mean a lot to me,' she begged.

'I haven't even looked at any of it myself,' he said. 'No, no, I really don't think so.'

'Please?'

'That's it, leave me alone now.' His voice had taken on a deeper, more commanding tone and he held himself upright. 'I'm sorry.' He did not sound sorry. Straight-backed, his stature was imposing. Under the duress of his glare, Freya stood. He walked her back down the corridor and opened the door.

'Okay, well, I'm sorry to have intruded, Mr …' She realised, too late in her urgency to be polite, that she could not remember his surname. Marie was just Marie to her. She must have seen it on her hospital records once or twice, but now, at this crucial moment, her memory failed her.

He did not miss the significance of her pause. His head snapped around, his lips pursed into an astute smile. He knew he had got her.

'Please leave my house,' he demanded roughly. He placed his hand between her shoulder blades and shoved her out of the door. Freya looked back over her shoulder, up each stair to the door at the top. At the last moment before Marie's father slammed the door in her face, her gaze fell upon a purple wooden M, laden with glitter, hanging lopsidedly from a wire.

As she walked down the road back towards the tube station, Freya thought back to her brain scan that morning. It had been less eventful than the last one, a year ago, in which the neurologist had calmly pointed out the areas of her brain that were showing signs of degradation. The helmet that took the scan was so uncomfortable and heavy that after the hour-long session, her neck still ached. She rubbed it now, pushing her thumbs into the knots at the tops of her shoulders.

There was every reason to be pleased with the results this time. The neurologist had said he could see no marked worsening since the last scan, which had come as a pleasant surprise. Had she been having migraines? Any problems with coordination, digit or limb control? He had looked confused as he peered at the screen over his spectacles. Freya had replied affirmatively and he then looked perceptibly relieved. *When I'm tired,* she had said, *at the end of a hard week at work, or if I've been to the gym and not eaten properly.* He had nodded and tapped some notes into the computer. *Well, that's to be expected,* he had said.

Freya had merely stared at the screen. Despite the seriousness of the situation, she never tired of seeing her brain appear before her, first in two dimensions and then in three, digitally overlaid with fluorescent colours so that it ended up looking like something that belonged on the wall of a nightclub rather than inside her head. It always looked so strange, so otherworldly in its folds and holes, like the topography of a long-lost land.

She had nothing to compare it to though, not really. *Each brain is different,* her neurologist had told her, which initiated the spark of a thousand questions she had wanted to ask him but had not, afraid to break the silence of the room. Hers, apparently, was just too different. Different enough that it would be her end.

After getting off the bus, Barney ambled in order to look aimless, scattering himself across streets haphazardly. It was not characteristic behaviour; he was a very deliberate, methodical man by nature. At home, the cutlery drawers were meticulously ordered, and the front door was repainted British racing green every year on the same day: 4 January. If any of his friends or family had been watching him, they would have been immediately suspicious. But to strangers, this sweet-looking old man, as Barney had finally accepted he was, just appeared to be meandering with no real purpose. A waitress might pause and watch him for a moment, her hand rested on her hip, wondering whether he had a wife at home or whether he was alone, wandering the streets seeking the company of strangers.

A few streets before reaching his destination, he stopped for a sandwich and a carton of apple juice in a little café and sat there for half an hour, reading the news on his Index. He even rang Joe to see if he did want to meet for lunch, wanting to cover his lie, but his old colleague was taking his girlfriend out for her birthday. Barney felt even guiltier and ordered a slice of carrot cake to take away, wrapping it carefully in a napkin and placing it in his satchel for Leila.

Finally, he got up and walked on—more directly this time—to the address, no longer recorded in his Index, but memorised. He slowed down as he approached the big house and glanced around. The street was quiet. It was one of those huge houses that looked as though it might have been stolen from the set of a suburban American drama series. Overlooked by statuesque oaks and surrounded by a wooden veranda, it was grand but poorly kept and in need of a caring hand. Curls of discoloured paint were peeling from the struts of the veranda so that they looked like the trunks of a birch tree.

Barney walked up the few steps of the stoop and rang the doorbell, feeling rather calm. Perhaps this was some kind of self-denial, he thought. A few shouts came from within, their words inaudible, and then footsteps rushed to the door. He noticed there was a little spy hole in the centre of the door and he imagined the person inside was observing him through it. He smiled and felt immediately like an idiot.

'What's your name?' The voice was polite. It might as well have been asking him if he would like sugar in his tea.

'Barney North. I'm here to see Angie. We made an appointment.'

'Angie!' the voice shouted. 'What does Barney look like?'

Barney could hear the call echoing down a hallway. He supposed that if he were younger, he would have heard her reply.

The door opened and a young man, possibly still a teenager, held out his hand. They shook hands firmly as the young man peered up and down the street.

'Hi, Barney. Angie is down this way.' He led the way along the long corridor, talking as they went. 'She's been looking forward to meeting you. We don't have that many people coming by, so it's always good to see a new face. I hear you're a psychologist—I've been told that I'd be good at that, it's really ...'

Barney had stopped listening. He was trying to take everything else in, glimpsing into side rooms and assessing pictures hanging on the wall, but it was all astoundingly mundane. He wondered to himself what he had expected. The walls were covered with peeling flock paper, dotted with pink geraniums that looked to be desperately clambering up the wall away from the ugly royal blue carpet. The woodwork had been painted white many years before. It was clumpy and thick; Barney could tell that no one had sanded it down before applying a new coat, and he almost clicked his tongue aloud.

'Here she is!' the man announced, disappearing up the stairs, and left Barney standing in a doorway.

Barney looked into the room. A woman, presumably Angie, was sitting with her back to him at a modern glass desk that looked out over the rear gardens of this street and the one running parallel to it. It was a lovely view, scattered with protected trees too old to clear for crop space. The yellowing blooms of late-flowering courgette plants blanketed the nearest section of ground. The sun had briefly appeared from behind a cloud and was shining in the window so that the reddish-brown henna in Angie's hair glowed. She looked at him over her shoulder and smiled. She was made up and well dressed with a grey woollen jacket on over a camisole. She had sharp, strong cheekbones but was soft around the edges, healthy-looking apart from the darkness under her midnight-blue eyes. He guessed she was in her forties.

'Barney,' she murmured.

She continued to beam at him graciously, and Barney began to wonder whether he had misjudged the whole thing and she was actually some long lost relative who had finally found him. She swung her chair around and gestured to a small sofa behind the door.

'Do sit down,' she said. Still seated, she scooted on the wheeled chair towards the door and closed it, using her feet to manoeuvre. She looked at him and tapped on her neck with her index finger.

'I'm pleased to say that we are free to talk here. My team have been working on some cutting-edge firewalls and fortresses that keep our conversations private. If a Sentry asks why you were here, you can tell them that I'm a clairvoyant. It's worked so far.'

Angie looked proud of herself as she gestured around the ordinary-looking room. 'So, why do you think I asked you to come here?' she continued. She had a similar tone of voice to that which he had used for his patients; calming and soft. He felt immediately younger than his seventy-three years.

'You knew Sal.' As he spoke the words, Barney sobered up slightly from his adventure. He saw something, some veiled emotion, flicker across Angie's eyes as she heard Sal's name.

'And ...?'

'And I think you probably have something to do with the Anti-Genetics Movement. I think you might know why Sal did what he did. That's why I'm here.'

The corners of her mouth curled up into a sad little smile that Barney took to be an agreement with his statements. He could see that he would be doing most of the talking. Something occurred to him then, and he looked back at the door through which he had come as he formulated the question.

'How did you know what I looked like?'

'We met once, sort of.' She laughed a little, a trill that rolled confidently off her tongue. 'I was in prison at the same time as Sal. You came to visit a lot. More than anyone else did, in fact. More than my own husband and daughter.'

She turned away and pulled a little notebook out of a desk drawer. Barney could see the drawer was full of similar books. She turned to a page in the middle and read aloud.

'I don't believe in any of it any more, Sal,' she read slowly, pausing and meeting his eyes. She was mimicking him— rather accurately, Barney felt—how he might have spoken the words himself. 'In the system, in birth diagnosis, in Backgrounds. Not in any of it.'

She sat back in her chair and rested her chin on her fist, waiting for the words to take effect. A knowing smile flitted across her lips. Barney looked past her, out of the window, beyond the rows of courgette plants, and breathed deeply. He remembered the moment of revelation, the mistaken conversation he and Sal had that day. He realised for the first time how it must have sounded to Sal: a slap in the face to an already condemned man. He had no words to respond with.

'We're on the same page—you, Sal and I,' she said quietly.

The comparison made Barney shudder. 'One hundred and thirty-two people? Robbing that many innocent people of their lives? No we're damn well not!' He heard the anger judder through his voice and it shocked him slightly. He felt his fingertips quiver with adrenaline he had not noticed before, and rage-sodden tears readied themselves behind his eyeballs.

'I think the toll is actually more than that now. But what is it that you no longer believe in again?' Angie was clearly not going to accept an attack. She leant forward now, her eyes narrowed.

'It's more a question of what I *do* believe in.' He sat firm, shoulders back. They had reached a deadlock. Angie poured water from a jug into glasses.

'Drink?' She held it out to him and he took it. 'Barney.' Her voice was syrup again. She was clever. 'Listen, Sal clearly trusted you. I've put a lot of trust in you to bring you here today. As you know, Sal was a very damaged young man. I saw in him the things I think you probably saw in him. I can assure you that he *wanted* to do what he did; there was no talking him into it. And we needed to build our profile, so ...'

She could have been a businesswoman, discussing her stake. Barney could tell she was poised to continue what seemed to be a rehearsed speech, but he did not want to allow her the privilege.

'So much for the profile-building,' he said. 'The official news corporations won't publish a word about your organisation claiming responsibility. The State will never allow your opinions to see the light of day.'

'I didn't expect they would; words can be so easily bought and hidden these days. But there *is* talk. It is already beginning.'

Barney stared at her, incredulous. 'Why are you doing this?'

'Why? Because what I do means something. I'm in a position, for the first time in my life, where I can effect change.' She paused and looked straight into his eyes. Her pupils were tiny, the muscles tightly contracted.

Barney knew what was coming next; he had a way of reading people that meant he knew when they were about to place their heart on their sleeve. She blinked as if to hide them, but she was about to reveal her deepest thoughts.

'I'm respected here,' she said. And then she shrugged and sat back as though it meant nothing.

But those three words mean everything, Barney thought. There was an emotional trigger concealed in them. For her, as all things were for everyone, this was personal. He nodded lightly, as if she had told him nothing of much interest at all. He had forgotten how much he enjoyed these games; it had been a long time since he had last played them. He gulped back some water and stood, walking behind her desk to the window. He would be in charge of this conversation now.

'What do you believe in?' he asked, levelly. He did not look at her, but stared out through the glass, to an oak tree, spreading its middle age across the back gardens. The low-lying winter sun shone from behind it so that it burnt golden-green.

'Let me tell you, I don't have the first clue about the actual genetics. It's really not my strong point. It could all be perfectly correct, as far as I'm concerned … although I don't think it is. If you want to talk about belief, what I *don't* believe is that people, born or unborn, should be judged on the basis of their genes. It's like people are blind to it. They just can't see that they're all in some kind of caste system and that it's like apartheid all over again.' She paused momentarily, gathering her breath and trying to swallow back some of her passion. 'I think you cared very much about Sal and that you want to understand what happened. And you want to know it wasn't your fault.'

It was a cunning tactic, but Barney avoided looking at her, putting her attempt to infiltrate his emotions to the back of his mind. He heard the desk drawer open again. Angie stood across the desk from him and held out a battered black notebook. Where her sleeve was drawn back, he could see the unmistakeable scars of a serious burn, but he quickly averted his eyes. He settled on the windowsill and took the notebook. Slipping his finger under the elastic, he opened the cover and began to read the frenzied sentences.

As he absorbed the contents, Angie spoke quietly. 'This came to us from one of my girls—one who sleeps with people in high places. A man on the scene of the bombing handed it to a pair of Sentries last week.' She paused and smiled sardonically, waiting for them both to acknowledge that there was no way anything had been given away so freely to the sleazy representatives of the State. 'He had some sort of connection to the woman who wrote this account, and she, it seems, had some sort of connection to Sal, however brief.'

As Barney read, an unofficial version of Sal's Background leapt from every page. Every sentence was familiar, and the hardened vulnerability rang true to Sal's voice.

'I thought you might want it,' she continued. 'Maybe it's just a keepsake, but I thought … well, I don't know, maybe you'd want to find out a bit more about it.'

Barney took his eyes from the paper to watch her speak, his brow furrowed. She was difficult to read but he had no doubt she was using him. She was barely making an effort to pretend otherwise. Did he really want to get caught up in all this?

'If you do, the man is called Kane Ong and he lives here.' Angie placed a scrap of paper on the table. Barney sighed and picked it up, slipping it inside the book.

'Maybe,' he replied. 'What's the woman's name?'

'I don't know.'

'Where is she now?' he asked.

'She's dead,' Angie sighed, as if this was awfully inconsiderate and unhelpful of her.

'In the bomb?'

Angie nodded. 'Well, if you do find anything, let me know,' she said, more brightly.

'Why, so you can blow some more people up?' Although he felt like throwing it onto the desk, he thrust the book into his satchel. He did not intend to return it, or to come back here. He walked towards the door and opened it.

'No,' he heard her say, quietly, as he walked out. 'So we can give people back their freedom.'

Barney's heart pounded in his chest as he let himself out and walked down the street. His feet fell over each other in a rapid pace and he admired the ability of his body to still carry him where he needed to go, as quickly as he wanted to leave. He needed to get home, to sit in his chair with a cup of tea, away from the world. He usually loved to open the door and see Leila there, but for once he hoped that she was out so he could be alone and without questions for a little while.

His neurons tangled over each other, new knowledge and old memories binding together. The connections fizzed off each other, messily. He felt stupid to have been so

unprepared. The woman could well be mentally disturbed—
she could have been armed. Why on earth had he gone? Was
he now complicit?

He felt the extra weight of the notebook in his otherwise
almost empty bag. He had gone because of Sal. And the
anger festering in his stomach finally found its source: The
boy he had tried so hard to nurture, to help along a path.
The teenager who had promised that he would always try his
best, and would try to break the mould set for him. Barney
had obviously been so wrong about him, to only realise now,
too late, that he could do such harm, such evil.

And then, from nowhere, Angie's damning words floated
to the surface, as Barney had known they would when she
said them: *You want to know it wasn't your fault.*

He clenched his hands into fists by his sides. He would
not be deceived. She wanted him for something, but
whatever it was, she would not get it. He strode so fast that
his sides ached and his mouth grew dry. He marched like
that all the way home and, relieved to find Leila's note on the
kitchen table saying she had gone shopping, placed her slice
of carrot cake in the fridge, ran a bath and read the
notebook, not once or twice, but over and over again, tears
running down his cheeks until he felt sick with dehydration.

After Barney left, Angie took a very deep breath. It was not
often she met new people. In fact, she spent most of her
time trying to avoid people. She found such meetings
exhausting; her new easy, workmanlike attitude was one she
was still cultivating. It did not come naturally to her. *But then,
what did?*

She stood and walked around the room twice, dragging
her fingertips along the walls and pacing in deep thought.
Exiting her office, she walked up the stairs to the biggest
bathroom. She closed the door and locked it. She put down
the toilet seat and sat, resting her chin in her hands. She felt
tired and tearful but continued to breathe deeply, swallowing
the feeling back into her stomach where it would be
dissolved by the acid. She acknowledged to herself, for the
first time, that she had felt this way, had been this tense, for

many months now, in the build-up to the bombing and ever since.

She pushed up her sleeves and unconsciously rubbed her palm over the damaged skin of her arm. Turning her face to the right, she gazed at herself in the loose, wonky mirror tiles covering the wall above the bath, speckled with rust patches. She looked at her own hair, similarly flawed with strands of white. The rest was glossy enough, and shiny. She liked being back to a brunette. It felt all right now, to be back to looking how she was; it did not mean that the same things would happen, that the same mistakes would be made. It was fine to be herself. She ran her hands over her face. Her skin looked tight for her age but it was strained, stretched rather than youthfully taut. Her restraint, as always, shrouded the tiredness beneath her eyes. Angie knew that hers was a face that had seen too much. It had seen the old world crash and burn.

Angie had been seventeen when the Takeover happened. It was unexpected to all but those in the government and the financial sector, who had known for many months that the whole continent was bankrupt, that there was no other way out without everyone in Europe starving to death. However, that year was more heavily imprinted upon her mind for running away from home to escape the abuse that had changed from rare to routine. It had been the poverty, perhaps, which had pushed them over the edge. It was the same year she met him. He had revelled in the Takeover; he knew all the right people, and at first it was intoxicating to feel so safe. She remembered the day he marched her to the clinic and paid for her genetic diagnosis, his way of having control over her.

His plan worked—the tendency to severe depression it revealed made her feel weaker, and it convinced her she needed his support, whether it was in the form of fists or finance. After he threw the acid over her in a fit of rage, she left. Falling pregnant by another man, she was at least able to give birth and leave her daughter in safety before her former boyfriend managed to convince the State she was violent and unstable. She was tagged with a curfew and put into his primary care. Two decades later, she found herself serving a prison sentence on his behalf during which she discovered in herself the beginnings of a dream: The imagining of a world with free will, without State control, without the invisible chains she could feel rubbing at her skin every time she moved.

Angie deliberately neglected her own emotions so that when people asked how she was, she could lie more easily. It was a habit—*but not necessarily a bad one*, she thought. She rarely told anyone anything about herself, and she stared her reflection in the eyes now as she ran through the personal history she could barely herself believe, watching her pupils widen. She wondered why she had been so dangerously close to honest with Barney. He had seen something in her, his gaze had been so precisely focused, as if he had homed in on something and latched onto it. She continued to study herself, running a finger over the scar on her cheekbone; faded now and papery soft. It crinkled under her nail like tissue. *What was it that she had said? I'm respected here.* She shook her head, firmly chastising herself, and slapped her palms onto her knees.

'This won't do,' she said to herself. 'Not at all.' She stood again, flushed the clean toilet in case anyone had seen her go in and washed her hands under icy water in the sink. Flicking her hands to the floor, she watched droplets scatter and sink away into the floorboards. Angie left herself behind as her body departed the bathroom.

12

Kane walked back from the hospital through the pouring rain. As the ground drank it up, sucking it in through the cracks in the pavement, he remembered that the last time it rained was the night of the bombing, two weeks ago. He knew it was two weeks because the dressing had just been removed from his arm. He looked down at it now, the skin shrivelled and insipid. The arm felt colder than the rest of him, as if it was unsure if it was still welcome, whether it still belonged to the rest of him. He swung it out from under his umbrella into the rain, feeling the drops fall on the skin.

Kane was relieved that he would be able to paint properly again; he had felt useless these last weeks, being little more than an annoyance in the pub and unable to create anything of merit with only his left hand to work with. This creative block had led him to researching handedness on the web. He had discovered that the left hand had once been considered evil and that good Christian parents had forced their left-handed children to write with their other hand. He was not surprised to find out that like seemingly everything else, handedness was strongly genetic. However, the discovery that those children, even as adults, still found it more comfortable to write with their natural hand rather than the one they were forced to use was one that had settled in his mind. *It just showed you, you can't fight what you're born with.*

He felt satisfied with this conclusion and had kept away from his canvasses, waiting for his arm to heal. He had been to the gym a lot instead, in an effort not to think. He could feel the difference in his leg muscles and they ached now as he walked. Hours of running on the treadmill or doing abdominal crunches had numbed his brain; if he started to think about the bombing, of Freya or Marie, or even of that guy he had met and whether he was still alive, he pushed the thought away and made himself run an extra kilometre as punishment. Before this routine had taken up his days, he had considered getting in touch with a counsellor, just to talk things through. But he knew they would download his Background and get a copy of his birth diagnosis, and he would feel that he could not be completely honest, so he quickly gave up on the idea.

Listening to the time, he realised he was running late for his shift. He was not too concerned; he had warned them he might be late, and besides, he did not think they valued him for his timekeeping anyway. He was more of a good-time lad, and an efficient worker, unlike the cash-hungry students that came and went. The Stag's swinging sign and blackboards finally came into view above the umbrella-laden crowds scurrying along the street. Testing out his healed arm, Kane pushed gently against the pub's main door that curved elegantly around the corner of the street.

Today he was working the afternoon shift; it was quiet inside. A few office workers were clustered around the wooden tables finishing late lunches and a couple of the regulars were sat at the bar with pints of ale. It was warm inside and Kane shook himself out, winking at the girl wiping down the bar as he passed her by and slipping into the back room. He furled his umbrella and hung his damp jacket from a hook on the wall, taking the fake fur one from beneath it first. He held it out as the girl poked her head around the door.

'Hello, you! Is it my home time at last?' She grinned at him. She was a little elf of a woman with dark cropped hair and a mischievous dimple on her left cheek.

'Yeah, sorry I'm late, Rina. I was having the dressing taken off.' Kane offered the coat to her, draped over his wrinkled arm. She took it gratefully.

'Oh, sure. Wow! It looks gross. But all better now, huh?'

'I guess so.'

Kane took a spare black apron from the back of a chair and wrapped it around his waist, tying the straps in a knot at the front.

'Okay, so I'll be off then,' she said. 'Everyone is paid up apart from the guys in the far corner, who have a tab down. Marcus has just nipped out somewhere to see a man about a dog. Probably to see a woman or do some dodgy business deal, I'd imagine.' She grinned again and slipped on her coat, waving as she disappeared.

Kane yawned and stepped out behind the bar. He logged into the till and checked that the ID scan for the tab was a real one. He had seen a few obvious fakes recently, although he had no idea how anyone did them. How tiresome—to spend your whole life pretending to be someone else, risking prison or deportation, just to get a few free drinks. One of the old men seated at the bar grunted at him and pushed the pint glass in his direction. Kane took it and started to fill the glass with ale, waiting for the nitrogen bubbles to finish swirling, staring and waiting as it turned from milky brown to a ruby-tinted darkness. As he topped it up, out of the corner of his eye he saw another man enter and sit, dripping wet, at the opposite end of the bar by the toilets. He handed over the glass and the Index reader took the money. The group in the far corner were still finishing their food and complaining loudly about their boss, their words shooting aggressively upwards to the red-varnished ceiling.

Kane frowned and ambled along the bar to the new arrival. He was an older man, almost drenched through by the rain in a light cotton jacket and a smart checked shirt tucked into jeans. He was cleaning the water and steam from his glasses with a handkerchief.

'Horrible out, isn't it?' Kane offered. He liked chatting to the customers, or if they were not up for any banter, just observing them. He enjoyed hearing about the minutiae of their lives. Sometimes, if he thought he could get away with it, he would stand at the back of the bar and sketch them from their shoulders up. He had likenesses of all the regulars perfected now. He knew every mole, every line, like a lover would. Some of the more friendly ones had even bought the sketches. He had got lucky a few months ago; a rich businessman had spotted his sketchpad lying on the bar and had commissioned a portrait on the basis of it. He tried to leave it out more often these days.

'Indeed—not on the forecast either,' the man replied politely. 'I thought they were supposed to be more accurate these days. I wasn't at all prepared, waiting around in the rain.'

Kane laughed. 'As I can see!'

The man smiled. 'Touché.'

'So what can I get you?'

'Maybe a ginger beer, if you have it? With a slice of lime and some ice? Non-alcoholic.'

Kane nodded and turned away, reaching for a glass from the racks above his head.

'So ...' The man waited for Kane to glance an acknowledgement before he continued. 'So, you're Kane Ong, aren't you?' The man pushed his glasses back up his nose and waited for Kane to return his gaze, an unconcealed expression of surprise on his face. 'I've been waiting to speak to you.'

'In the rain?' Kane exclaimed, laughing it off. He hoped this sweet-looking old man was not a new addition to the list of pub oddities. He took a can of ginger beer from the fridge.

'I was standing under the shop awning next door, actually, but it has a lot of leaks.' He paused, looking out the window and back to Kane again. 'My name is Barney North. I'm here to ask you about the night of September Twenty-Fifth. I thought it would be better coming to your place of work rather than your home.'

To ease Kane's confusion, Barney pulled the leather notebook from the inside pocket of his jacket and laid it on the bar. As mundane as it was, Marie's notebook was immediately identifiable from its worn-down corners and scratch along the top left edge.

Kane placed the drink next to it and leant down, folding his arms on the bar. 'This was taken from me,' he said, his voice unusually serious. He ran his fingers slowly across the fading marks on his neck, tipping his jaw upwards to display them clearly. 'I can't afford to discuss it.'

'I know—but as you can see, it has found its way to me.'

'How?' Kane might have been more unsettled by a younger man, someone who looked more official. But this man's grey eyes beamed at him, leaving him with a feeling of intrigue. This was no Sentry. He was not being tested.

'It seems that Sentries aren't too careful about who they let into their beds. I have it because *this* man'—Barney flipped it open and tapped the first few words with his fingertip—'was a patient of mine. Well, more than a patient, really. I used to be a child psychologist.'

'The bomber?'

Barney nodded, lowering his head, and Kane saw a shadow flow over his face for a moment, wrinkles looking momentarily deeper and eyes darkening. He continued to talk more quickly, dropping the notebook back on the table.

'I came to ask you: Did you know the girl whose notebook this is?' Barney took a pencil from his inside jacket pocket and placed it on top of the notebook.

'I'm sorry, I really can't talk about this,' Kane said, quite loudly. Loudly enough to be heard.

Glancing around to check for waiting customers, Kane wondered for a while what to write. He ran his hands through his hair and imagined Marie's cold little fingers lacing through his, her sparrow's whisper of a voice in his ear. He thought about what Freya would say. She would say that yes, she did know her and that yes, she had been a friend. He thought of the numbers encrypted within his Index under Freya's name and felt a pang of guilt. *Oh, Freya.* His mind began clambering, scrabbling towards her and bit his lip firmly, tearing his thoughts away again as he began to write on the first blank page.

she died in the bombing—very strange, what hapened that night. hard to explain.

He stopped to survey the pub for empty glasses and plates. No one needed serving.

i was sposed to be in the club but got sidetracked. got chatting to a woman in a bar while i gues Winstan was planting bomb. we left, walked down street back towards the club and a girl ran up the alley. seemed a bit crazy! she wanted to get inside—knew what was gonna happen and thought she could stop it. before she died she gave me this

Barney made a gesture that Kane took to ask whether he had read the notebook. He nodded in response and Barney started to flick through the well-thumbed pages.

Barney wrote: *Do you think she knew him?*

Kane shook his head. He glanced around again to see if any customers were waiting. He was glad they were not. He cast his gaze out through the windows. No one seemed to be standing still, watching.

There was some kind of bond between him and Barney now, a tangible momentum. Barney continued to write. *I think she'd only just met him, but I can't imagine the circumstances.*

Barney shrugged and chuckled. Kane looked at Barney sternly, worried he had made too hasty a judgement of character.

he killed a lot of people for no real reason!

I'm sorry. He was no longer the boy I knew.

Barney's face was a picture of apology. Kane saw that this man felt he held some degree of blame. Sensing that it was misplaced, he nodded and smiled a little, kindly.

This must be difficult for you.

They faced each other for a few quiet moments. Neither seemed sure where to go next and Barney looked around cautiously. He eventually turned a page and wrote: *Can I trust you?* He waited for the nod he expected before continuing. *With some dangerous ideas ... ideas about how our lives are laid out for us ... ideas about genetic birth diagnosis, Backgrounds.*

Kane felt the laughter burst from his mouth like old-fashioned popping candy.

'Why are you laughing?' Barney asked aloud.

'Because that kind of thing, my friend, is what I've spent my whole life trying to avoid! And suddenly in the space of a few weeks ...' Kane trailed off. He was not sure where to begin explaining it to Barney, who looked mightily confused.

Barney bit the inside of his cheek. He seemed to be finding it hard to decide whether this was going well or not. In the end, Kane held out his hand and Barney shook it, and they both broke into broad smiles. The partnership was made, however loose, however ignorant.

'I trust you and you can trust me,' said Kane, resigning himself.

'I seem to remember that this is what we used to call fate,' said Barney, grinning in the way old people do. They're always so keen to show you they know something you don't, thought Kane.

Barney stood and spread his hands on the bar top, his fingers splayed. Opening the notebook again, he wrote: *We can't talk properly now. I'll write you a letter. Reply in the same way and we'll take it from there.*

Barney showed the words to Kane, reclaimed the notebook and walked out. Kane suppressed the urge to laugh as he watched the door close on the man's back. It was surreal.

13

Freya sat on the wall at the junction, marking schoolwork on her Index. Since visiting Marie's father, she had been coming here most days after work, apart from the times it had been raining. Every day it was getting colder. From where she sat, with her back to a blackberry bush, she could look over her left shoulder and see the house. She was hidden, unless he broke his usual route and turned right upon reaching the end of the road, or looked closely around him. So far, he had not. He always paced as quickly as his frame would allow, his gaze fixed on the ground, but she had worn a selection of hats so as not to compromise herself. Even Freya found herself vaguely comical. Today it was a black fedora dug out from the back of her wardrobe, set with a cut glass brooch.

She finished marking the spelling tests—she would add encouraging comments later—and thrust the Index back into the bag on her lap. She placed the flat of her palms on the wall on either side of her thighs and stared down at her feet; even when she pointed her toes downwards like a ballerina, they did not quite reach the pavement. The stones of the wall were cold and it was slowly seeping into her through the woollen fabric of her skirt and thick tights.

If only Kane could see me now, she thought. It was unlikely he would even recognise her without her clinging clothes and make-up. Her hair was tied back into a bun at the nape of her neck; she wore only a slick of mascara and colourless lip balm. Her cherry-red scarf was wrapped tightly around her neck, pulled up over her chin so that she could nibble at the edge of it comfortably. She looked back over her shoulder at the house again and then listened to the time. It was ten to five. Perhaps today was the right day. For weeks now, he had left after five and been gone for roughly the same amount of time, probably to the local pub. He often came back with a takeaway or a bottle under his arm. It had occurred to her more than once that it was a deadly weapon, a heavy glass bottle. She closed her eyes for a few seconds and they felt glassy against her lids; winter was beginning to set in now. Soon there would be snow on the ground and her footprints would give her away. She thought of the purple, glittery 'M' hanging on Marie's bedroom door and wondered once more what lay behind it.

Freya's medication had been increased recently, since she had turned twenty-nine. She was now taking two different pills a day. She tried not to look too closely at the packets, only reading the pharmacist's instructions and following them to the letter. The details did not interest her. She had already admitted to herself, many days before, that this endeavour of sitting outside a stranger's house every evening was purely a distraction, something to divert her from the dullness of her day-to-day life, from thinking about the bombing, or of Kane, to distract her from his pills and from her pills, from thinking that this coming year could possibly be the last normal one of her life. Since the bombing, she had regularly awoken in the middle of the night to the same dream in which she saw herself kneeling in the middle of the street, facing the club, and being unable to shout at herself to move. She knew the bomb was going to go off at any moment, but although her mouth was open and her lungs were straining, she could not scream. And there was only ever one other person there; sometimes it was Marie, others it was Kane. Marie would always try to help her up, but Kane would just stand there and laugh, like she was doing something funny, trying to wind him up. These past few days, Freya would go to bed at night and determinedly think of Marie until she fell asleep, hoping to influence her subconscious, praying that she would dream of her instead.

She heard a door slam. Hunching her head into her shoulders and peering back through the tangled branches of the blackberry bush, she saw him walk down the front path and out onto the street. Marie's father took his usual route, and soon he turned the corner and was gone. Freya jumped to the ground and swung the strap of her bag across her body. The street was quiet apart from a few kids on bikes at the far end, shouting at each other, far too absorbed in their own world to notice her. She already knew the French windows at the back were her best bet.

She skirted quickly down the side of the house and let herself in through the unlocked wooden gate into the back garden. The doors were shut but he had obviously been gardening. A soiled trowel and secateurs laced with slices of leaves lay on a blanket in the paved area. The open blades glinted and she shivered as her eyes caught on them. The roses were now in hibernation; where only weeks ago there had been huge blooms, they now were just tangled thorns. She turned away from the secret, illegal garden and looked in through the glass. The sun was rapidly setting, and inside the house it was gloomy. As her hand reached for the door handle, she tried to talk herself out of it, but the handle moved down and the door opened, welcoming her in. Freya felt tightness in her chest. Until this moment, she had convinced herself that the door would be shut and that it would be unethical, not to mention dangerous, to actually break in. That would be that. But yet, here she was. The door had opened and she was now walking through it. She wiped her feet on the mat and whispered an apology both to him and to herself.

She left the door ajar and ventured further in. *What if someone else is here? What would I do then?* She looked up at the vodka bottle on the kitchen shelf, in the exact same place it had been before, and smiled to herself. Taking it, she took a gulp and placed the bottle back, turning the label so that it faced towards the pepper grinder again. Calmed, she stepped forward through the kitchen diner and along the corridor towards the front door. Through the translucent glass panels, she saw movement and froze to the spot, her heart racing, but the figure was on the street, passing by only briefly. Breathing in and out deeply a few times, she regained her composure and walked more quickly up the stairs into new territory. Staring and pressing her finger to her Tag, she captured an image of the letter hanging on Marie's door and let herself in.

She had expected a treasure trove, perhaps, a room full of stuffed toys, boxes, chests and photographs in gilded frames. The glittered M had held so much promise. She released her breath, disappointed. The room reminded her of her bedsit at college. The walls were painted white but were yellowing with age. A pale blue blind was half-open over the window and a single bed and bare mattress occupied the far corner. A faded brown carpet covered the floor. There was nothing else.

But Freya felt the presence of something: she felt close to Marie. She had waited for weeks. There must be something to be found. She thought of her own room at home that her mother kept set up for her. She thought of the diaries she kept as a teenager, hidden under the bed where she naively thought no one would ever think of looking. Her brothers found everything, of course. Oh, how she had died of embarrassment when they discovered she was in love with the boy who babysat them. Freya felt herself blush now with the humiliation of it.

She knelt on the floor and peered under the bed, but there was only dust. But up through the struts she could see something beneath the mattress. With some effort, she pushed it up and there, laid out in neat lines, were assorted sizes of papers, notebooks, Indexes and some memory cards. On top, there was a handwritten note, marked clearly in capitals:

DAD, I KEEP THESE THINGS HERE FOR SAFEKEEPING. IF YOU FIND THEM, PLEASE DO NOT THROW THEM AWAY. THANKS, MARIE XXX

The three kisses were clearly an afterthought, because they were squashed into the bottom of the paper. They could be read as a sort of apology, perhaps a request for or an offering of forgiveness. Freya ran her hands through the papers, spreading them apart with her palms. She had hoped that Marie's birth diagnosis profile would be here somewhere, but there was nothing else; this was it. Perhaps she could look for that downstairs somewhere, if there was time.

Freya gathered everything together and crammed it into her bag excitedly. She closed the door behind her as she left and looked again at the M. It was all Marie's father really had left of her now. She pushed the thought away but felt suddenly tearful, thinking of her own mother being left with no memories other than a stupid, piece-of-tat door hanging. She traced her finger across it and found herself placing a kiss on it. *Had he known about the things under the mattress?* She ran down the stairs and back towards the kitchen.

Even before she saw him, she knew he was there. Lifting her eyes from the carpet, she saw Marie's father standing in the garden, reaching out for the open French window, the secateurs in his hand. Freya's mouth fell open and her eyes widened with the sudden pulse of adrenaline. Within a split second, his face contorted from confusion into anger and Freya's body left without waiting for her, running back down the corridor and out the front door, slamming it behind her, as in her mind she was frozen to the spot, still staring in shock and guilt at Mr Lane. She knew he came after her, because she heard him yelling, but she ran as fast as she could down random streets until she was completely lost but had left his hefty frame far behind.

She stopped and gathered her breath, quite amazed that she had run so far and so quickly. She looked down at her legs, taken aback by the power of her own body. Her muscles had been pretty damn well coordinated just then. She allowed herself a grin. Perhaps her decline would come next year rather than this year after all.

Later that night, Freya sat in bed in her freshly washed, stripy pyjamas, her legs crossed beneath the duvet. She was still warm from the brief heat of her three-minute daily shower allowance and her cheeks burned with a rare mixture of warmth and excitement. She had laid everything out in front of her; the memory cards and Indexes in one pile and the notebooks in another.

She turned to the books first, opening one at a time. They were full of writing and what looked to be algebra. One was packed with a number of poems and what might be chapters of a book. Freya had promised herself she would give them each individual attention, but she found herself scanning them rapidly, flicking through at random. She stopped to read one of the shorter poems. It was outlined with a border of biro stars and bird shapes singing tiny quavers. She skimmed through more poems at random. Some of them were about love, and she found herself pausing to read more of them; they tugged at her in a way that the others did not. They were sad, pained. They spoke of frustration, confusion, rejection, of different kinds of unrequited love; the kind that tears you up and spits you out. Clearly, Marie had suffered. Here and there were descriptions of physical abuse, of love making its mark in the form of a bruise or a cut.

Freya sighed deeply and leant back into her pillows. She took her hot tea from the bedside table and held it against the ribs between her breasts until it stung her skin. She stared at the wall and thought of the tiny, frail girl that had ran wildly towards certain death. She was beginning to understand something of the desperation and the passion in her eyes.

She placed the notebooks down in a pile by the side of her bed. She slipped the memory card out of her own Index and slotted in the first of those in the pile on the duvet. It was unmarked. Her Index automatically started to download a program she had never heard of—HubbleStat2—and a little logo of starry constellations, each star lighting up in turn, appeared on the screen as it started to open the documents on the memory card. Freya yawned and settled herself down under the covers, holding her Index in one hand. It was after midnight; it would be hard to get up for work in the morning now.

She switched off the lamp and the room sank into darkness, but the screen from her Index pulsed with a green light as it thought over the task in hand. Pulling the covers up to her chin, Freya rolled onto her side and held the Index in front of her face. After a few more moments, the documents opened, each eclipsing the other until a series of about twenty different pages could be swapped in and out of the main view. She flicked through them quickly with the tip of her finger. Zoomed out, as they were now, they all looked the same: indistinguishable typed scribbles filling the screen. She wondered whether the files were corrupted, until she noticed that some of the scribbles were actually tiny numbers.

'One hundred percent,' she whispered.

The screen flashed and Freya blinked a few times, taking in its contents. She had never seen anything like it. Almost more numerical symbols, diagrams and signs filled the pages than white space remained. Each page was crammed with algebra of a kind she had never seen. It was like a Jackson Pollock painting, or the seat upholstery on a commuter train. Again, unbidden, she thought of Kane with a paintbrush in hand. Crazed and yet ordered, the algebra filed across the pages in straight rows, black and white but for a few areas that were highlighted in a yellow tint. It was completely unfathomable. *It's clearly mathematics of some kind,* she thought, *but what?* At the bottom of one of the pages was a typed list of contacts by name, location and email address. One, Dr Andrea Ziemberg, had a smiley face drawn next to it and a list of dates, ticked off.

Moving back to the landing screen, Freya looked again at the logo for the program. *Hubble—like the old telescope?* The stars in the image certainly suggested so. She had learnt about it in school once; their teacher had switched off the lights in the classroom and activated the screenboard, and they had watched, unusually quietly, as the sky zoomed in and in upon itself in ever greater detail. Distant specks of light became galaxies and then solar systems, full of stars and planets and nebulae. It was a forgotten revelation to realise that the night sky was full, fuller than could be seen, of bright, undiscovered things, and all of them billions of billions of light years away. Too far away to ever be of interest, she had dismissively thought at the time. Science had never much interested Freya, and yet Marie must have found it intoxicating. *So that was what it was perhaps, some kind of physics, something about space.*

Freya was asleep before she could finish her train of thought. For the remainder of that night she dreamt not of being fixed to the spot in the middle of Frith Street, her mouth gaping open with horror, but of moving through the darkness, plucking planets and stars from around her and putting them into her pocket. She was Marie and she was flying.

14

Dear Kane,

It was very good to meet you the other day—I hope I didn't surprise you too much. You seemed to have recovered reasonably well from the terrible trauma you must have suffered several weeks ago. I hope I'm right.

The notebook and your address came to me via someone I should probably not name at this stage but I'll refer to as 'A'. As we both know, Sal detonated the bomb that fated night (I still shock myself to write those words). The official State news expanded very little on the incident at all—the reasons for which I think are as obvious to you as they are to me. As you'll know from reading Marie's notebook, a body known as the Anti-Genetics Movement are attempting to claim responsibility.

It seems Sal was working with them to carry out the bombing, which, I suppose, makes them a terrorist organisation. As the name suggests, they are violently opposed to birth diagnosis or the creation of Backgrounds. It clearly makes them angry enough that they are willing to resort to mass homicide if a weak, easily influenced and willing martyr (perhaps not quite the right word but I can't think of how else to describe it) steps forward. You can find out more if you search for them online, of course, but I probably wouldn't recommend it, unless you want your activities monitored for the next year or so.

I'm not sure I completely understand why A wanted me to take the notebook. I suppose it wasn't much use to them and I think perhaps they're hoping I might find something, some further ammunition for their cause. I feel in some respects that I've been 'recruited,' but I might as well say quite clearly to you, as I did to them, that I'm a pacifist and always will be.

So let me introduce myself properly: My name is Barney North and I'm 73, although really, my age ought to be irrelevant! I mention it merely so that you realise I am far too old to have a Background myself. I barely use my Tag, to be honest. I am recently retired, but as I think I mentioned when we met, I used to be a child psychologist. I did private work for the last years of my career, but half of my time was spent in State work, dealing with children who had various issues highlighted in their Backgrounds. The idea is that my work was a preventative measure to minimise social disruption. We all of course are told, somewhat reluctantly you might say, that much of genetics is not completely cut and dry. We are all taught that certain aspects of our Backgrounds are to some extent malleable. It was my responsibility to use that plasticity to steer the children in my care towards a better life. In Sal's case, and now I think of it, in probably many others that I never followed up on, I failed. There were very few of them I followed up on as adults—it was simply out of my remit. But certain characters—like Sal himself—endeared themselves and became almost like my own children.

Sal's Background was an albatross around his neck. As you might've read in Marie's notebook, it quite strongly emphasised that he was prone to violence, criminality and anger management issues. His father had great difficulty dealing with the shock of his birth diagnosis, which certainly aggravated things and made Sal feel abandoned and useless. Eventually (inevitably, I would say), he committed a very serious assault when he was nineteen and was imprisoned for three years. He got off lucky, really, considering he beat the man to a veritable pulp. It was a low-security place for younger people and first-time offenders.

I think three things happened during that period that tipped him over the edge. Firstly, I think he felt that his dreams were ruined—he was a teenager, heartbroken and hormonal, and he knew that having a criminal record on top of his miserable Background had scarred him for the rest of his life. Secondly, it seems he met A there (yes, the same person who gave me the notebook), who seems to have influenced him at a very fragile time for his mental state. And thirdly, with regret, I mentioned to him some of the things I'm going to tell you now.

Several years ago now, I started working with a little girl of seven years old. She, like Sal, had a strong tendency towards violence. She was a tomboy, a bit boisterous, but very sweet and polite. A few weeks after I started sessions with her, she was killed by her nine-year-old brother. It turned out that he talked her into hanging herself from the ceiling fan of her bedroom. A lesson about birth diagnosis and genetics at school had got out of control. He said that he had to make her do it because all the boys at school were saying that people with criminal Backgrounds should be terminated before birth. I got caught up in the whole thing along with social services; the parents went to court for abandonment of duties and so on. It struck me at the time that no one else seemed to see the horrific irony that she was the one with the tendency to violence, and yet it was her brother—an angel in terms of his Background—who had done something so terrible. It was all hushed up, of course, because what would people have said if it had got out? The family were moved away and it got written off as a freak one-off, but as I'm sure you can imagine, it rocked me to my core.

You will have read in Marie's notes what I said to Sal that day when I visited him in prison. I think the words are the exact ones I used, in fact. He obviously must remember it very clearly. By then, I had thought about it a lot, I'd done research, and I *didn't* believe any of it anymore, but I had never dared voice those words out loud. I had never really acknowledged them to myself, let alone to anyone else. I think I had been trying to make him feel better, trying to encourage him. I felt very strongly at that moment that Sal had been brainwashed by the system, pushed towards a criminality that might never have otherwise reached the surface.

Since then, I have tried not to think too much about such

things, but these events have come along and I suddenly feel that I ought to act, not in the way A or Sal have done, of course, but in my own way. There are people like Sal everywhere that are being condemned at birth: I can't feel the way I do and not do anything about it. So I'm going to see what I can find out.

What I need from you is whether you know anything else about that night, or any more about the girl who wrote the notes.

I am a scientist of sorts, and I shall keep going with this until I've figured things out. Despite the atrocities he's committed, I feel that I owe it to the sweet little boy Sal once was.

Yours faithfully,
Barney North

barney,

cheers for yr letter. your a good writer! im more of an artist really, but ill try to do my best so its not a big pain to read! its hard to know what to say or were to start …

it sounds like your caught up in a lot of stuff here. it must be tough for you, knowing sal so well. he must of had a hard life but I still cant understand what would drive anyone to do someting like that.

so, you alredy know that marie died in the bomb. i tried to save her but it went badly wrong. i just broke my arm and scratched up my face and she died. there was another girl there with us. her name is freya and if you want to speak to her I can probably put you in touch. but she doesnt know any more than me really, which isnt much—i only knew both of them for a matter of hours at most so the whole thing is quite strange. marie never got a chance to say any more about the notes, or add to them in any way. i do think when she gave me the notebook she knew she was going to die. i felt like she wanted me to do something with it, but honestly barney, i read it once, just breifly, and then the sentrys came for it.

when i think about it now, marie seemed pretty taken with sal. she wanted to dive right in there, to drag him out, which i thought was pretty strange at the time. it must of taken her some time to write all those notes—an hour or so, id guess. he must have said something that meant something to her, or maybe she just fancied him. but other than that, i really dont know.

an anti genetics movement huh? im not surprised that something like that exists. but i dont think this world can oprate in a state of doubt anymore; we only know how to make snap decesions, follow paths and rules. maybe its easier not to get caught up in those things when your retired!

i did like reading your letter. it feels good in a way, to know what was at the heart of the bombing—a sort of closure.

ive had my own issues with my background over the years, but im sorted now, and happy. i do kind of see where your coming from, but I dont know how else i can help you. all i can say is that i hope you find what your looking for.

sorry and best wishes
kane ong

15

One cold Sunday in December, in the run-up to the festive season, Barney took the train into central London on pretence of shopping for the grandchildren. He would actually have to buy some gifts at some point so that Leila would not tear her hair out, but first of all, he wanted to make the most of his early start. Yesterday, it had snowed a little and the last frozen flakes still crackled underfoot. The weather was bright and the sun glowed in the sky. It was one of those wonderful winter mornings that made him happy to be alive, that sparkled across his clothing like the frost.

He walked across the paved square towards the offices, shivering against the cold. He had already spoken to an old colleague, ensuring that a pass would be ready and waiting for him. As he reached the old concrete building, the doors opened and he walked in. The lobby had been redone since he had last been there. It was now decked out in tiny but powerful organic LEDs that glittered like constellations across the ceiling so far above him, casting overlapping spotlights onto the floor. The building was virtually empty, as he had hoped. Where two friendly ladies had once sat and gossiped on the reception with steaming cups of sugary tea, there was now only a black two-metre column of stone. Within the frame at its top shimmered the hologram of a smiling Chinese woman.

'Hello, sir. Please hold up your pass or give me your name.'

'Barney North.'

'Thank you, sir.' She smiled blankly as his photograph was taken and matched to the one his old colleague had already provided. A credit card–sized piece of plastic appeared from a slot.

'Please take your pass, Mr North, and keep it on you at all times. Place it in the recycling bin on your way out. Have a good day.'

Barney took the pass and slipped it into his pocket, moving through the unlocked glass door. At the top of the stairs, he walked straight into the data room. The doors closed automatically behind him. He took a seat at one of them, near the wall beside a window, and looked down at the square he had just crossed to get here. Stubborn crystals of last night's ice laced the glass and rendered the view over the sculpture-strewn piazza picture-perfect. It had the appearance of an American holiday snap.

He laid his pass on the table and the computer instantaneously blinked into life. 'Search,' he commanded.

The screen remained clear and white. He frowned and looked around. He would have thought that these machines would be voice-activated, but he tried touching the screen instead, gently with his middle finger, and a list of options appeared. It was a library, after all; perhaps the touchscreens allowed people to work more quietly. His heart buzzed in his ears over the quiet of the room. If he closed his eyes and listened for it, he could hear the traffic moving down on the street. He yawned and stretched his palms out to the sides. The end of the yawn invaded his ears, but not completely; not enough that he could not hear the footsteps. Three footsteps, taken briskly and sharply; nails on a keyboard.

Barney looked over his shoulder, scanning the room and the door through which he had come. He realised he was holding his breath. He waited, but no one entered. They had come from the floor below, perhaps, or had not been steps at all but a bird at the window. He ran his hands through his hair and turned his attention back to the screen. He selected the advanced search option and then paused, placing his hands in his lap as he decided where to start. With Sal, of course. He typed in Sal's complete name and date of birth, adding in specific details he knew, and then requested the birth diagnosis. The concise version appeared without delay in a new window and Barney requested the full, State-disclosed version and dragged it to fill the screen. He took his Index from his jacket pocket and laid it too on the table.

He selected the option to upload and the document saved itself into his private files. *This was all on the very edges of professional and legal acceptability,* he reflected, *considering I no longer work here.* And it would be noticeably odd, in the very least, that he was digging into the Background of a suicide bomber that had killed one hundred and thirty-two people—a suicide bomber that he used to treat and was known to have been close to. All these data transactions would be recorded and checked, of course, he knew that, but he would deal with that later if his old colleague could not sort it out.

Barney pressed on, skipping over the first bit—family background, ancestral links—and wondering briefly how Cherry, David and Tiane were, and moved to the later pages in the second half of the document. His eyes caught the familiar words written early on in *Section 4: Attributes.*

4.2: Personality
4.2.1: Aggression
The gene signature (see Appendix C) on the X chromosome points to a highly enhanced tendency to violence and criminality.

Taken in concordance with the comments in 3.1: Sexuality, the individual is unlikely to exert this aspect of his personality on women specifically and the threat posed is not necessarily of a sexual nature.

In this weighty version of the document, these life-defining words were seemingly buried amongst thousands of others. It was people's jobs now, those with medical training, to disseminate these detailed reports into the more concise birth diagnosis; a summary of the main points. Understandably, there was much regulation and each report was checked by up to three or four people to ensure clarity and balance. Although it was available to them, many parents still never read the whole of their children's original document.

Barney remembered making his own notes on this section before meeting Sal for the first time. He had read more around it, adding scribbled thoughts around the borders of his notebook. He had been careful, over those early years, to assess the evidence for Sal's aggressive streak; that had been his job, after all. He remembered watching carefully as Sal fought with his sister, noting his blatant contempt of her. But his relationship with his parents had cemented whatever was written in his genes. To Sal, it was evident from early life that his mother was a goddess, his father a brute. Barney had never suspected David of physically abusing Sal, but it had been upsetting to see such hatred between a father and son. The memories came back to him now as he shivered in the cold library. Sal had felt written off by his father from as early as he could remember; as a young teenager, he had confided in Barney that the level of disdain had been unbearable at times. It was an emotional abuse of sorts, at the very least, and over the years, despite Barney's pleas for peace, it became fully reciprocated.

Barney looked away from the screen for a moment to look out at the ice-blue sky. It looked cold enough to crack, to shatter between the cement of the clouds. Barney was amazed now, in hindsight, that Sal had never inflicted any physical damage upon his father. It was a small miracle in many respects—and a shame, really—that Sal could not have taken out his anger on the man Barney could not help but consider largely responsible for it. And there it was again, Barney slipping into these private convictions, blaming not the offending gene sequence in Appendix C but instead circumstances or bad luck, as if he were a seaside fortune teller.

He sat back and folded his arms, allowing himself a few minutes of reflection in the silence of the data room. *What if Sal's parents had both loved him, unconditionally, as he loved his own children? Would things now be different?* Barney already knew what he thought. It was written in freshly oxygenated blood in his mind. His attention skipped, briefly, to the case of the little seven-year-old girl murdered by her own brother. He tried to refocus on the computer screen as his brain was pulled towards morbidly recollecting the scene: her limp body hanging from the ceiling, the spare cord coiled loosely around her body, falling to her white-socked feet. Barney shuddered at the little horrors of the memory.

He moved back a few pages to the medical section. As he already knew, Sal had been predicted to have a largely healthy life—an intermediate risk of developing diabetes and heart disease if he allowed himself to get overweight in middle age, but nothing to worry too much about if he kept himself in shape. And Sal had always been so slight, so keen on walking everywhere. The maximum lifespan section, always brief and to the point, had Sal down as a centenarian, but as ever, the surmising narrative cross-linked the reader to Section 4.2.1, quoting some widely used piece of statistical analysis:

Please note that this section (3.5.3) should be read together with Section 4.2.1 (aggression), in that individuals with high aggression levels and criminal tendencies live on average around only half their maximum lifespan.

Barney sighed and felt the sadness spread across his face until it hummed mournfully in his ears. It was a cool, calm sadness, though. He was done with crying. In many ways, it felt to Barney as though Sal had been dead for years, not months. He worked it out in his head; Sal had lived to be twenty-eight, twenty-two years less than his birth diagnosis had so optimistically predicted. The State had won there, saved some unexpected cash.

Barney felt himself bridling with fresh contempt for the document in front of him and skipped back to the front cover. The network of boxes, ticks and signatures were familiar, each one with the same layout: At the top left was laid out the individual's personal details, and at the top right, the details and signature of the medical professional signing off the final diagnosis.

This was never really of much relevance, it was merely a contact to go back to if anyone handling the document had any questions, wanted to address any ambiguities or consult for further opinion. Those completing and issuing the birth diagnoses were geneticists by background who, after substantial training, were licensed by the State to specialise in this field. There still were not many genetic diagnosis executors operating in this country, although the training courses were popular. It was a good field to get into; you could expect enough time to carry out your own research projects one or two days per week, and after ten or so years, you could put your feet up in a private practice and issue genetic diagnoses to people too old to have had it done for free at birth, or increasingly to foreigners, many of whom flew into London for this exact purpose.

At the time of Sal's diagnosis, nearly thirty years earlier, it was all very new. There were perhaps a couple of dozen fully qualified practitioners then; now there must be several hundred, perhaps more. It was not a boom that would last, though. As the generations passed, soon everyone in Europe would have a Background, as well as in many other continents. The State was spreading its influence wherever it could.

Barney looked at the name to see if it was anyone he had met. He had known quite a few of the executors who worked nearby; he would often call them up with random questions and they would laugh good-naturedly and explain as best they could. Sal's profile had been completed by a Professor Elin Nagayama: not a name Barney recognised. He was surprised, too, as Sal had been born and diagnosed here in Euston, at what Barney still considered to be the 'new' hospital. He sat back in the chair and frowned, squeezing his brain for answers as he knotted his brow.

'I *must* have called her,' he murmured aloud. He recalled that he would normally try to call the executor of the diagnosis even before he met a new client, to talk it through, mull over any shared concerns or discuss queries about some of the statements within. He looked out the window again; a man was walking across the far side of the square with a child in one hand, and festively coloured shopping bags in the other. He thought of his own long grown-up children and how he used to walk with them like that when they were young, them always holding onto him tightly. His mind wandered to thoughts of the presents he must buy and he nibbled on his lip nervously. He ought to push on, really.

As he stared at the father and child, the memory of the phone call to Sal's executor suddenly entered his head, and he was pleased that he was not losing his marbles. Sometimes Barney wondered if he would like to know whether any errant genes were lurking amongst his neurons, ready to steal away everything he had ever learnt, but the thought would disappear as quickly as it had come and he thought no more of it, until the next time he forgot something.

So, the phone conversation: *Yes,* he thought, *I remember it now.* It had been brief, and Nagayama herself—based in London, he thought—had been hard to get hold of. She had moved into another field of work a few years earlier and spoke measurably, somewhat vaguely, he recalled. Barney closed his eyes and clasped his hands together. He must have called her from his office downstairs; they would not have spoken for long. He had wanted to gain more understanding about how the different parts of Sal's diagnosis interweaved and overlapped. Sal had exhibited complex personality characteristics as a young child, and it had taken Barney years to unravel them into a rounded picture he was happy with. But strangely, she did not seem to be able to add anything that was not already on file—or perhaps, looking back now, it was that she was reticent to. Normally, he would have had a chat and a joke with the executors; it would have been collegiate, light-hearted, but if he remembered correctly she had been brusque, and he had thought her strange.

He sat up straight now, his full attention back at the desk, and flicked back through the layers of documents to the original search screen. In place of Sal's name, he put Dr Nagayama's, and he cleared the other fields, selecting 'executor' from a drop-down field. One result appeared, opening itself automatically. It was a brief, partially completed record of her professional biography and status as a genetic diagnosis executor. Born in Japan, Nagayama had lived in the UK since she was a teenager and had graduated from Edinburgh University in 2006. That placed her in her late sixties now, around forty when she had completed Sal's diagnosis. There were links to her qualification certificates and other personal details, but Barney reminded himself that everything he accessed could be tracked, and he hesitated.

A series of options down the left-hand side of the screen offered to link Barney to a list of the individuals she had dealt with in her role of executor. That seemed less private somehow, and so Barney selected it and a two-page document appeared. He was taken aback at how short the register of names was, listed by surname in alphabetical order. He scrolled down it quickly and back to the top again; he estimated it was no more than a few hundred names.

He stopped and thought for a moment. At that time, there were relatively few executors, and yet it appeared that she had only done diagnoses for a small number of people. That was very odd. Barney felt sure there must be some explanation but he could not see any notes or amendments. He scanned once more, slowly, through the list of names and the main details next to them. Even more unusually, the birthplace of the individuals varied significantly. Apart from a cluster in the Central and Greater London regions, there were individuals born in York, Exeter and Manchester, amongst others. Most executors, at least these days, would be linked to one hospital or two, only completing other diagnoses if the demand was there and deadlines needed to be kept. Barney furrowed his brow and pinched the bridge of his nose, deep in thought. It also appeared that all the diagnoses had been completed within a two-year period. This, in particular, presented Barney with lots of questions, and they burst out of him with such urgency that he had to start talking aloud.

'Why would she do all that training only to be an executor for two years? Did something better come up?' he asked himself. He felt a strange sensation creep up on him, the feeling he got when he realised something was not quite normal. It was a feeling he remembered from his working life; the unforgettable moments he could count on his fingers when a child had looked at him in a certain way and everything had become clear, their disturbed characters had finally presented themselves.

For the third time, his eyes ran down the list of names, straining over his glasses in deep concentration at the rows of tiny characters. He felt so peculiar that when he first saw the name jump out at him from the page, he did not feel a sense of shock; it seemed to make complete sense, albeit a sense he did not yet understand the reason for. *Kane Ong.* It sat a hundred or so names up the page from Sal's. It was the right age, and he recalled Kane telling him he was a Londoner, born and bred. Neither was it a common name.

A spurt of energy overcame him and before he knew it, he had downloaded the list of names onto his Index, then opened the link to Kane's diagnosis and downloaded that, too, before even reading it. He sent both documents to Kane accompanied only with the words:

Is this you?? Barney.

It was impulsive, but he hoped it was the right thing to do. Barney pushed back his chair and stood up. He needed to mull this over, and he wanted to wait for Kane's reply before he did any more. He glanced outside. An hour or more must have passed; it was barely after lunchtime and already the sun was beginning its homeward journey to the horizon. He would still have time to pick up some presents. Leaning over the desk, he closed down everything and picked up his satchel. He could always come back another time. He walked quickly out of the room, then took the lift down and left the building. He felt ten years younger suddenly, buzzing with excitement like a naughty schoolboy who had let the school guinea pig out of its cage.

The adrenaline blurred his senses so much that he did not notice the man follow him out of the building and fall into step behind him as he retraced his steps towards the square.

Travelling home by the most direct route, absolved of his worries and wanting to reach Leila and his late Sunday lunch as soon as possible, Barney was foiled by the last section; his most travelled. The ten tube stops home became eleven and then twelve as his senses dulled to his internal workings. Along the last smooth stretch, where he normally had to fight to stay awake, he stared unseeingly out the window, thinking nothing. He noticed the sign for the twelfth station a few seconds too late, as the train pulled away, and he ended up getting off three stops beyond his own. Leaving the carriage, he scolded himself under his breath and stubbornly walked the distance home as a form of punishment, refusing to clamber aboard a passing bus or hail a cab.

Leila rolled her eyes when Barney arrived home at seven o'clock, tired and hungry. Having told her he would be gone all day, he was pleased to find his dinner in the oven, the plate hot and the meat—one of their own chickens—only a little too dry. The hot gravy soon cured that problem. Leila sat watching him eat, her head rested on her hand at an angle.

'The kids were sad to miss you,' she said.

'That's sweet of you. I bet they didn't really say that.'

'They did! I told them that you hadn't seemed well lately, that you were acting a bit odd, a bit out of character.'

'Did you indeed?'

She nodded, her eyebrows raised, knowing that Barney himself was fully aware of his own unaccountable strangeness. 'But you seem brighter today,' she added, narrowing her eyes probingly, making Barney think that it might be time to begin his admission. But before he could begin, he felt his Index vibrating in his pocket. *Fate comes knocking,* he thought wryly. He fished it out and immediately wondered why he was surprised to see the source of the incoming call. It was a number he did not want on his Tag; it was not saved in his contacts underneath any name, pseudonym or otherwise. He put down his knife and fork and glanced apologetically at Leila as he walked out onto the balcony. She looked frustrated to have been interrupted at such a crucial interval.

'Hello?' he said, wearily, disabling the video link.

'Barney—you said to call.' Her voice was treacle.

'I'm quite sure I didn't.'

He stared out across the darkening horizon. Birds danced in the dying light. London was darker than he remembered as a child, especially tonight; it was murky, almost soulless. This small, bulb-like extension of his working life, this minor obsession with his own mistakes, was growing into something beyond his own comprehension. It had already ceased to be his hobby, now enveloping people that had become close to him, lives that were both long gone and yet to be. He could feel it coming. He had thought he could walk away.

'Tell me,' she said.

The birds were gone into the blackness; the sun had long since set. The line between him and Angie, wavering somewhere in the invisible cloud around his head, was silent, had been that way for over a minute. Angie was waiting, patiently, for a response, and he had the feeling she would wait forever, if that was what it took.

16

London, 2042, ten years earlier

It was the end of a hot summer and Marie had just turned eighteen years old. It was before the time of unforgettable betrayals, of being homeless and alone. In hindsight, and despite the subsuming anger that throbbed at the back of her throat, this short period of time was among the happiest parts of her life. She had the freedom to walk out of the house whenever she liked, college was more interesting now she had narrowed down the subjects she studied, and her father was going through a peaceful period: no vodka bottles lined the path to the rubbish bins. It was night now and she could not sleep, although she kept reminding herself that she had college early in the morning, a double dose of maths and then cross-country, if she had the energy. She would probably skip it and walk up to the tuck shop, and maybe sit on the grass in the park for an hour or two.

Marie was sitting cross-legged on her bed. The street light down the road, the bane of her life, glowed orange through the edges of the blinds. Lying on the bed in front of her were university brochures, scattered where her father had left them. The options he had chosen for her, probably all chemistry degree courses, were circled in thick black marker pen and she refused to look at them on principle. Her fury manifested to the ends of her fingers and she twisted them deeper into the duvet cover, her neatly filed nails curving and breaking as they pushed through the cotton and back into the flesh of her palms, hard enough that it hurt. Her father had left in a rage five minutes before and eventually, as the slam of her bedroom door stopped ringing in her ears, she managed to tear her eyes away from the photograph of her mother on the bedside table and looked up at the sky instead.

She had always been the girl at school who cried on vaccination day, causing a fuss. She remembered always being sickly. A mere cold had laid her up in bed for a week. Her genes—just like everybody else's—were far from perfect. Her glass had always been half empty, but she could never change her attitude: her father deplored that in her, and she deplored it in herself but never felt capable of filling it up. There was no fighting spirit in her. There never really had been. Only when it came to the stars, those distant lights that meant so little and everything, all in the same twinkle. She found it romantic that one day, she would go back into the matter that they were all formed of, back into the black anonymity of the cosmos where she belonged, merely to be part of life, but not to participate.

Unravelling her hands from the sheets, Marie reflexively reached into the drawer of her bedside table to pull out her Index, keeping her eyes on the sky. Soon, the street light would turn off and she would have the stars to herself. She was lucky to live in an area where the State's energy-saving measures were quite extreme, she reminded herself, or else this monstrosity might have stopped her from ever pursuing her true talent. Every year, with the increasing light pollution controls, it seemed that more stars could be seen.

She had been on a school trip once, when she was around fourteen, on which her whole class travelled to Scotland for a week. She and her best friend had slipped out from the dormitory one night, coats over their pyjamas and trainers on their feet, and had walked down to the loch. They had sat on the freezing banks and shared a joint, staring up at the sky. It had been a revelation, aided by the rush of sneaking out and the cannabis firing off dopamine inside her head. The sky had been alight; Marie had never known there could be so many stars. She had found out afterwards that the mist that snaked across the centre of her view like the trail left by a giant intergalactic aeroplane was the Milky Way. But here, back in London, there was less to see and more to hear: an urban peace of never-too-distant traffic hum, bluebottle-like sirens, echoing screams and shouts, the airborne effervescence of electricity, muddying her horizon ochre.

Marie unfurled her Index, carefully smoothing it onto her bed with her hands. She had saved for this model for months, paying for it by working as a waitress at a local café after school. It had been fun at times, despite the terrible pay. As she held her fingertip flat to its reader, it switched on and opened the program where she had left it.

The speed of light in a vacuum is denoted as c, because it is constant. It is the fastest thing in the whole universe, at 299,792,458 metres per second, faster than anyone could ever imagine. Every single photon departing the Sun takes eight minutes and nineteen seconds to reach the back of her retina.

Except Marie had, in recent weeks, decided she no longer believed this; she instead wanted to believe something quite different. *Who cares about special relativity?* All of it was a convention that no one dared break, but Marie possessed a destructive, aggressive need to smash it to pieces. It was a convention that was already teetering, like a simple penny balanced on its edge. If it fell, the whole textbook of the universe, every rule of physics, would need to be rewritten; it was a gripping thought that had whispered around the corners of her mind for a long time, ever since she had first understood a scientific paper in a journal her teacher had loaned her.

All her teachers were very aware of Marie's Background. Each one of them liked to believe that Marie would be their star pupil, that she would come to excel in their field and that they might be the ones to have inspired the direction of her genius and they would feature, perhaps, in her Nobel Prize acceptance speech. Marie had come to find that the concept of genius was one that attracted attention. Like gravity, it pulled people in. Everyone wanted to be near it, to experience it, to feel they played some part in it.

Sleepily, Marie stared down at the university brochures in front of her, scanned the bare walls of her still-childlike bedroom, and recognised that her need to take this thing apart, to demolish this long-held belief, was her form of teenage rebellion. She picked up her scribing pad from the floor as the street light finally flickered off. With her stylus, she began to add to last night's notes with pleasingly pencil-like electronic ink. No scientist writes in anything but pencil, she had remembered reading somewhere once, and she held it to be true. She closed the papers she had been reading a few days earlier; Moffat, 1992 and Albrecht & Magueijo, 1998. They too, believed, for probably quite different reasons, that the speed of light was not constant. Instead, she opened her email and was pleased to have received a reply from the research scientist she had written to a couple of weeks before.

Marie—thanks for your interesting email. You're in London, are you? You must tell me more about yourself next time!

Anyway, you had asked me for my thoughts on your ideas and queries, and I've finally found a quiet moment in which to write back to you. I'm at a rather dull conference and there are so many coffee breaks I don't know what to do with myself. Anyway, to address your questions, these are all things that have come up before, and I'm sure lots of researchers, including myself and a few others at my institute, are steadfastly asking themselves the same things. On the other hand, there are plenty of people out there (the vast majority) who would think that we are crazy for doing so.

First of all, and most importantly: I know you know this, but don't allow yourself to forget that the speed of light is a ratio of a distance travelled and time. If one person claims this ratio varies, then another can just as easily claim the alternative: that it is distance and/or time that are being stretched and/or bent. This, of course, is the wonderful basis of Einstein's theory of General Relativity—where gravity is the 'thing' which bends space–time.

You could also do the reverse and model the bending of light via gravity as refraction due to varying speed of light. I'm not sure how far this can be pushed. But as I recall, you can view the varying metric of GR as a tensor expressing varying light speeds in various directions. This is all 'off the cuff' and I'll think about it some more and email you when I get a moment along with some good references, perhaps in the

next coffee break!
    Yours,
    Andrea

The next coffee break must have been and gone, because the email had been sent several hours before. However, Marie smiled and felt pleased to get a response. She had sent out quite a few queries, trying to spark a conversation, but they were either dismissed by a secretary's brief response or left unanswered. This time she had found the right person. If only Dr Andrea Ziemberg knew the sender of the email was a teenage girl in her bedroom. Or perhaps she did have an inkling; perhaps she was once that girl herself.

Marie chuckled to herself quietly and read the email once more, making notes on her scribing pad as she did so. She would come back to this. Tonight, she was going to try and focus on the fine-structure constant and the evidence that suggested it was changing over time. Only when she truly understood all the physics, all the arguments, could she begin to put forward her own ideas, and there was still some way to go on that front. If she was going to reply to Andrea's email and really start a conversation with a quantum physics heavyweight, she would have to be prepared with all the facts.

She opened the research paper she had been looking for and started by reading the related blog entry, which was usually an easy introduction to the deeper content. It would be a late night.

17

2052

It was late on a Tuesday afternoon, a fortnight before Christmas. The sound of the fist hitting the door was definitely more of a thump, less of a knock, and Leila jumped. Peeling off the yellow washing-up gloves, she felt suddenly like her mother, refusing to answer the door to a stranger with anything less than a perfect manicure. She opened the door to their flat with a welcoming smile upon her face.

'Oh,' she said. A young man was stood there, one arm resting against the door frame above his head. His expression was tense. The dark freckles across his nose and cheeks jarred against his Asian features.

'Hello. I need to speak to Barney, please.'

'I'm sorry, my love, he's not here.' Leila's automatic lie slipped off her tongue; she felt chilled by the evident anger on the man's face.

At almost the same moment, Barney called from the utility room, where he was looking for an extension cable: 'Who is it, darling?'

As the young man burst into a grin and chuckled, raising his eyebrows at her quizzically, Leila experienced a sense of confusion. She felt as though she had been caught handing out sweets in class and smiled meekly at him. Now that he was grinning she could see that he was handsome, and very well groomed. His green eyes were wide and almond-shaped and were fixed upon her, taking her in.

Then the broad, toothy grin fell away again into a stern frown. 'How did you get hold of it?' Kane demanded over

Leila's head, and she turned to see Barney standing there. 'Do you get off on this, prying into other people's lives, or what?'

'Ah,' Barney said, wincing. 'You'd better come in.'

As they walked to the sitting room, Leila closed the front door and put her hands on her hips. 'Barney, my love, what's going on?' she asked. She was sure to say it kindly, softly. She knew, after forty years of marriage, that this was resoundingly the best way to uncover her husband's secrets.

The men both sat down around the coffee table and turned to face her.

'I'm sorry, darling. Kane and I go back a bit. I used to counsel him and we have some things to talk through,' Barney said smoothly.

'No you didn't,' Kane said, turning back in his seat. 'I only met you a few weeks ago.'

Barney sighed and shrugged at Leila, as if he didn't know what to say. She shook her head and narrowed her eyes. She would deal with him later.

'Fine, I'll leave you to it. Kane—can I get you a warm drink at all?'

'Oh, that would be lovely, Mrs North, a cup of tea would be great. Milk, one sugar, please.' He cast her another one of his dazzling smiles and then switched it off as he turned his attention back to Barney. He slammed the flat of his hand onto the table.

'So?' he demanded.

Barney leaned forward in his chair, folding his arms over his knees. He put on his softest, most honeyed voice and made his body language open, spreading his hands in defeat.

'I'm sorry, Kane, I didn't mean to alarm you,' he replied, squeezing the bridge of his nose. He waited until Kane had nodded and sat back in his chair, his anger beginning to visibly subside. 'As you already know,' he continued, 'I'm a retired psychologist and counsellor, and I'm able to access such documents as part of ongoing consultancy work.'

'But I've never been your patient. You had no right.'

'You could say that.'

'I *do* say that.'

Leila brought over a single mug of tea and placed it on the coffee table, looking pointedly at Barney. She smiled at Kane and walked out of the room to pick up where Barney left off with the hunt for the cable. Closing herself in the utility room in the corridor, she closed her eyes momentarily. Forgetting the missing cable, she fixed her attention solely on the heated voices of Barney and Kane.

'Why did you read my diagnosis?' she heard Kane continue. 'We haven't even exchanged Backgrounds yet. This isn't right. It's not the right way of doing things.'

'I didn't read it. It was an accident, really, a bizarre one,' Barney began.

'I thought you were just interested in Sal,' Kane retorted, spitting out the words.

'I *was* reading up on Sal's records principally, and then I got onto the person responsible for completing his diagnosis—a Professor Nakayama—and I fell upon something most unusual. I found that she had done the genetics for a relatively small number of people. I was studying the list for commonalities, trends, and by complete coincidence, I saw your name. I wanted to know if it was the same Kane Ong, and so—'

'And so you just thought you'd read my most intimate details, before I'd even had the opportunity to tell you my Background?'

'I'm sorry, again,' said Barney, dropping his voice so low that Leila could barely hear him through the wall. A silence followed, and Leila imagined the two men staring at each other's faces, emotionally squaring up. She knew how reticent Barney usually was to apologise. But his words had sounded heartfelt, and she thought that Kane must be able to sense that, too.

'So what you're telling me, Barney, is that the same person completed both mine and the bomber's diagnoses?' Kane's voice was immediately more level and his words were spoken steadily.

'In short, yes. Which isn't anything particularly bizarre in itself, but it felt like … I don't know, like a strange fluke when she had done so few.'

'Right.'

Leila heard them pause, then a dull sound as, presumably, Kane placed his mug back on the table after taking a sip. Kane sighed.

'And in your letter,' Barney said, 'you suggested that you've had problems coming to terms with your Background?' He spoke haltingly. Leila recognised his tone as the one he would use with his patients. He was exploring, stepping carefully, as if crossing a river on rocks that wobbled in the current.

'Did I?'

'Yes, I think you said that you had experienced some issues.'

'Well, I would tell you my Background, but ...' The edge had returned to Kane's voice.

'Kane, I didn't read all the contents of your birth diagnosis,' Barney said, his voice truthful. 'Only enough to know it was you.'

Leila pressed her body closer to the wall as she heard Kane move the mugs and place something else onto the table. Whatever it was tinkled as he moved it: small things chiming against metal.

'I take one of these pills every day,' he said, his voice thick with emotion. Leila's fingers danced over her own throat as it constricted in empathy. 'I've taken them for so many years that I daren't stop.'

Leila knew that Barney wouldn't interrupt. His ability to actively listen was one of his best qualities. 'I'm gay,' continued Kane. 'When I was a teenager, I thought I'd fallen in love with a girl. I was young, confused. I felt for a while that my Background was wrong, that by some freak of nature, some misunderstood aspect of genetics, I was heterosexual after all. But I went to a specialist and she prescribed me these. And since then, luckily everything has been alright.'

Leila, now sat on the floor in the utility room listening intently, imagined that he was frowning sadly. She heard him tip the pills back into the box.

'And that's it, really.'

'So do you have a partner now?'

'I don't really see how that is relevant to you.'

'No, sorry, that's fair enough.'

So that's a no, Leila thought. Even through the wall, she could feel Kane's unhappiness starting to seep out from behind the thin veil of self-assurance.

'But I was born in South East London and Sal was born in Euston,' said Kane. 'Don't the executors normally just do the births from one hospital, or at least from one Trust?'

'Yes, they do. That was one of my first thoughts and another odd thing about it all. Here's the whole list.' Leila heard Barney's rough palm flatten his Index against the table.

'List?'

'The list of all the people your executor diagnosed.'

Barney made a small grunt of displeasure. 'Hang on,' he muttered.

The fabric of Kane's coat grazed the leather chair as he leant back. He chuckled and Leila imagined him folding his arms in defiance.

'You can't find it, can you?'

'Just let me check.'

'It's gone, Barney. They've wiped it remotely,' Kane explained. 'Mine's gone, too. I scanned through it—for a matter of seconds, when I first opened it—and then pop.' He clicked his fingers. 'It disappeared from in front of my eyes.'

'Oh, my God.' Barney stood up, and Leila knew he was walking away from Kane, and further from her, too. Perhaps he was standing at the window, pressing the tips of his nails into the glass as he often did when thinking. He was in trouble.

'But I saw something in those few seconds, Barney. I saw Freya's name.'

'Freya?'

'In my letter, I told you that besides the girl who gave me the notebook—Marie—I met another woman that night. We had chatted in a bar and we ended up taking Marie to hospital together. Well, she was on that list. Our surnames are close enough in the alphabet that they were listed on the same page. And I know her birthdate because it was her birthday the night of the bombing.'

'How can she be on the list?' Barney asked, disbelief sharpening his voice.

Kane shook his head. 'I don't know, Barney. It's as if someone picked us all up and put us together on Frith Street that night.'

'What do you know about her?' Barney asked. He walked back across the room and sat back down.

'She's due to develop early-onset Huntington's,' he said, flatly, after a short pause. 'Christ, this is so, so weird,' he continued. 'Look, I'm going to go now. I'll be in touch.'

Leila heard him stand up and walk towards the door. She stood up herself, suddenly conscious of how long she had been listening to their private conversation. She moved a few things about on the shelves, deliberately chinking old tools against the vase she and Barney had received for their wedding anniversary.

'Go carefully, Kane,' said Barney. 'They may be watching you.'

It was some time later when Leila entered the room. She walked to the front door and gazed into the alarm's sensor to set it for the evening before settling where Kane had been sitting.

'I should probably be angry with you, but you usually do things for a good reason,' she said. She took his hands across the coffee table and held them in hers, stroking his gold wedding band with her little finger. 'I'm not even going to ask you to explain, as I have a suspicion that you wouldn't know where to begin.'

Barney grinned back, the burst of love and gratitude visible upon his face. These open-ended statements were often effective in prompting him to explain everything. But this time, it seemed that he would let the challenge go.

She looked at him knowingly. 'Just promise me you're not doing anything dangerous,' she said.

'No, no, I'm just curious,' he replied. 'Did you listen?'

'I'm in the same flat, Barn. Of course I heard some of it.'

'Oh, Leila,' he sighed. 'It's just so … confusing.'

'Why?'

'Because why would these three people all appear in a list of three, four hundred names? What are the chances that they are so intimately connected as to have the same executor?'

She loved the calm reasoning of his voice, harmonious even in distress. She half stood and leant towards him, kissing him tenderly on the cheek.

'Well, they're about the same age, born in or near London. It's not absurd. Besides, it sounds like they don't even really know each other.'

'Yes, but …' he started.

'But what? What could it even mean, anyway?'

'I don't know. I just have a feeling.'

'About what?' she asked. She laughed softly and shook her head at him as she wandered off towards the kitchen. 'You think there's more to it, don't you?' She glanced back over her shoulder as she reached the door to see Barney nod, chewing his lip.

'Oh Barn, you always have to have a *reason*, don't you? Something solid, with an explanation that can be written down. It was the nature of your work, I suppose. You forget that sometimes, things just happen, like magic.' She shrugged and looked away from him, out of the window, before continuing. 'Our parents talked about destiny, didn't they, like there was some mystical power that intervened in people's lives to make something happen, something that was intended by a greater force? If nothing else, it was a way of accepting things and moving on. I don't think that idea is so ridiculous, Barn.'

'Oh, Leila, I love you,' he sighed.

'I love you too.'

18

Freya glanced to her right, through the little windows that looked onto the terrace and playground. Most of the parents were already out there waiting, gossiping amongst themselves. She cast her eyes back over the children scattered in front of her, a few of them actually trying to finish their spelling practice for the day, most of them chattering in barely concealed whispers. She burst with love for them.

'Alright, that's it! It's been a long enough day—get out of here, you lot,' she called out. Freya cleared her throat and rubbed it; today had been a tough one. She felt drained.

The bell sounded at last but they were already out the door, a tangle of screaming and shouting limbs, bags flung over their shoulders. She gathered the things from her desk and stuffed them into an already overflowing drawer. She would sort it out after the holidays. She sat down in her chair and took a deep breath. Looking up, she noticed that one of the boys was still stood at his desk, packing his bag slowly, sighing heavily as he did so. He looked across at Freya and smiled a sad little lopsided smile.

'Is your Mum coming to pick you up, Robin?'

'No, Miss, me Dad is coming today.' He sat down, zipping his bag up across his lap.

Freya walked over and perched on the edge of the desk, flattening her woollen skirt across her knees. 'Is everything alright?' she asked softly.

'Just a bit of trouble at home, that's all.' He shrugged, his eyes cast downwards.

Freya knelt on the floor in front of him, feeling the playground dirt from the children's shoes dig into her knees.

She held out her arms and grinned at him. 'Come here; give me a big cuddle before you go home.'

He smiled and fell into her arms, burying his head into her shoulder. She ruffled his hair and felt that gut-wrenching reminder that she would never know what it would be like to have her own child. It was far too late now, it would not be fair.

He squeezed her neck tightly and sniffled into her cardigan. They stayed like that for a few minutes before he pulled away.

'I feel better now, Miss.'

She nodded and he ran out. Freya looked around her classroom. She would soon have two whole weeks off. She was looking forward to spending time with her mother and with Matt, his wife and their kids. She was looking forward to mince pies, red lipstick and carols sung quietly at home. There was no longer a Church of England, let alone a monarchy to uphold it, but there was something about the spirit of the tradition that the State couldn't take away. The festive holiday was one thing they seemed to have relented on.

Cool, piercing winter sunlight broke through the clouds and shone through the skylights above her. Now Freya's concentration was broken, she felt chilled. She started to fill her bag with the things she would need for the evening. She pulled out her makeup bag and mirror to spruce herself up for the walk home, but just at that moment, her Tag sounded. She pressed her finger to her neck. It must be her mother calling about their plans for next week.

'Hello?'

'Freya?'

The voice was immediately familiar, smooth and masculine. She jolted with sickness. As Freya unrolled her Index to accept the video link, she vainly wished it had come thirty seconds later so that she would have already applied her lipstick and let down her hair.

Kane's face appeared in front of her and he looked almost the same, except that the cuts on his cheek had healed and his expression was more serious than the face in her memory. She found herself feeling all kinds of things at once: delight, anger, and confusion.

'Hello, stranger!' she replied, cheerily, trying not to sound nonplussed. 'How's that arm?'

He held it up and waved it in front of the camera, grinning. 'All good now! I had the cast off a few weeks ago.'

Freya smiled into the camera and then shyly looked away, out of the window. She saw Robin run towards his father, a tough-looking guy who met him halfway across the courtyard and swung him up into the air. She found herself blinking back tears and shook her head at her own sentimentality.

'Um, look,' he started to say. 'I'm sorry I haven't been in touch. I've been—'

'Busy, I'm sure you've been really busy,' Freya cut in before he could finish, without looking back at the screen. 'I have been too, like you wouldn't believe, sorting out everything here with the kids and trying to organise Christmas.' She smiled politely, irritated with herself that she had not just let him squirm. She always seemed to find herself making other peoples' lives easier and hers harder.

'I can't believe it's December already,' Kane said. 'It's been what? Nearly three months?'

'Yeah, it's hard to believe, isn't it?'

'So how are you?' he asked.

'Okay, thanks. I'm just getting on with things really.' Freya thought he looked more handsome than she remembered. He was sat in a poorly lit room and his face looked darker, more rugged than it did in real life, up close. His hair faded into the darkness behind him. She wondered whether to tell him about her exploits, her trips to Marie's house. He would probably think she was crazy.

'And how are you?' she asked.

'I'm fine. It's good now the dressing's off because I can get on with some work. I've got a new commission. A portrait.'

'Great,' she replied. She desperately wanted to ask why he was calling, but she held back.

'Actually, the man is someone I met recently. That's why

I'm calling, really.'

'About a guy whose picture you're drawing?'

'Well, no, not as such. Look, could we meet up somewhere, in person? Now?'

Freya suppressed the desire to say yes. 'No, not tonight, I can't,' she lied.

'Tomorrow? The next day?'

'What about this time tomorrow? I'm going out in the evening but I could meet you on the way home from work.'

'Okay, that works.'

'Five-thirty?'

'Yep, that's fine.'

'On the north side of the Millennium Bridge.'

Later that evening, as Kane relived Freya's image retreating into his Index, he realised his whole body was rigid with tension. He tipped his head towards each shoulder in turn and pressed his hands firmly into his face, forcing his fingertips into his hairline. He did not want to think; he wished it was late enough already that he could just climb into bed.

He looked across the room at the portrait he had just started working on, standing on an easel beyond the kitchen table. It was based upon an old photograph Barney had posted him. Already the old man's half-formed face was beginning to emerge from the canvas. At the moment, only the base colours, a taupe and pale grey, formed the image. The contours of the nose, the masculine cheekbones and the heavy brows dominated it, slabs of colour that would appear to a casual onlooker as haphazard, sloppy. Later, Kane would begin to add the detail and the tones, the personality of his subject. The face looked ghostly for the time being and Kane knew he could not do any more work on it today.

He glanced down at the drying remnants of paint on his hands. It would have to wait, lurking in the gloom of the winter's dying afternoon and the cold of the night until his concentration returned. It was not in his nature to leave a painting half-finished. Normally, he would spend weeks making the initial sketches and plans, but once started on the actual piece, he would work right through for two days or more; stopping only to make some toast, pour himself some juice or answer important calls on his Index. He felt it was bad practice to stop, and he was scared that he would forget or somehow lose track of the person he had become so closely attuned to over the preceding weeks. Kane's skill lay in how rigorously he created a character, and when clients were reticent or simply boring, he would invent his own version of them. And they were the ones that needed reinvention; subconsciously it was this they paid for, rather than the portrait itself. Away they would walk, their new acquisition under their arms, praising Kane for 'really capturing the essence of their character' or 'hitting the nail on the head.' Kane would smile and nod knowingly; he himself knew that he was a master of reinvention. He had been since he was fifteen.

Kane had joined a community group to help paint a mural along the side of the destroyed and derelict church in the centre of his district. It was there that he had fallen in love, as hard and as fast as is so typical of first love. Destined to be forever unknown to his family or anyone else he knew, her name, for all it mattered, was Gemma. They talked very briefly each Sunday as they stood next to each other, daubing the wall, and for the rest of the week Kane could barely think of anything else. He spent the summer overwrought, avoiding answering questions about his Background at the club, keeping to himself. It was exhausting; someone would ask and he would have to excuse himself, either to the toilet or for a fresh brush or paint. The others thought he was strange, that there must be something wrong with him, and eventually left him alone, but Gemma was drawn to him in what he felt afterwards must have been a sense of pity.

One day, she walked over to his end of the mural, dripping paintbrush in hand. It was hot and her baggy, paint-covered T-shirt was tied at the side, exposing a sliver of tanned stomach. The paint from the brush dripped down her calf, running like veins over her skin. Kane found it hard not to stare.

'Hi,' she said and smiled.

He stared back, speechless.

'Do you need any help over here? You're always on your own, at the end.' She tilted her head to one side, and raised her brush to start painting part of his rainbow. 'You need some purple here.'

'It's shadier here. I get too hot in the sun,' Kane lied, shielding his eyes from the dappled light falling on his face.

She glowed; her skin looked so soft, her eyes so gentle.

'You can help me if you like,' Kane continued. 'Here—what about this bit? I don't know what to do with it.' He pointed to a section of the wall where someone else's rainbow had ended.

'A pot of gold, obviously!' She laughed and sat cross-legged at his feet, starting to draw an outline. He watched the stretch of delicate tendons in her neck as she leant over. After a few minutes, she looked up at him and he knew what she would ask. It would have been rude of her not to.

'So, what's your Background, Kane?'

'Oh, next time, maybe,' he blurted out, panicking. 'I've actually got to go now. See you tomorrow maybe.' He dropped his paintbrush on the floor and away he walked, as Gemma stared curiously after him. He did not return for two weeks.

Enclosed in the privacy of his bedroom for most of that fortnight, he would sit on the chest beneath the window, his knees drawn up to his chin, gazing out on the playing fields, deep in thought. It was a period of time that even now he remembered with painful clarity. He would run imagined conversations with her through his head, over and over again. In them, he would always be the one in control, leading her through their verbal exchanges, guiding her through their shared unknown with a strong hand, pulling her shoulders towards him and kissing her hard on her mouth. Until the last children left the fields, until the summer sun finally tore itself away for the day, he would think of her.

As an adult, Kane keenly remembered these feelings, although he kept them bunched up and hidden away, like a locket implanted somewhere beneath his skin. Looking back now, he realised that these daydreams had focussed far more on him than they had on Gemma. Although necessary, her presence was secondary to the fantasy of himself as a masculine, heterosexual young man, a person who knew his place in the world, who was able to demand what he wanted. They were desperate dreams of an alternative reality and, through some sort of mental association, she became the route to achieving that. She was, he thought at the time, his deliverance.

Kane's fantasies were to some extent played out as the summer had turned to autumn, although, in sharp opposition to his daydreams, it was Gemma that had done the chasing. She had first invited him to come round for tea one evening. He told his mother he was going to a friend's house and she had packed him off with a chocolate cake. As he sat with her family around the table, nervously picking at his food, he had been relieved when her parents hadn't asked him about his Background; she must have briefed them about this strange boy who refused to talk about himself. That night, on the doorstep, it was her that kissed him for the first time, twice fleetingly on the cheek and then on the lips. Kane wandered home in a daze as if drugged. Arriving home, he pretended to be suffering from a headache and slipped straight upstairs to lie on his bed, staring at the ceiling with a stupid grin upon his face.

For the last few weeks of summer, they saw each other most evenings. They would have been inseparable if Kane had been able to walk with her in public. He had declined offers to join her and her friends on days out and he had put off another meal with her family. She had never met his school friends or his family. It was a temporary, secretive life that was fine by him, but Gemma was becoming increasingly agitated. The ground beneath them was shaking but Kane tried to ignore it, desperately pretending that it would work. At times, he convinced himself it was the stuff of Shakespearean romance, a modern Romeo and Juliet, but, hopefully, with a better ending. But eventually he realised he would have to be honest with her.

It had come to the night he had planned to tell her the truth, and they were sat on the bench at the top of the hill, London rising up to reach them. The evening was chilly and Gemma lay curled up against his chest, looking up at him, her green eyes glowing in the dark. Kane leant down awkwardly and kissed her on the lips. His courage stumbled around shakily in his belly, trying to find its legs.

'Maybe I could come round for tea sometime this week?' she asked.

It was a question she had asked a few times now and Kane was running out of excuses. He sighed heavily.

'Are you embarrassed of me or something?' Her sweet little voice trickled over him like freezing water as he worked his fingers into her hair. It was now or never.

'Gem, I've got to tell you something.' He felt his lips tremble as he spoke.

She nodded and giggled in response, as if expecting a surprise present. He swivelled her to face him and held her hands.

'I don't know what we're gonna do about this,' he continued. 'But I'll figure something out.'

She looked confused now, crestfallen. 'What is it?'

'I've never told you my Background, and I know you've stopped asking, but …'

'It doesn't matter, really,' she interrupted, and for a moment he wondered whether he had to tell her at all.

'There's a reason why I haven't said anything. I'm not weird, but there's something I can't …' he paused, struggling for the right words. They never came. 'There's something in it I don't agree with.'

'What do you mean?'

'Well, for a start, it says I'm gay.' Some nervous laughter slipped out with his words. It sounded odd, he knew. Gemma slipped her hands away from his, folding them under her armpits, and sat up straight.

'What?' she asked. Her voice was tiny but hostility was written across her face.

'My family, my friends, everyone I know apart from you thinks I'm gay. It's written in my birth diagnosis. Apparently the genes are all there.' He laughed nervously. She was still there, he reassured himself. He felt emboldened. 'But I have never really *felt* that way. And now you and me ...'

He reached for her hands again, but she did not move or speak for a small piece of forever. His internal organs were squeezed together so tightly that he could hardly breathe. He bowed his head, trying to look into her eyes, but she evaded him, turning her head to the side and blinking rapidly. And then, finally, she looked up, and he realised in that one cold glance that what he had said simply did not compute and never would.

'Why have you strung me along like this? How could you do it? I knew there was something up with you, not telling me about your Background. Who does that?'

'Gem, I'm sorry, I'm sorry. Look, I haven't said this before, but I love you.' He tried to kiss her but she pulled away. He could feel fault lines tearing through his chest, a tsunami building like a swallowed scream in his stomach.

'You *love* me? How can you? How can you just string me along on some ridiculous teenage phase?'

'Because I don't think I'm gay. I'm not, I'm not gay.'

She gazed at him incredulously as he spoke, and her last words still stung at him, the same patronising ones his mother had used. He felt intensely frustrated in a way that he never had before, an unsurpassed emotion that drove him, weeks later, to seek help.

'But of course you are! You're crazy. You need help, Kane. Get away from me. I never want to see you again.'

'Gemma!' He tried to hold onto her hands but she pulled away and ran, her pale calves slicing down the hill through the darkness until he could see her no more.

Kane did not run after her. He felt like he should have sat there crying for hours or until daybreak, like a deserted lover from a romantic film. But after a few minutes he stood and walked home, in the opposite direction. He felt, very acutely, that nothing would be the same as it was before, and equally, that nothing would ever be what he dreamed of. There was a sudden emptiness inside him and he was bundled into some awful kind of limbo from which there seemed no escape.

When he reached home, he walked straight past his mother's concerned face up to his bedroom and climbed fully clothed and shivering beneath the blankets, falling immediately into a void of deep, dreamless sleep.

Kane blinked back the wetness in his eyes at the memory and blew the air from his cheeks. Walking over to the kitchen diner, he started to fill the kettle, wondering whether to give one of his brothers a call. He needed something to stop him from thinking. Ignoring one trail of thought, he focussed for a few minutes on wondering why he chose to live alone. It really did not suit him; he hated being alone, apart from the rare times he had a painting to do. Perhaps he could find a flatmate that would go away occasionally, at just the right times, to allow him to paint in silence. It might be better for him.

As the kettle boiled, he watched the steam drift upwards, dense in the cold of the flat. It whirled around, dispersing across the ceiling randomly. His mind was being obscure now. *How many cups of tea have I drunk in my whole life? Would it be in the thousands? It must be.* As the steam formed into lines and broke apart again, he found himself staring at his fingerprints, remembering something he was once taught in school. They were unique to you, your fingerprints; entirely environmental. Assuming you had fingertips in the first place, nothing genetic influenced them at all. If your father or mother or cousin had whorls, it did not mean you would not have loops. He inspected his own thumbprint. It was a whorl, but a triangular one, with lines that were quite straight. *Not bent,* he quipped to himself, *but straight.*

The kettle clicked off, but he continued to stare at his fingers as if he had never seen them before, stirring milk in with the teabag. He squeezed it out, but before he could reach the bin, it fell from the spoon onto his bare foot. Swearing, he kicked it off and hopped on one leg as he rubbed the reddening patch above his big toe. The teabag lay on its side in the middle of the floor, leaking brown juice into a crack in the tiles. He was so clumsy. He was so many things that it was easier not to think about until the minutiae of life forced him to. The teabag oozed at him, sad and lonely.

'Fuck,' he said to himself.

Kane left the room without picking the teabag up. He strode into his bedroom and pulled the drawer fully out of the bedside table, tipping its contents onto the duvet. He swore under his breath repeatedly as he rifled through the items: headache pills, tissues, last month's sports section, unused condoms well past their use-by date, little sketches on the backs of receipts. He gathered together the blister packs of his pink pills and threw them in a pile on top of the dishevelled duvet. Gathering everything up, he walked back into the kitchen and paused to pick up the forlorn teabag. He dropped everything into the bin, slammed the lid and picked the whole thing up, shaking it so hard that the leftovers from last night's dinner covered the pills. He stood over it for a minute or two, staring at his reflection in the stainless steel, until his breathing calmed and he could no longer hear his heartbeat.

19

The winter sky hung heavy with clouds. Here and there a star struggled through, exhaustedly delivering a pinprick of light that had travelled so far that its source might already have been extinguished. Freya's eyes fell from the transient sliver of moon to rest on Kane's face as he jogged up the steps towards her. He smiled shyly and as he reached her side.

'Hello,' she said as he came to a standstill.

'Hello.'

People bustled past and they naturally began to walk along the bridge together, slowly, keeping close to the barrier. Unspoken words clattered about them, bouncing off the rush hour traffic. Despite the background noise within her own head and from the bridge, Freya felt a naturalness envelop them. She took a deep breath.

'It's nice to see you,' she said, quietly. The words came out without her volition and she tried to erase them by hardening her face and looking beyond him to the people rushing up and down the steps.

Kane nodded, looking uneasy. 'It's good to see you too.'

'And you wanted to meet me because …?' she asked.

'Yeah, that's right,' replied Kane, faltering. 'Thanks.'

'About the guy whose portrait you're painting?'

'Well, I'll try to cut a long story short. Marie gave me a notebook in the hospital before they took her away,' Kane said quietly, not once taking his eyes from Freya's face. She looked straight back at him, trying to decipher the enigmatic shadows of his face. He looked around nervously, as if he was searching out a face in the people streaming past.

'Really?' Freya could hear the mock casualness of her tone

and she feared it was not very convincing. 'You didn't mention that before. But then, you were in quite a rush to leave.'

'I forgot all about it until I got home, to be honest.'

Freya only nodded in response, biting the inside of her cheek.

'From reading it, it seemed like she had spoken to the bomber,' Kane said. 'It was strange, right? We saw how keen she was to rescue him, and then in this notebook, she had written all these things down about him—his Background and stuff.'

As she listened, Freya realised how desperate she was to find a lasting attachment to Marie, to find out more about her. She struggled to remain detached and felt her face flush with anger that Kane could be so nonchalant about everything. As he spoke, she looked away from him over her left shoulder towards the office blocks, still lit by busy workers, and the darkness of the plane trees lining the river. This was her favourite view of London, the curve of the river allowing all its greatest monuments to be seen at once.

'Are you even listening to me?' Kane asked.

'Yes, of course I am. Marie had written all this stuff about him. And so where is it now? Have you brought it?'

'No,' Kane replied, shaking his head. 'It was taken from me. By force. By Sentries.' He paused, as if waiting for Freya's eyes to show concern, but then he sighed and went on. 'But then, somehow, it ended up back in the hands of this guy Barney—the guy I'm talking about. It turns out he was the bomber's psychologist when he was a kid. I think he was quite fond of him.' Kane paused again, as if he was anticipating Freya's snort of contempt. 'Anyway, so he found me at work, at the pub, because he thought I might know more about the notebook and Marie and everything.'

There was silence for a few moments as Freya processed the series of events. She finally turned away from the river to lean against the railing, her body next to his. They stood there silently for a few moments, watching the red of tail lights on the next bridge upriver intensify as the sky gradually darkened.

'Does that make sense?'

Freya nodded. 'But you didn't have anything else to tell him, really?' she finally asked.

'No, obviously not,' Kane said, dropping his voice and leaning in more closely to Freya. 'But see, that's only the beginning of it. He is pretty against the idea of birth diagnosis—I think he feels more strongly about it than he's even let on to me. He's been digging around, and get this: He found out that the bomber, you, and me all had the same executor.'

Freya was silent. She stared straight ahead.

'Freya, did you hear me?' He touched her on the shoulder.

She nodded almost imperceptibly. 'How did we get to *me* all of a sudden?'

'Because Barney gave me the list of all the people this particular executor had done birth diagnoses for. The Winstan guy was on it, then Barney noticed that I was on it, and then I saw that you were on it. Our surnames are so close together alphabetically.'

Freya frowned at him.

She realised that Kane could not bring himself to say *Sal* instead of *Winstan*. A surname was far less intimate, far less humanising. She reflected that perhaps that night and its aftermath had disturbed him more than he was willing to accept. But before the empathy flooded her, she pulled back, letting the feeling of rejection return.

'Are you following this?' Kane continued. 'Look at me, Freya.'

'I'm surprised you even remember my name, to be honest.'

'Come on ...' Kane reached out for her hand, nestled in the pocket of her coat. She let him hold her wrist, clamping her palm into a fist.

'But it's not *that* unusual, is it?' she eventually said, meeting his eyes through her lowered lashes. 'We're both about the same age, both from London. Those executors must do thousands and thousands of birth diagnoses every year.'

Something was simmering inside Freya's stomach but she refused to acknowledge it. It was the beginning of an excitement, that she and Kane might after all be in some way more deeply connected, linked to each other more strongly than by just one bizarre, life-changing night.

Kane was nodding now, his eyes widening. His enthusiasm was contagious. 'Yes, but Barney thinks there's something more to it. Our executor—some British-Japanese doctor—only did a few hundred kids, which he says is really unusual. In fact, it's kind of weird. He has all these theories.'

'So why are you telling me this?' Freya dragged her hands down her face and left her fingers covering her lips. She let her annoyance show, too exhausted to do otherwise. Kane looked away from her, straight across the bridge, through the passers-by, and to the far handrail. His eyes tightened into a slight squint and Freya followed his gaze. A face there caught her eye: a man's face, a bloated head atop a striped red and white tie, looking directly at them. She immediately dropped her gaze. They were being watched. Kane ran one of his hands through his hair, hiding his face from view for a short time before looking straight back at her. His expression was hard to decode. Freya wasn't sure if it was anger, or fear, or both making his lips quiver.

'Why am I telling you? Because I want to believe in something other than this,' Kane said at last, his voice lowered and curdled with frustration. He pulled at the tight white T-shirt exposed at his collar between his thumb and forefinger and let it go, the material falling, slightly stretched, back against his chest.

Freya could barely hear his words, but the simmering in her chest began to bubble. 'So where do we go from here?' she asked.

His face glazed over and he looked away from Freya, back towards the Sentry. She noticed his clenched jaw, and his hands curled into fists on the rail behind him. He seemed defiant, now, and it unnerved her. 'I don't know. The State wiped the files Barney had got hold of. And we're being watched, right now.' He paused. 'Don't look around.'

'I know, I know.'

'There's more I wanted to tell you,' Kane said. 'But I can't now.' He pointed back up the bridge at the cathedral. 'It's kinda ridiculous when you think about it, isn't it?' he said. 'I bet our parents would never in a million years have thought they'd see ads on the dome of St. Paul's.'

Freya said nothing, only raising her eyebrows and nodding. The whole dome was covered in a scrolling Coca-Cola advertisement, ruby red and harsh white sharply in contrast to the soft elegant pearl of the building's stones. The pillars supporting it had been temporarily wrapped with red and white fabric to make them look like giant candy canes. The structure's beauty, its meaning, was no longer sacred; there was no longer any such thing. With the end of organised religion, churches were little more than real estate. Beneath the brick, builders were converting the chapels into apartments for the rich and genetically superior.

'Look, I guess you'll need some time to process the things I've told you. You need to go home and be with someone,' Kane said. Freya rolled her eyes. 'This evening, I mean. I don't like the look of him.'

Freya felt something inside her snap. Her defences crumbled again.

'Kane. Maybe you know how I feel about you. If you want me to come with you, just say it, but don't pretend that I need you, that I need *anyone*, because I don't.' Freya folded her arms and pursed her lips as she would with her students. She fought to keep her voice calm but knew the anger was sweeping across her face. She felt tears pricking at her eyes.

Kane stared back at her, stuttering. 'I—I just meant that ...'

She shook her head, exhaling sharply through her nose, and started to walk away.

'Freya, wait,' he called after her. 'I'm sorry. I do think you should come with me. Or I can go with you, if you want. I don't mind.'

She looked over her shoulder coolly; her anger had already faded. 'Come on then, stupid. Let's go to your pub.'

Kane held open the door of the Stag for Freya. She grinned

as she walked past him into the pub and her eyes flickered admiringly up at the lacquered red ceiling. It felt like home: warm and cosy on a winter's evening. Dashing to the bar, she stood on the brass rail running around its base with both her feet and waved at the bartender.

Kane walked in slowly behind her, looking around for Marcus. He felt slightly uncomfortable; he normally only ever brought his brothers here. It was early evening now and the pub was heaving with customers ordering dinner. He looked at Freya's figure from the back, strands of her long hair slipping awkwardly out of the woolly hat on her head. He realised for the first time, guiltily, how she must have felt when he walked out of the hospital that morning. He then acknowledged how he himself had felt at the time; his petty avoidance tactics had made him schizophrenic and self-sacrificing.

Joining her at the bar, Kane smiled at the bartender, who was already pouring out a glass of English red wine for Freya.

'The usual please, Josh. Is anything off the menu already?'

'There's mash, but no sausages. I think Marcus completely forgot to send somebody to get them today.' The two men rolled eyes at each other and chuckled.

Kane pointed out the food menu, chalked in white above the bar. 'Anything you'd like, Miss Passingham?'

'Mmm, this wine's lovely,' she murmured, briefly lifting her lips from the wine glass. 'Let me see. Oh, a veggie lasagne would go down a treat, actually!'

'Okay mate, one vegetable lasagne and a goat's cheese salad, please. Put it on my tab, will you?' Kane asked.

'Might do, might not.' Josh grinned and shrugged his shoulders jokingly as he handed Kane a pint of local ale, still swirling in the glass like watery gravy.

Kane followed Freya to a corner of the pub, a semi-private alcove surrounded by columns from floor to ceiling. He slid along the bench to sit next to her, swiftly shifting back a few inches as he felt their knees bump together.

'The fire's nice,' she said, nodding towards the open fireplace across the room.

'And we're tucked away from the draft here,' Kane added, his words falling into what felt like a vacuum between them. 'We were lucky to get a seat at all, it's so busy. My privileges only go so far.'

'Not far at all, I'd imagine,' she said, smirking.

'Cheeky! What does being a teacher get you?'

Freya stared at the flames as if she had heard nothing, her hands tucked beneath her thighs, shoulders hunched up to her jawline.

Kane took his eyes from her glowing face, leaving her alone with her thoughts. He took a long, cool sip of his beer and collapsed back into the cushions. Out of the corner of his eye, he watched her take off one shoe and tuck her foot up onto the bench. She rested her drink on top of a cushion on her lap. The diamond ring he had noticed when they first met was still on her finger, its angles catching the flickering light. Freya noticed him look at it and turned her head away from him.

'That really does look like an engagement ring, you know. Are you deliberately trying to scare men off or something?' Kane knew his tone was combative, but even as he tried to soften the final words, Freya turned to face him and he saw a fiery spark in her eyes.

'Thanks for the observation, Kane, but I don't need a psychoanalysis session, if you don't mind.'

'It's just ...' he paused, letting his own thoughts catch up as he raised his eyes to the ceiling. 'I'm sure we've both pushed people away because of who we are. We must both be guilty of that.'

'Guilty of pushing people away? Wow, this just gets better.' Her sarcasm cut through the pub's warm atmosphere. She moved forward on her seat and slowly spread her palms on the table. 'The man—or should I say boy—who gave me this ring wanted to marry me before he knew the truth about me. He was an idiot. It was *his* guilt that was the problem, Kane, not mine.'

'So why do you wear it then?'

'Why do I wear it?' She looked furious; her lips curled. Her eyes betrayed her confusion. 'Because it's all I've got,

Kane. It's all I'll ever have. And at least with this I've got a reminder.'

Tears stung at Freya's eyes but she did not wipe them away. 'There's nothing to remind me of Jim. Even my memories of him are fading.'

'Jim?' asked Kane, softly. He could see emotions swirling to the surface of Freya's face. Anger and sadness seemed to diffuse out from her skin. She gazed at a fixed point beyond the table, as if she could see the person she was talking about, standing right there in front of them.

'My brother. My oldest brother.' She felt the anger disperse out from her belly as Jim's face entered her mind. She glanced at Kane and saw concern in his eyes. 'He died when I was seven. He was eleven.'

'What was he like?' asked Kane, finally daring to rest his hand upon hers.

'He was stupid,' she said, smiling to herself ruefully. 'He had the kind of Background anyone would dream of, but we always knew he would need a new liver at some point, when he was older. The only thing they told him to do was to avoid alcohol.'

'So what happened?'

'He and a friend stole a bottle of whisky. They drank it all. They were only little. Just kids.'

'I'm so sorry.' Kane squeezed her hand.

'It was a long time ago. We hardly talk about him anymore.' She sighed and tipped back her head, shaking out her hair. 'I'm sorry, I'm alright. I have this!' She tapped a nail on her wine glass and half-smiled.

For a couple of minutes they sat in silence as Freya's expression faded into blankness. Kane looked over his shoulder out of the window, thinking about the nature of tragedy. So much was known now; so much could be predicted, possibly even prevented. But there were still accidents. *Did Freya's brother's death cut her deeper because he should have lived a long, relatively healthy life?* Perhaps it was that it was harder to be philosophical about such things these days.

The snow from the morning was melting already and turning to sludge beneath people's feet. A few passers-by stopped to peer in through the windows of the pub. Seeing no spare tables, they invariably continued on, their faces still cold and miserable. Kane felt safe here, tucked into this corner. Freya was staring around the pub and scratching on the surface of the table with her fingernail. Kane knew that he should be similarly preoccupied, but he recognised that his mind had switched the thinking part off temporarily; he was often relieved by his innate ability to stay awake but muse over nothing, to let his thoughts drift carelessly above his consciousness like cirrus clouds over a factory. It was in his Background of course, his inner calmness. He had inherited it from his mother. To the disapproval of the State, some people spent years trying to attain that kind of enlightenment against the insistence of their genetics; lives were spent trying to learn the art of meditation and relaxation. That kind of dedication to nurture often worked, but to him, finding inner calm was as natural as sneezing in a dusty room.

Kane glanced at Freya again out of the corner of his eye. She appeared to be calm again; her face had taken on the taut youthfulness he remembered from their first meeting, as if she had been ironed out and all of her concerns extracted out of her ears. He acknowledged to himself that he had felt nothing less than normal since the afternoon he had thrown away the pills. In truth, apart from a brief bout of nausea, he had otherwise felt no different since and had lain in bed at night trying to decide if the physical indifference he felt ought to be a relief or a worry.

Until today, until he had met her and she had smiled at him with that sunbeam of a smile he did not feel he deserved, he had not known whether he had made the right decision. There had been an incessant tapping in his chest and stomach for most of the day; he had barely been able to focus on anything else. Sitting on the tube on the way here, with her head on his shoulder, he had been afraid she would hear it vibrating up through his skin and clothing. He had sat back and imagined that all of the pills he had ever taken, lying like stones on the bottom on his stomach, had finally broken apart and had hatched tiny birds that were now trying to fly out, all in one go. He had kept swallowing to keep them in and now his throat was dry and sore from the strain of it all, although the ale was helping.

Their steaming-hot meals appeared on the table and Josh plonked down a bucket of condiments and cutlery before dashing back to the bar.

'Wow—this looks amazing,' Freya said, pulling the plate towards her with one hand and grabbing the pepper with the other.

'I'm so hungry I already want to order another one!'

Freya laughed as he dug into his meal. 'Have you not eaten today?'

'I think it's just,' Kane said through a mouthful of food. He swallowed before repeating himself. 'I think it's just all the thinking I've been doing.'

'About?'

'Well, about whether something's going on with us.'

'You mean, *between* us?' Freya put down her fork and wiped her mouth, her eyes wide but coyly averted to the ketchup bottle.

'No, you know, *with* us. With you and me being on that list with the bomber, with the State wiping that information from mine and Barney's Indexes.'

'Oh.'

'I just keep asking myself why they would wipe it if they didn't have something to hide.'

'Do you think we can even talk about this?'

Kane shrugged. 'It's nothing they don't already know.' He felt himself wanting to protect Freya and he studied her face carefully for signs of distress. Her eyes moved quickly, randomly, over the table, as if she was chasing lines of thought and then losing them again. She pursed her lips. She seemed confused, but not upset.

'Then yes, I think so,' she said, slowly. 'I think something is going on.'

'I think so too. But what?'

They held each other's gaze for several seconds before returning to their dinner, the heat from the fire reddening their cheeks.

'Kane!' The call came rolling in with the draught from the front door, billowing coldly around their table. 'Thank God you're here.'

'Barney!' Kane squeezed his shoulder with genuine affection. 'This is Freya, actually.'

Freya grinned warmly and Barney offered her the briefest of smiles. As if he hardly dared, as if he was supposed to be anything but happy. He sat on the spare chair, adjusting it so his back was facing the window. His woollen coat steamed against the roar of the fire, and Barney pulled a note from his inside pocket, carefully unfolding it with shaking hands in the shadow of his hunched shoulders. He did not speak. He flattened it out on the table.

The words were small and so neatly written they could have been printed, yet the ink leaked into the paper, creating veins at the point where the pen had paused.

IF YOU GO BACK THERE, YOUR BODY AND THAT OF YOUR WIFE WILL NEVER BE FOUND.

Freya looked up at Barney's face with horror, her fork clattering to her plate. Despite Kane's disconcerted state, he saw the youthful beauty of her parted lips and her eyes swimming with fear.

'Shit.' Kane sighed deeply and shook his head, looking briefly around them. 'I think someone was watching us tonight, too.'

'I found it inside my pillbox with my medication,' Barney whispered. 'I've got no idea how it got there. With one thing and another, we've hardly left the house in the last few days. Leila's at a friend's house, but I had to find you. I had to warn you.'

Kane could tell Barney was going to say very little more. His spritely spirit was gone; his face was grey and tired. It was the first time Kane would have described him as an old man. He had no idea what to say.

Barney stood again. He crossed the room and threw the note onto the fire. Returning to the table, he slid his hands over Kane's, leaning over them like a spectre.

'We have to—all of us—forget all this. All of it. I'm sorry.' He clamped his lips together and stared back at Kane's shaking head before he turned and was gone as quickly as he had arrived, out into the darkness.

20

The man watched from across the road as Barney paused on the steps of the Stag to button up his overcoat. It was already after the early curfew and the street lights were dimmed. Soon they would be turned off completely. Barney stopped moving, as if hesitating, caught by his thoughts. He half-turned, as if to walk back in, but then seemed to change his mind once more.

Barney visibly frowned as he looked up and down the empty street, probably looking for a taxi. It was cold, and each exhaled breath hung in the air around him like ghosts of unspoken words. The man tensed as Barney stepped to the edge of the pavement, his fingers darting across the screen of his Index without shifting his vision. The street had fallen strangely silent and he feared what was coming. Barney didn't know about the invisible road blockades beyond his range of vision; it only took one Sentry to hold a crowd to ransom with a single glance.

Finally a black cab came along, driving slowly, and Barney waved it down. The man struggled to keep his eyes on Barney's face as he climbed in and mouthed instructions to the driver.

The door of the taxi slammed shut and Ivan Msembe broke into a run.

Tumbling out onto the street, Kane remarked that the air felt warmer, wrapped as they were in an aura of red wine and ale. To fill the shocking void left by Barney, they had gone on to spend hours talking about things of relative inconsequence: work, family, the other people milling around them. He had spotted in Freya the qualities he had noticed the first time they had met in Raith's, the same carefree, youthful banter escaping from beneath the veil of her carefully manicured personality. The rawness had faded and it was almost as if they were as comfortable as strangers again.

They walked in silence now. Kane could feel the alcohol still seeping from his stomach into his bloodstream, circling in ever-increasing concentrations through his heart and his brain, bouncing off the dopamine receptors and causing a cascade of miniature firework displays in his wandering thoughts. They walked through the little park, cutting across the grass to reach the station. Kane kept his eyes about him, looking for shadows. Nothing caught his attention. The Sentries had either given up for the night or were less keen on making an approach than he feared. Perhaps they had seen Barney's warning. Something told him they were safe for now.

As Freya and Kane walked down the hill, he felt his insides glowing like the remnants of a bonfire, scattered across a distant beach. They walked shoulder to shoulder, and Kane held his arms folded across his chest like Freya. He was fully aware of their closeness and found it hard to think of anything else. When they reached the entrance to the tube station, the awkwardness between them became tangible. Kane felt it could be pinged like an elastic band, as if he could watch it recoil and vibrate as they spoke.

'It's late, Frey.'

'I know, it's fine. I'll be fine. It's only a short walk on the other side.'

'If you like, you could come back with me. I've got a sofa bed in the lounge,' Kane said, his chin tucked cautiously into the collar of his jacket. 'I promise to cook you one of my famous fry-ups when you're hung-over tomorrow!' He broke into his most charming smile.

Freya rubbed her nose and smiled politely, looking around them. There were couples walking all around them, holding hands or laughing and joking. Kane saw her eyes fall upon a man and woman, standing at the end of the ticket hall. The woman was half-turned to step onto the escalator, the man resolutely holding onto her outstretched hand, his head leaning pleadingly to one side. As Kane watched, fully aware that Freya had not yet replied, the man pulled the woman gently into his body and they kissed so passionately that he almost had to look away. The way the man wrapped his arms around her shoulders, the way the angle of the woman's inclined leg revealed the shortness of her skirt under the long, open coat tickled at him. It took Freya's voice to tear his attention away.

'Yes, maybe we could talk. About everything that's happened. I haven't really had anyone to share it with.'

'Okay, it's only fifteen minutes on the tube.' Kane was pleased, although his thoughts immediately turned to concerns with the state of his apartment; the dishes still piled up in the sink, the lacklustre state of his allotment, the portrait of Barney still unfinished on its easel.

He glanced back to the escalator; the couple had gone. Their decision had been made, for good or bad.

Barney collapsed back into the leather seats of the cab, letting his head tip back onto the headrest. He closed his eyes and willed away the rest of the journey. The radio was tuned to a foreign station and the lilt of the song was Arabic, or Indian or something. There was a strong scent of aftershave, mixing incongruously with the jasmine he'd seen strung in a garland around the rear-view mirror. As he tried to switch off, the soaring notes of the music tugged at his consciousness, demanding his attention.

Something was not right. Barney felt his heart slip downwards, hanging precariously above the turbulent pit of his stomach acid. His insides churned suddenly with sickness and his eyes snapped open. The driver was Caucasian, he had spoken with a slight Cockney accent as he had confirmed the destination, and now Barney could see his blond hair was slicked and neatly parted to the side, and that he wore a silk tie clipped neatly against his shirt with a shiny silver pin.

This was not his taxi. The doors were locked. Their eyes met in the mirror and the driver's coldly triumphant smile fuelled Barney's panic. At that precise moment, Barney also realised they were driving in the wrong direction.

'Where are you taking me, and why?' Barney asked,

desperately trying to force the wavering from his voice. Reason was his only defence.

The driver ignored him. Barney turned to gaze out of the rear-view mirror but the glass all around him blackened before his eyes. In seconds, he could no longer even see the driver on the other side of the screen. The darkness choked him. He scrambled for his Index in his pocket, but that too was like a stick of slate. His breathing became loud in his ears, ragged and irregular, tangling against the thumping of his heart which now boomed through his arteries. Even the smell of the jasmine faded and he could barely feel the air on his tongue as he inhaled.

Sensory deprivation sank around him like a blanket that offered no warmth. He could feel time stopping, his brain stopping. He was going to die just after he had decided to quit this stupid endeavour. The irony made him buckle with a sudden, painful laugh that doubled his body in two, forcing his head onto his knees.

Angie's message had been unequivocal: Msembe would have to go further than he had gone before. Getting the motorbike was easy. He grabbed the collar of the pizza delivery boy before he could acquiesce. *No location data available,* the electronic voice of his chip repeated insolently in his head as he threw the boy to the pavement. The taxi was masked. Msembe looked up and down the empty road, calculating the distance to the roadblock he had passed on his way to the pub. He was wearing a balaclava but he could still be scanned. Speed and the brick shoved hastily into his deep coat pocket were his only weapons. He kicked down and revved, pulling out into the middle of the street. The streetlights were out already. If you wanted to drive at this time of night, you drove slowly, carefully.

Msembe hit seventy kilometres per hour as the roadblock came into sight. The bike's headlights illuminated a Sentry on either side of the road and Msembe squinted to try to see what they were armed with. One spun a slim handgun through his fingers, and the other ...

It was too late. Msembe kicked down hard, and his chest

exploded with a fear unmatched to anything he had felt before. He felt the bike wobble underneath him and steeled his arms, gripping the handlebars more tightly. The Sentries raised their arms in unison.

Msembe glanced upwards, wishing he could fly. The stars seemed to snigger at him, and the moon was hiding its face behind a cloud. He had studied Stephen Hawking in his last year of school, and the quote which had formed the concluding sentences of his coursework rang out into the swirling, half-lit night: *I have noticed even people who claim everything is predestined, and that we can do nothing to change it, look before they cross the road.*

Msembe flattened his body to the bike, shut his eyes and swerved as sharply as he could manage without losing control.

On the tube, Kane drifted in and out of sleep, his thoughts such a cacophony in his waking seconds that they quickly exhausted him to the point of drowsiness again. In a lucid moment, he looked down at Freya's head resting on his shoulder, her hands folded primly in her lap. He could feel the steady, gentle expansion and contraction of her chest against his. Kane struggled to keep his own eyes open in order to bathe in their closeness as she slept.

As the tube pulled in to his stop, he ventured his hand on top of hers, stroking the skin of her knuckles with his fingertips. The train came to a halt and Kane shook Freya slightly to wake her. She opened her eyes almost before he nudged her and beamed at him, knowingly. She had not been asleep at all, he realised, and he felt stupid to have been caught. *What am I doing?* He recalled suddenly the fleeting kiss they had shared on the floor of the hospital that night and he felt inexplicably close to doing it again—simply leaning across and pressing his lips into hers—but also sick; a nausea filled his chest and he breathed out.

Freya stood abruptly and joined the queue of passengers filing out of the carriage. 'Come on, slowcoach,' she teased.

Walking beside her towards the tube station, Kane felt a game was at play, one that he did not know the rules of. He felt out of his depth but he needed to stay with her, he wanted to talk.

'Can you believe we're both on that list?' he exclaimed, as if the information was brand new to his ears.

'Yes and no,' Freya replied. 'It's weird, but I just had this feeling. I've wondered if Marie is on there, too.'

'Well, that *would* be odd.'

'You probably think it's daft, and I'd almost be inclined to agree with you, but I think something brought us all together that night.'

Kane stayed silent, only raising his eyebrows by way of a response. Freya seemed surprisingly serious, as if the past few hours had slipped down off her shoulders and into her pockets and were now knotted up inside the palms of her hands. How easily her mood could change. As they left the station and walked down the road to the tower blocks, he became consciously aware of the fact that he was running his eyes over each person walking in the opposite direction, focussing on the buttons of their coats or the hair on the back of their necks. His eyes fell on a man of a similar age walking towards them, a briefcase in his hand. Diamonds sparkled at his cuff. Eventually they reached home.

'Sorry,' said Kane. 'The lifts are switched off after nine p.m. to save energy.'

'Not ideal for coming back from a night out!' Freya laughed. 'It's okay, I don't mind.'

'It's only on the third floor.'

They walked up the stairs to the little apartment and Kane dashed in, pulling the cloth over his easel and pushing it to one side as Freya sat down on the sofa.

'Coffee?' he asked as switched on the lamp. His words sounded so clichéd and he winced slightly at himself in this situation he did not recognise, barely felt himself to be part of.

'I won't sleep if I have caffeine. Maybe a nightcap?' She grinned and he felt relaxed again.

'What would you like? Whisky?'

Freya nodded and he walked over to the kitchen, reaching for the bottle from the back of his top cupboard and pouring it into two glasses.

'Does whisky go off?' he joked, winking at her.

'I wouldn't know!'

Handing Freya a glass, he tucked himself into the opposite end of the sofa. They were both curled into balls, feet hidden beneath thighs, facing each other. Although he drank it rarely, whisky was one of the few drinks that really grounded him, prevented him from floating away with his thoughts.

Freya took a few sips and sighed heavily. 'It feels like we've known each other for ages, doesn't it?' she asked, tonelessly. Kane found her meaning hard to decipher.

'It does really, yeah.' He sipped his drink deeply.

'I want to tell you something, and I want you to promise you won't think I'm weird.'

'Can I think it but just not say it?'

'Okay,' Freya said, smiling. 'I went to Marie's house.'

Kane stuck out his bottom lip and nodded slowly. 'I wasn't expecting that.'

'You're thinking I'm weird.'

'No, not weird, just …'

'Just what?'

'I'm just not sure why you'd do that.'

'I'm not sure why either.'

'And what do you even mean? You went inside? Said hello? Had a chat with the family?'

Freya paused for a while before continuing. She rested the glass on her belly and tapped the glass with her fingertips. 'That night we all met—the bombing—it felt like everything was coming together by being blown apart. Do you know what I mean?'

Kane was still thinking about her words as she continued.

'It was like everything in my life was coming to a head, as if something was *happening*. I can't explain it. You spend so much of your life with nothing happening.' She stopped for several moments, her eyes hanging on the easel in the corner of the room. 'I felt a connection to her and it's like I can't shake it away.'

As she shook her head, as if in disbelief, Kane noticed

her eyes were teary. He did not feel the same about Marie, but he recognised the sensation she had described. She might as well have been talking for him, explaining how he felt about her. Little did she know.

'So what did you do?' he asked.

'I just knocked on the door and spoke to her father, offered my condolences.'

'The poor man. What did he say?'

'I tried to be kind but he was … I don't know … *malevolent*. That's the best word I can think of.'

'Really?'

Freya nodded, her eyebrows raised in assurance. 'It made me even sadder. He wouldn't let me see anything of hers. I don't think he trusted me.'

'But who'd trust a stranger turning up out of the blue to ask after their dead daughter?' As Kane spoke, he was not sure if it was a genuine question or his lame attempt at a joke. Freya looked offended, and he wished he had not said anything.

'So I went back. I broke in.' She seemed to be emboldened by Kane's ridicule. 'I broke in and I took some of her things; her writing and stuff.'

Kane opened his mouth to speak and then changed his mind.

Freya's eyes flashed at him. She seemed to be challenging him, but it quickly subsided. She rearranged herself, crossing her legs beneath her and twisting her hair down over one shoulder. Her forlorn face looked beautiful in the lamplight. Turned to the side, the soft, fuzzy hairs covering her cheek were backlit and the curve of her eyelashes played shadows across her delicate nose. Inside Kane, the last of the little pink eggs split apart and its little bird burst forth, hammering excitedly at his chest, trying to break through between his ribs.

The bullet came like a kick in his shoulder blade, but instead of rapidly fading to a dull ache, the sharpness of the impact intensified as the shouts were swallowed into the darkness behind him. Msembe heard more shots crack through the night but felt nothing. His teeth started to chatter and his back began to go numb, as if he was pushed up against ice. He tried not to slow down as he flexed his right arm. Pain volleyed through him, bouncing off his bones. With a burst of relief, he saw the taxi switching lanes up ahead; a few other cars lay between them. As his body sank into chaos, clarity descended on his mind and his spirits rose as he moved his left arm to feel the brick still sitting heavily in his pocket. As Msembe pulled closer to the taxi, he glanced in his wing mirror. Their speed had forced them ahead of the other cars. Far enough, he hoped. The driver's window came down and a slim handgun emerged. Quickened by the pain in his shoulder, Msembe dropped back and swung around behind the taxi, darting up on its inside before the Sentry had time to react. Horns blared behind him. The taxi swung to the left, trying to force him against the pavement. Msembe dropped back again and, without hesitating, revved hard, pulling forward in front of the taxi. Now this was his game.

Barney felt only movement. The taxi spurted forward, pushing him back into his seat. His hands grasped at the seatbelt across his chest. He fought the nausea that came with the jerky movements he could not align without his senses. He did not even hear the windscreen shatter or see the blood spray against the glass divider. The taxi was a gyroscope and Barney cradled his head into his chest as the wall came up to meet him.

If the State did not already want to arrest Kane, or even kill him, they would soon. It felt as if he had little left to lose. He leant forward, his voice a hoarse whisper. 'I did what you asked me to, Freya. I threw the pills away. They're all gone.'

As soon as the words were out, Kane was released; the bars of his life felt as if they had that moment been wrenched apart, like he had bent cast iron with his bare hands. He had known so long ago, always really known, that there had been some kind of mistake, that one of those infallible machines had somehow missed a base pair, misread a sequence or doubled a copy-number.

Freya was visibly staggered; three parallel lines appeared across her forehead.

'I'm not gay, Freya. And do you know what? I never have been.'

'But ...' She looked around nervously.

'Come on—things can't get any worse. I don't need anyone to tell me—I *know*.' He studied her reaction but her face was blank. He paused, daring himself to continue. 'I thought that maybe that was what you wanted to hear.'

He watched as she collapsed in upon herself, tears suddenly wracking her. He moved along the sofa to hold her, pulling her head against his collarbone and resting his mouth and nose on her hair as she shook.

'What? What's the matter?'

'I wish I felt the same about myself,' she managed through her sobbing. 'But I know it's not true. I know I have such little time left. I can't keep dreaming. I have to start planning what I'm going to do.'

'Shhh,' Kane whispered into her ear. 'I'm sorry, I'm sorry.'

Freya breathed deeply, trying to starve the sobs that had taken control of her. 'You don't need to be sorry.'

'I do. My problems are nothing—nothing—compared to what you've had to deal with, what you've had to go through.'

Freya sniffed and wiped beneath her eyes, looking away from Kane. He took her chin and turned her around to face him and kissed her on the lips, cradling one hand behind her head. For a few seconds, Kane let himself fall a little deeper, shimmering into her embrace. Then she pulled away.

'All of this ... it's just a distraction, an amazing distraction,' she whispered, tear tracks drying down her cheeks. Kane did not know what else to say. Shocked, he could only nod at her, trying to reject the anger stirring inside him. Gathering a pillow and blankets from the bedroom he brought them out to her and laid them on the sofa.

Freya tried not to absorb his confusion; raising her barriers, she turned in upon herself. Watching Kane, hearing the power of his newly found conviction, had made her realise that she could not imagine feeling the same. She thought of her weaknesses: her terrible balance, the increasingly bad headaches, the tiredness she felt at the end of the days now. A jelly still trapped in its mould, she felt surrounded by glass. She pulled the blanket over her and stretched into the sofa. Like she had with Jim's death so many years before, it was easier to shut down than to face the pain of the present. She closed her eyes to dismiss him and listened to the padding of his feet as he walked away.

'I hope you meet somebody, Kane, somebody wonderful. But not me,' she said.

He paused on the threshold of his bedroom before slamming the door shut.

21

I'm sorry to interrupt,' Angie said as she walked across the room. Her heels clicked loudly on the cream marble floor and brought Barney's attention back from the high-rise view out over Elephant and Castle. Squinting, adjusting his eyes from staring at the squares of tower block windows, he recognised her immediately through the vestiges of his shock. She was dressed smartly in a tweed jacket and black trousers, a heavy winter coat lying over her arm. Angie sat down in the chair beside him and arranged the coat over his shoulders. To Barney's surprise, he let her.

'Msembe said to give you this.'

Barney stared back at her, wide-eyed. There was little more strain that his body could take. Worry swarmed through him, tangling in the webs of his anger.

'Is he ...?'

'He'll be okay. The bullet went in below his shoulder blade and out below his collarbone. We'll sort him out. He's a brave lad. He's lucky. You're lucky. I'd have felt terrible if ...' She dropped her eyes to the floor before raising her gaze to look at Barney again, licking her lips and tipping her head to the side. Her eyes perceptibly narrowed. 'So, how far have you got?'

Barney shook his head in disbelief and ran one hand through his hair, resting it at the back of his neck. Her very presence made him feel accomplice to her and Sal's crime; he felt muddied by her sitting next to him.

'Maybe I didn't make it clear when we met before, but I don't want your help,' he said firmly, gesturing to his swollen, bruised face. 'This is where your help has got me.'

'That's a little ungracious, Barney,' she said softly, reaching across and sweeping her fingertips across the dressings on his cheek. 'I've just saved your life. And that of your wife's.' Her palm was cold.

'She's safe? Where is she?'

'She's fine; we have her in one of our safe houses. She's absolutely fine,' Angie said before standing and walking to the window, her back to him, arms folded. She pushed the half-open curtain back against the frame and leant on it. Barney so wanted to believe her. He closed his eyes in the absence of her gaze and pictured Leila asleep in their bed, her hair shining on the pillow. Tears welled up behind his lids.

'I accept that we are different and I understand that you do not support what we do,' Angie said. 'Sometimes, I hate myself, too. Believe me when I say that I cannot sleep for thinking of it, for thinking of the people who lost their lives.'

'They were blown apart, limb from limb, or burned through to their bones. They didn't all just expire like that,' Barney clicked his fingers and the room became colder. Angie turned as she spoke, and Barney was surprised to see that tears had sprung into her eyes and collected above the dam of her lower lashes. He struggled to believe they were real.

'You don't think I know that? I didn't know so many people would die. I—I don't know what I thought …' She trailed off as her voice began to wobble and Barney studied her face, deciding that her misery was real. He felt no need to comfort her or to further berate her; she would become her own punisher in time, and he suspected a good one at that.

Angie was silent for a few minutes as she composed herself. Barney watched her as she took deep, even breaths, letting the emerging tears crystallise around her lashes. He pondered that everything, even her own sorrow, must be fuel for the cause.

'Why do you need me?' Barney asked wearily. 'Just let me go home. I'm not interested anymore.'

Barney watched, now transfixed, as the colour drained away from her cheeks and she pursed her lips back into the same narrow line.

'Barney, I think we both want the same outcome here.' Her voice was businesslike again. 'We want to see real change; we want the State to think twice about all of this.'

He could not help but laugh. 'Maybe you haven't noticed, but I've got a death warrant hanging around my neck. And who knows where Kane and Freya are.' He paused momentarily, thinking back to earlier that evening. 'Precisely how many of my conversations have you listened in on?'

'Oh, easily as many as the State has. Maybe more. Enough to know that you've found something that doesn't add up. Am I right?' She rested her chin on her clenched fist and smiled that triumphant, conspiratorial smile.

Barney shrugged in response, reflecting for a moment that she was wasting her time, that she could have been a leading politician, a formidable businesswoman, rather than fronting a half-baked guerrilla movement. He found himself frowning once more at her apparently middle-class uniform, the bizarre, hypnotic blend of tweed and terrorism. His expression ended her smile and she extracted an index finger from within her fist, directing it firstly to her thin lips and then towards him. She narrowed her eyes as she pointed.

'I know you can't get hold of those files you so desperately want to see.'

She was calling his bluff, Barney thought, but he could see no point in lying. He was a terrible liar, as it happened. He sighed heavily, letting his cheeks puff out and the air run noisily through his lips.

'You're right. I have no idea how I can get them.' He instantly regretted it. Angie cocked her head to one side, like an animal that had heard the call of an unusual bird in the darkness of the forest. She did not speak for several moments.

'A huge part of you wishes you'd never got caught up in this mess, I know that. There must be times when you want to leave it all behind you, don't you?' she asked. She had his emotions backed into a corner now. The upper hand was hers and he was starting not to care. 'And maybe you're right. Let me take it from here,' she said, her voice danced around, rising and falling. 'I know someone on the inside, the kind of guy who could get his hands on these things with no trouble at all, without any unnecessary interrogations. Don't pull that face—I can keep you safe if you just help us a little bit. This can all be done very easily without recourse to any kind of coercion or violence. I promise.'

'Remind me again what it is you're trying to do?' he asked carelessly, being sure to avoid eye contact with her, focussing on the buckle of his satchel. He would run if he knew where he was starting from. He could not remember getting here. Nearly everything from the moment of the crash was blank. All he could recall was the soothing voice of his Tag whispering directly into his brain. *Vital signs functional. Vital signs functional.*

'Barney, listen to me,' Angie continued. 'The first thing is that you have to forgive me, and you have to forgive Sal. In hindsight, it was a huge mistake, something I would never play a part in again. But I think what we have here is the beginning of something revolutionary. If we could find some evidence, all those people whose lives have been governed by a faulted system, a flawed technology—'

'Faulted?'

Angie ignored his interruption. 'We could change the world for the better, I'm sure of it.' She paused, waiting for her words to take effect. 'I have contacts that can get it to the media, to the right people. All I've ever needed is one strong story, one mistake, backed up by evidence, by real lives, to start to take this system apart.'

The strength of the passion in Angie's voice made Barney's skin tingle. She walked closer still, visibly swallowing back the emotion at the back of her throat. She was on the hard sell. 'I will do it, Barney, if it's the only thing I ever do with my life. I will do it with or without you.'

Barney nodded. He found the corner of his mouth twitching, and as she beamed back at him, he knew that she had spotted the smile in his eyes. The threat in her voice was understated but Barney already understood the extent of her ruthlessness.

'But do not ever mention my name to anyone,' she said.

'It would be a mistake. We will know where it came from. We will keep each other safe: that is the deal.'

22

Freya awoke early, with a start. Two successive shocks washed over her as she firstly realised where she was and, secondly, felt a sharp pain shoot between her temples. *The alcohol or the disease?* she asked herself, pressing her eyelids back over her eyes, banishing thoughts that should not be forming so early in the morning. Freya was angry with herself for what she had said the previous night, frustrated that she had no ability to throw even the smallest amount of caution to the wind, to have a little belief.

After a further five minutes of laying on the sofa bed, half asleep and fully dressed, she sat up with a start, a high-pitched whine coming from her throat. She braced herself, holding her breath, as she stole a glimpse at the screen of her Index.

'Fuck it,' she exclaimed. It was Friday, the last day of term. It was nine-thirty. Her pupils would have been in school for nearly an hour. By now, somebody else would have scanned them in, somebody else would be teaching them their first lesson of the day, or at least supervising them as they coloured or read. This was not like her; she had never even been late for work. At least she had that in her favour. Freya groaned and, upon doing so, realised she also felt violently sick. Dashing to the bathroom and bending over the toilet, she prayed that Kane was still fast asleep.

As she wiped her mouth and splashed her face with water, Freya considered using the tragedies of her Background for positive use. It would not be the first time.

She sat down on the toilet seat and leant forward over her thighs, pressing her hands flat against the cold, tiled floor

195

and resting her chin between her knees. Her head throbbed viciously, her agitated heartbeat bouncing back and forth off the walls of her chest.

She thought back to her teenage days, doused in the throes of puberty and capable of doing as much winding with her little finger as she liked without even having to question her morals. Her mother, so terrified by her daughter's fate, was very easily misled. Faked headaches, shaky limbs—there was a time when one of those complaints alone would have got her out of any unwanted situation. It was a terrible habit she had grown out of long ago, but perhaps just this once …

But of course not, she thought, sadly remembering. In less than a year her employment contract would be handed over to her doctor, and the head teacher of her school would have to inspect her state of health and decide whether to renew her employment or whether to extend it by six months at a time, pending disintegration of her health. This was not a time to report collapses or migraines. She wanted another year, at the very least; otherwise all her training would have hardly been worth it. Tears rolled down her shins and she shook herself, pressing the hand towel into her face and rubbing her eyes. It smelled of lavender and her mind wandered to Kane, to the words they had exchanged the night before.

Kane laid in bed listening to the sound of Freya vomiting in the bathroom. He was glad he had gulped back a pint of water before bed, although even now the taste of whisky was still coating his tongue, sucking it free of moisture. He thought about getting up to pour a drink but worried that Freya would be embarrassed to be seen as she was. He reminded himself of his shift at the pub later and realised that Freya ought to be at work. He groaned; he did not want her to be any more upset. He rolled over onto his back and rested his arms beneath his head. His eyes lingered vainly over his arms before he shut them again; those hours spent hauling around the barrels at work were paying off.

His mind skipped to Barney and imagined him eating

breakfast, at a very reasonable hour for a proper grown-up to have his first meal of the day. Kane himself probably would not eat anything until he rolled into work at midday. Perhaps Barney was eating muesli now—no, eggs on toast—thinking nervously about the warning from the previous day. Kane looked around cautiously, almost expecting to find a threatening handwritten note of his very own lying on the pillow or tucked under the bedside lamp.

As he became fully awake, his thoughts focussing, something buzzed around him like static electricity. It was something akin to excitement, an eager adrenaline pulsing through his veins. Kane heard the shower start to run and immediately, selfishly, realised that Freya would probably consume this morning's hot water ration. Rolling out of bed and steadying himself before he opened the bedroom door, Kane headed to the kitchen to make a pot of tea.

'I have to go,' Freya announced as she strode into the room minutes later, pulling her sweater over her head. Her hair was damp but wound back into a long plait, black with water. She barely glanced in his direction. 'I used one of the towels hanging up in there. I hope you don't mind.'

'No, of course not—I've been rubbing myself down with that towel for the last three weeks.' He laughed a little at his own joke but Freya ignored him, starting to tie up the laces of her boots as she sat on the sofa.

'I'm sorry. Are you late for work? I was making us a cup of tea.'

'Yes, Kane, I'm very late and I've got no idea what kind of excuse I'm going to give. I've got to go.' Her eyes squinted, sadly, as if it was painful for her to leave.

Kane watched her, dumbly. He wanted to stop her, but he knew he could not and that it would not be appropriate to even try. Her cheeks flushed and her eyes flashed, but there was always that vulnerability seeping from beneath her skin, that girlish skittishness that she probably did not realise she possessed. He revelled for a brief moment in these feelings, a gift he was still unwrapping, ever so slowly. He fought back a smile. He tried to think of something that would make her stay.

There was a knock at the door. They looked at each other and Kane ushered her away, back into the bathroom.

'Who is it?' Kane called as normally as he could manage, edging closer to peer through the spyhole. A man dressed in plain clothes was holding a police hologram badge in front of his chest.

'You're both in danger,' said Msembe. 'You need to come with me.'

23

Freya paced angrily around the small room, pausing occasionally to scratch her nails down the peeling, textured wallpaper, tossing narrow strips to the floor. Barney and Kane watched her wearily from the sofa.

'The Anti-Genetics Movement?' She demanded it again, as if it were a meaningful question with a simple answer.

Barney nodded gravely.

'I don't understand what you're saying, Barney.' Freya frowned, looking from one of the men to the other, seeking clarity.

'The same people who planted the bomb,' Kane repeated quietly. He was speaking to Freya but seemed to be directing the questioning tone of his voice towards Barney.

Freya's eyes were wide and she moved to the window, the fury slipping off her in waves. 'So what you're telling me is that you've been working with the same people who nearly killed us, who murdered Marie and all those innocent people?'

Barney was still, composed. He smoothed down his shirt where it crumpled across his stomach, as if to flick away her anger, direct it elsewhere. 'I know how bad this must look, Freya, and believe me; I've had my own doubts—'

'Doubts? About collaborating with terrorists? And with my personal information, my life! How dare you!' she thundered from her position across the room. Her arms were folded demurely but she spoke as if she towered over them, throwing lightning bolts with her words.

'And you! You conveniently neglected to mention that bit, didn't you?' she shot at Kane. Her wavering anger, oscillating over split seconds, spilled over both Barney and Kane, drenching them in her confusion, her fear, and the wistfulness of her hope. The tumult of emotions that had plagued her since the bombing, for so long hidden in the clouds above her, now rained down in a storm that she could not control.

'From the moment I met you, it's all gone wrong.' She walked over to Kane and, pushing him from the arm of the sofa where he sat, showered his chest with blows using the sides of her fists. He stood up but let her continue; shoulders back, his arms hanging by his sides.

'Listen!' Barney shouted. His voice sounded strangled. 'Please, please listen, Freya.'

Freya stopped and looked at him in surprise. She had not imagined him to be the kind of man to ever raise his voice. She saw the kindly face of an old man, every wrinkle and each age spot beseeching her. And as if by some sort of magic, his calmness spread to her across the chasm between them, an invisible finger laid itself across her lips. A sense of resignation gradually overcame her.

'So, what can I do?' she whispered, sinking back into the chair. 'Tell me everything.'

Barney nodded thankfully. Kane remained standing, pressing his fingers to his temples.

'She—I can't tell you her name—asked me to come and see her. I didn't know who she was, but she promised me information about Sal. I *had* to find out what it was. Her contact in the police—the man who picked you up this morning—had given her Marie's notebook and I think she knew I would know what to do with it, would have an idea of where to start. She gave me Kane's details and suggested I ask him some more, which, as you both know, I did.' He paused, nervously smiling. Freya mirrored him with a slight smile of her own.

'Yesterday, just after I left you, they saved me from God knows what,' he continued. 'She had been listening; she knew we were onto something and she knew I was in danger. She's told me that her contacts can get us the rest of that material, things I could never have got hold of. For all it's worth, she's promised us safety. I thought of you both, and all I could think was that you deserved the truth, whatever that might be.'

'Didn't you just do it for Sal?' Freya asked, her face stony.

Barney sighed deeply and leant forward towards her. 'Of course I don't condone what Sal did, what the Anti-Genetics Movement has done, but he was like a son to me.' He blinked away dampness in his eyes. 'I might have started this journey on Sal's behalf, perhaps even to go some way towards quelling my own guilt, but I promise you that I will finish it for you—for you and Kane.'

Freya and Kane looked at each other and then back at him, each with their lips folded together solemnly. The atmosphere in the little room was beginning to clear; the storm clouds were slowly retreating.

'It must have been rather terrible, that night,' Barney ventured.

Freya shifted her arms about against her chest awkwardly. It was true that she had tried not to think about it very much, and it was a few moments before she spoke.

'It's surreal, you know, to look back on it. Me, Kane—we all could have died, just like Marie. It's a very strange feeling: like you've cheated death somehow, you know?'

'I can't imagine how it must feel. And you didn't know any more about Marie than Kane?'

'No,' she said, 'but she was so sweet.'

Freya noted the tenderness in her voice. Barney nodded in response; a gentle smile on his face. She could see that he must have been very good at his job. His presence alone was reassuring. His eyes took her in—all of her—and whatever he saw, he made no judgement. 'Actually,' Freya said, 'I went to her house afterwards to see her father. I don't really know why. I just wanted to know more about her, I guess.'

'That sounds like fairly normal behaviour after something so distressing.'

'Really? I felt like I knew her and yet knew nothing about her, all at the same time. I wanted to offer her father my condolences, although I'm not sure he really wanted them. She had no next of kin listed, you know. I don't know anything about her Background, but she told me, in the hospital, that she studied the stars. I thought that maybe if I could see her things, I could get a better idea of what she was all about.'

'And did you?' asked Barney. Freya noticed that Kane's eyes were downcast again; he was frowning.

'Yes, I have some of it at home. It seems really good.' Freya was not sure it was, but it felt like the right thing to say, in case by some miracle Marie could hear her. 'There were mathematical things that I really don't have a clue about. I'm going to have to find someone to ask about them because it's crazy stuff. God only knows what it all means.'

Barney grinned, and Freya realised she had not seen him do so before. He didn't seem like the sort of man to grin. He smiled often, yes, but calmly, vapidly, not widely enough to suggest that he was anything less than a sophisticated gentleman. He seemed to break the grin as soon as he realised he was doing it and Freya almost laughed aloud.

Freya stole a glance at each of her companions in the room. Were they imprisoned here, or were they being kept safe? Was there a difference? She noticed that Kane was dressed differently, wearing loose-fitting jeans and a hooded sweatshirt. She remembered what he had said to her only the night before, and recalled the bubbling in her stomach as he had voiced what she felt were old, buried doubts. And now he was uncharacteristically quiet. With his messy hair and three-day stubble, he looked like a university student. She found him even more attractive; he looked vastly more comfortable in his own skin. She turned back to Barney.

'So, Barney,' she said. 'After dealing with all those kids day in and day out, were you never tempted to get your own Background done?'

'Oh! Well,' he said, shaking his head. 'In the early days, when I was younger, I did think about it. I was in my forties then and having a bit of a midlife crisis in many respects, you might say. But it didn't last long. Leila, my wife, definitely didn't want hers done, and when you're already married— well, you sort of have to do such serious things together or not at all. So I never did. And now I'm glad.'

'Really? Why?'

'It's partly hindsight. Look at me—I'm still healthy,

happy. I haven't spent years worrying about what might have been. It's all worked out rather well!' He laughed a little and then stopped awkwardly. 'I'm sorry, Freya, that was insensitive of me,' Barney said quietly.

She turned around and forced a smile. 'No, it wasn't,' she said.

Barney shrugged and spread his hands in apology.

'It must be hard for people of your generation, even our parents' generation, to realise—even you, having worked with people like me—exactly what it's like,' she said. 'There's nothing but facts for us. I can't explain it, but there's such little prejudice, so much acceptance. So no, you haven't upset me. I came to terms with my fate a long time ago.'

Barney nodded, and Freya heard his voice catch a little in his voice as he answered: 'As did Sal.'

After what seemed to Barney like hours, Angie knocked politely on the door and walked in.

'You're going. Now.' Her tone was strictly instructional. No emotion leeched into her words. 'The three of you.'

'Where?' Barney asked, barely moving from the sofa.

'To get the data from where it's stored. You know where. We've tried, but we can't hack into it remotely—the State has really put its guard up on this one.'

Barney thought of Leila, of the horrific taxi journey from the night before.

'It's not …' Angie began, before catching herself.

It's not safe, Barney thought. *You were going to say it's not safe.*

'Msembe and I can't go,' Angie continued. 'But you can get yourselves in.'

'You were going to say it's not safe, weren't you?' said Kane, his voice low and steady.

'There's safety in numbers, and in being hidden in plain sight. They can't touch you in public, and besides, their powers aren't as strong as you're all led to believe. You're our map, Barney. You know what to look for.'

Barney stared at Angie as blankly as he could manage. She held his gaze, as if she was challenging him to defy her. It prickled over his skin like static electricity. She seemed to sense his submission before he had given it, turning sharply to leave the room.

'Get ready to leave in half an hour. As I told you before, you can talk freely here, but please try to limit any other forms of communication once we leave. Our blockades are good, but they aren't invincible,' she called over her shoulder just before the door slammed shut.

'You stay together at all times,' Msembe had repeated in the entrance hall of the apartment. 'You're not armed; you're not a threat. They know who you are, but you're just people. They can't touch you. You stay in full sight, yes?'

Freya had tried to speak but had found no words. The group's silence had been their assent. Msembe had told them they could be tracked from the moment they stepped onto the tube, which was why they had walked for twenty minutes already, following the directions in their heads. They were far enough from the apartment now to ensure Angie's location remained a secret. Freya, Kane and Barney did not recognise the area but judging from the landmarks in the distance, the Shard's spike and its sister tower's mock-pagoda roof, Freya thought that they must be north-east of the city. They turned the final corner and the familiar red and white Underground sign blazed like a beacon through the daylight.

'Burnt Oak; I can't say I've ever been here before,' Freya said. The other two shook their heads in agreement as they passed through the turnstiles. Talking had been at a minimum since they had left. An unshakeably sombre mood snaked between them, curling around their throats, tipping their faces towards the ground. Kane walked in front now, stepping onto the escalator and rolling his head to one shoulder with what Freya perceived to be a certain resignation to the task at hand. He led them to the Northern Line platform and they walked to its centre, standing next to one another with their toes edging towards the yellow line. Freya glanced at Kane. His eyes were closed and his head was tipped back slightly. The warm air current from the tunnel flickered across his face.

Hidden in plain sight, the woman had said. *Their powers aren't as strong as you're all led to believe.* Freya had not stopped wondering whether this was true. The woman did not have her trust, and neither did Barney or Kane, not really. In truth, trust was not a concept Freya was very familiar with. This fact bit at her now and she batted it away with the usual refrain: *So what, so what, so what?* The tube swept in past them, catching her off-guard, and she instinctively reached out for Kane's forearm as they pushed aboard the train. She released it again slowly, self-consciously, as she stared at it, remembering how that arm had been broken; how it had not saved Marie; how the night of the bomb had changed everything.

Kane deliberately ignored Freya's touch. He could barely meet her eyes without the anger intensifying at the back of his throat. He could not remember a time he had felt so strongly. This shedding of his former self, pills and all, was starting to exhaust him. Emotions he had long forgotten, the complexities of conversations and the interplay of his thoughts playing like a symphony in his head. It was so tempting to turn the volume down again. He knew what would do it. But then he allowed himself to sneak a glance at Freya. Her back was to him but he could tell she was gripping the pole, leaning into it to shield herself from the erratic movements of the tube. Her long hair swung with each judder and the breeze from the open window at the end of the carriage blew it into a scarf around her neck. This was real.

The tube shuddered along for a few more stops, just long enough for Barney to focus his mind on the task in hand. Years of practice meant he could slip into this meditative state in almost any environment now, focussing on a point on the floor and thinking first of all of absolutely nothing, and after that, of the particular thing his brain needed to work through. It was a skill he cherished more and more as the years passed. It made day-to-day life, and days like this, surmountable. He slipped out of the trance now as the doors buzzed and opened onto the busy platform. His eyes met

Freya's and Kane's, and he felt sure it was a look of confidence, of leadership, which he offered them.

They pushed their way through the crowds of Euston Station out onto the concrete square and then onto the street. It was a bright, sunny winter's day and dead leaves swirled between the passers-by. Freya and Kane followed Barney now, still in silence, hands thrust deep into their pockets and chins tucked into their coats. Looking over his shoulder, Barney could see that each of them was scanning the crowds, flicking from person to person, nervously searching. They reached the red bricks of the British Library's courtyard and walked off Euston Road to the side entrance. Suddenly the three of them were alone.

'We mustn't be scared,' Barney said, stopping and turning to face them. 'We're not doing anything wrong. Plus, we're safe here.' He turned to look up at the building behind him. 'It's hard to imagine anything bad ever happening here.'

Freya and Kane nodded.

'But how will we get out again? With the information?' Freya asked, her voice level.

'Today,' Barney replied, tugging down the scarf wrapped around his neck, 'I'm not Barney.' The mark of a small incision was visible beside his windpipe. From their expressions, Freya and Kane seemed to know immediately what he meant.

'But before we leave here, I need to be Barney again.' He pulled a pocketknife from his pocket and handed it to Freya. She took it, staring at it open-mouthed.

Kane was looking up and down the street. 'Come on,' he said.

In they went, Barney forcing a hacking cough from his lungs and pulling his scarf tighter as they passed through the entry scanners. The library was calming, a whispered buzz, the full lighting falling softly on their faces. Barney gestured to the soaring glass-walled internal library which stretched up through the heart of the building. Behind the rows of ancient manuscripts and rare-edition books of the King's Tower lay another library altogether. Behind the Age of Enlightenment was a section he had visited regularly before, the Library of

People. With no bags to check in, they jogged up the steps.

On the third floor, Barney stopped. He touched Freya's hand and raised his eyebrows. 'Ready?'

Freya allowed herself to look at Kane. He shrugged, and then he smiled. It lifted her, and perhaps it lifted Barney too, because he stood a little straighter and strolled ahead of them towards the entrance doors leading into the Tower. A lady sat at the reception smiled politely at them.

'I'm afraid our iris scanner is out of action at the moment,' she apologised. 'Could you please confirm your date of birth instead, Professor Hills?'

Freya nudged Kane. *The Anti-Genetics Movement did that.*

Barney paused momentarily before he answered, long enough for Freya to bite the inside of her lip.

The lady nodded, barely looking up. 'That's your access sorted. If you need more than two hours, just come back and I'll renew it. And these are your colleagues?'

Barney nodded and the receptionist ushered them in through the body scanners.

Freya looked around in wonder. 'It's amazing,' she whispered.

There were just three other people in the room, two of whom looked to be staff. Fully modernised, the data centre within the tower was now white and minimalist apart from the thousands of old books lining the four walls like bricks, hiding the glass. Mechanised robots were poised to recover specific files and documents when asked. Pods of desks set up with docking stations and screen surfaces were sprinkled across the room.

'So, where do we start?' Kane asked, sitting down at one of the terminals next to Barney. Freya did not respond, still gazing around the room. It felt safe; a cocoon.

'Here, I'll show you the list,' Barney said, touching the surface gently with his middle finger. A menu of options appeared. He called up the list of profiles created by Nagayama and highlighted Freya's, Kane's, and Sal's names with his fingertip. Freya pulled her chair closer, staring at the surface.

'Look at us—all there together,' she murmured. Kane looked straight at her and she met his eyes.

As Freya and Kane each appeared to privately struggle with their reading of the other's thoughts, for Barney the look they'd given each other was unmistakeable. He felt compelled to look away for a few moments as he spoke.

'Well, as I've said before, that's not what I find most strange. It was the early days, and you were all born within a year or two of each other, so it's nothing especially unusual that the same executor might have done your birth diagnoses. But it's the *number* this particular person did.' Barney scrolled up and down through the list to demonstrate. 'It's so few—a matter of only four or five months' work over the course of a year. I just can't think of any logical explanation.'

'Maybe she worked part-time or got ill,' said Freya.

'Maybe we're just weird,' said Kane.

'Maybe.'

Barney raised his eyebrows and opened up the front pages of Kane and Sal's profiles on the screen at the same time. He turned to Freya. 'May I open yours too?'

'Go on.'

'Now look, look very carefully. Is there anything either of you can see that makes these similar? Any reason at all that you might have all been processed together?'

They stared at the profiles as Barney slowly scrolled through them, one page at a time. Minutes passed. He reached the last page.

'Look at another one, a random one,' Freya suggested. Barney opened up the first one his finger fell upon from the list: Madeline Veena Nealcross, also around the same age as Freya and Kane. A red digital stamp across the top of the document read *DECEASED*.

'Oh,' said Freya.

Barney understood her tone. It felt wrong to be looking at the profile of a dead woman, a *young* dead woman, but he had a job to do. He scrolled down before she could stop him. He leant forward, hunched over the screen, squinting over his glasses to read the tiny text. Having briefly scanned it, he moved to close the document, but Freya touched his arm to hold him back.

'Wait,' she said. 'I wonder what she died from.' Freya scrolled back up to the notes to the medical section and ran her finger along the lines, following the text.

Barney watched her face as she did so, feeling pity rise up in his chest for her. She seemed so young, so full of life, and yet her life was focussed on death. Now, she was looking for someone else like her, someone else who had been dealt an unfair hand. Her face was alight with it. He glanced at Kane. He, too, was watching her face and the two men exchanged a regretful smile.

Suddenly, Freya sat back into her chair, staring blankly ahead, her mouth slightly open. After a few moments, she shook her head rapidly a few times.

'What is it?' Barney followed her gaze to the screen.

'Barney,' she murmured. 'She was supposed to live until she was in her seventies. How can that be?'

He followed the section of the document she had just read. The only medical issue listed for her was a high risk of Type 2 diabetes.

'She may have died in an accident, of course, as a result of something completely unforeseen,' he said.

'Oh yes, yes of course.' Freya nodded, sounding even more agitated. 'Can we check?'

Barney nodded. On autopilot now, he separately opened Veena Nealcross's medical records with a different program and gestured for Freya and Kane to look through it. Barney wanted, suddenly, to be at home with Leila. They would talk through their plans for next weekend and have a cup of tea in bed. He would forget about Sal and, over time, remember those he had managed to help, those who had fought against their circumstances and largely won through. He would become more optimistic; he would learn in his old age to look more often on the bright side of life.

'Barney?' It was the way Freya said it, cautiously, shakily, that reminded him he was in far too deep to be thinking of a cup of tea in bed. Kane was leaning back into his chair, his brow knotted.

'Yes?' he asked, hesitantly.

'She died from a brain tumour, a rare one.' Freya held one palm against her cheek as she spoke, her little finger dipped in the corner of her mouth.

'Look—why it isn't on her birth diagnosis is listed as unexplained. A complaint was lodged by her family but it seems to be unresolved.'

Freya could not lift her eyes from the display to look at Barney or Kane. She felt they were a million miles away, and it was as if she was alone in the room—vaster than it had felt minutes ago—talking only to herself. This woman had died from a vicious tumour that had grown to the size of a peach within months. The ugly scans, reminiscent of images of her own brain, appeared before her now. Undiagnosed until it was too late, Veena had suffered far more pain and unpleasantness than Freya's father or brother had done, far more than she herself could expect to experience. Freya sat back in her chair and stared at the fake-fur edging of her boots, the tiny fibres wavering in a draught she had not noticed before. She shivered.

'The cancer should have been in Veena's birth diagnosis,' she whispered, to herself more than to Kane and Barney.

This woman should have been screened every three months, more if she could have afforded it, and the disease should have been detected in time to be treated. But she'd had no idea.

Freya felt as if her own brain was working more slowly than she had ever felt it do; her thoughts were dragging their feet, unwilling to comply with the growing sense of clarity she felt moving up from her stomach.

'The life expectancy and medical data sections in her profile have asterisks at the end,' said Barney.

'Do they correspond to this?' Kane asked, pointing at a starred note at the top right-hand corner of the profile. He tapped the screen with his fingernail, highlighting the text. 'What's this? There's not usually a second report, is there?'

Barney blinked and shook his head.

'No, that's not normal.'

As he flicked back through Freya's profile, they saw the same note on every page in the top right-hand corner: *Project C–authorised personnel may access corresponding File C/34.*

'Is it on mine? On Winstan's, too?' Kane asked as he reached over and flicked to his own file, and then to Sal's.

Barney nodded slowly. 'That's the link,' he muttered.

Freya could sense that they were each moving to the same conclusion separately, silently. It was an aura that buzzed between them. She leaned forward as Kane took control; twisting the screen towards him and flicking quickly back to his own birth diagnosis.

Kane found the asterisk in seconds; he knew in which section of his profile to look for it immediately, and it was there. He could feel Freya's gaze following his navigations through the document.

There it was, in the sexuality section—a little star that you would not notice if you were just reading through it, if you were not looking for anything unusual. Freya clamped her hand over her mouth at the same time as Kane.

'Oh, my God,' she whispered through her fingers.

Kane smiled and nodded. 'The version I have doesn't have an asterisk, or a note corresponding to another file. I'd know, I've read it enough times.'

The vindication hit him like a tidal wave as he spoke. He thought of the pink pills still sitting in his overflowing kitchen bin, covered in cauliflower and baked beans. He thought of Dr Seymour and the expert he wanted to see instead, he thought of Gemma, he thought of his family, drowning him in a life he did not want. His fifteen-year-old self was thumping on the walls of his chest to be let out at last. *I told you so*, it shouted, *I told you so!* Kane felt tears springing into his eyes and bit into his lip as he stared up at the ceiling.

Freya hardly noticed as Barney glanced at her, briefly, seeming to seek some kind of agreement before he switched back to her birth diagnosis. She could barely look; her eyes bored through the desk as if drilling into the circuit boards beyond. The words became a haze, everything repeated twice. She held her breath. Barney found the little star where she hoped he would find it, buried halfway through the medical notes. He shook his head and breathed out with the beginnings of a smile upon his lips.

Freya's unfocussed stare saw two stars where there was only one, and saw overlapping repetitions of the word 'Huntington's.' Before she could register what she was seeing, Barney was back at the top of the document, where the note to the corresponding file lay. The file name was a link and his finger hovered over it. He glanced briefly over at the reception desk before pressing it.

'Barney wouldn't be able to open this,' he whispered, conspiratorially.

24

Freya shifted in her seat as the document opened. She heard Barney breathe a sigh of relief.

'We don't have long,' warned Kane. 'Can you save it all?'

'Better than that,' Barney said triumphantly. 'I'm sending it all directly to the AGM's encrypted databanks.'

'Is that really for the best?' Freya asked, turning her attention towards him and lifting her eyes briefly away from the screen.

Barney sighed. 'We don't have many other options open to us.' He flicked through the document, running his professional gaze over the text. Freya leant further forward. It looked, to her, like a normal Background. But, as they had already figured out, this was not the Background that she knew.

'There's a few minor notes. Allergies, that sort of thing, but ...' He paused, and Freya felt a creeping awareness that she wasn't prepared for what he was about to say. 'But this file records no reference to Huntington's disease.'

Freya felt her whole body relax as if into a deep mediation. She was close to falling, ever so softly, onto the cool marble floor.

Barney continued. 'The only thing I can conclude is that this second file is your real birth diagnosis. For some reason, it's been deliberately hidden and protected. Veena grew up eating healthily, keeping fit; whatever she did, she was always doing her best to avoid developing Type 2 diabetes—a risk she had been told about. But in reality, a ticking time bomb was growing inside her skull. And only a few people would have known about it.'

Barney paused, staring into Freya's eyes. 'For you, it's

been the opposite. This suggests that you're fine, Freya. For the most part, there's probably nothing wrong with you.'

'Are you okay?' Kane asked, resting his hand on her shoulder.

Freya bobbed her head slowly. Each possibility washed over her repeatedly, rippling across other thoughts, other memories, so that she could not decipher how she truly felt. In the face of so much fresh information, her emotions were shackled, unmoving. *It was a question,* she said to herself in her schoolteacher's voice, *of what she wanted to believe. Was this not what she wanted—for her birth diagnosis to be wrong?* She thought back to the day of the ballet class and saw herself, tiny, chubby in her leotard, desperately wanting to be as good as everyone else and, that same day, beginning to realise that she never would be.

From then on, it had been a death sentence that was part of her life. For so long, she had not wanted to accept it; she recalled those early days at school with her genetic counsellor, together deciding how to phrase her own Background, how to tell it with grace and strength. It was clever, if reprehensible, she thought now in hindsight, how her counsellor had made her start to cherish the drama of her genes. She had spent her life as the tragic heroine; it was a character—a huge part of her personality—that she realised now, with slight shock, had become an integral part of the person she was, the part that always pushed the fun-loving girl back into the shadows. And then she grasped at the key to her tangled emotions from the jumble of thoughts: it was the fear of not being this person any more, of having to be someone else, that made her anxious. Huntington's had been a dead cert and she had been told it was unavoidable and only marginally controllable. As a teenager, an extra year or two of life in her thirties was easily exchanged for half a bottle of vodka on a night out. Even now, she did not regret her choices, such as they were. A refusal to accept the tangible hope that her life could be her own crackled behind her eyelids.

'They're sent,' Barney whispered. 'We've got to get out of here. Now.'

Freya closed her eyes again for a moment. Marie's mathematical symbols scattered themselves through her thoughts and her tiny smile shimmered vividly before Freya's eyes. Freya's speciality, her ability to push back her own concerns in exchange for someone else's, came once more to the fore.

She thought of Marie's bare bedroom, her incomprehensible mathematics, and the black notebook she had never even seen. What was her fate? Who had she believed she was? Confronted by an image of Mr Lane, his fat hands wrapped around a vodka glass as emotionless as his expression, she realised for the first time in her life how much the lives of individuals are shaped by the people around them. She had sensed something radiating from him in waves, something she had thought might be disappointment, or more generously, a lack of understanding. His perception of his daughter must have, unwittingly to both of them, perhaps, created her persona as much as she had tried to shake him off. Even Freya's own mother had swaddled her in the cotton wool of her concerns, her eternal misgivings about what Freya could and could not do.

She found herself speaking words that surprised her, with a distress that leaked in from somewhere, wholly unbidden.

'Wait,' she said, gripping onto the back of Barney's chair as he stood. 'I want you to look on that list for Marie, Marie Lane.'

'Freya, I really don't think ...' Kane began, his words echoing Barney's heavy sigh. She stared at Barney and he stared back for a few moments. He shook his head and with a weary smile turned back to the list. He searched and scrolled through.

'Quickly,' he said. 'Do you know where she lived?'

'I know her father's house—Pennard Road, Shepherd's Bush. It would be a W12 postcode.'

'Well, I can't believe I'm saying this, but yes, this might well be her,' Barney said, shaking his head at the screen.

Freya smiled and nodded fiercely. 'I thought so.'

As the two men stared at her, she clenched her fist in a little display of triumph and put her hand on Barney's shoulder. 'Please, just send the file, would you?'

'Done. But that's it, we can't spare any more time,' he said, standing. 'Someone will already know these files have been accessed.'

He helped Freya up, letting her loop her arm through his. Kane gathered his coat and they moved, swiftly, out of the King's Library Tower. Barney pulled them down a corridor leading to the toilets. They walked past them both, stopping outside a door marked private. Barney reached into Freya's pocket and pulled out the knife, flicking the blade open. He looked expectantly at her.

'Barney, I can't,' she whimpered, feeling pathetic.

'It's okay,' said Kane, taking the knife from Barney.

There was the squeal of a door. They all dropped their arms to their sides, ready to pretend they were lost. Ready to run. Two women left the toilet without looking around, chattering, and the door shut behind them.

'Tip your head back,' ordered Kane. 'Into the light.'

Freya watched, transfixed, as he eased the knife under the skin where it had already been cut, lifting one side away from the other where it had already begun to heal. Barney slammed his foot into the wall behind him, squeezing his eyes shut.

Kane could feel the edge of the Tag. It would still be loose in there, not yet tangled amongst the fibres and tissue. He pushed at the far edge of it with his nail, forcing it back out the way it had come. There was a little blood and then it was out, glistening in Kane's palm.

'Whoever this is, that's who they'll be after,' said Barney, pressing his fingertips against the cut with one hand and winding his scarf back around his neck with the other. 'We need to lose it. Now, quickly.'

The three of them broke into a run back down the corridor, and soon they were out on the floor. Looking down over the mezzanine balcony, they could see several Sentries entering through the barriers, shoving people out of their way. Kane looked at Barney for instruction, holding out his clenched fist containing the Tag.

'Him,' Barney said, nodding in the direction of a passing man. He looked young, fit; able to take a bit of a tussle. Barney reached out and caught his arm.

'I'm sorry, sir; do you know what time the library closes?'

As the man broke his stride to answer, Kane moved behind him, dropping the Tag into the pocket of the man's coat. They did not wait for a reply as they all moved further along the balcony. Barney leant over the railing again, looking down onto the ground floor of the library. A couple of Sentries were still there, scanners in hand. The rest were closing in on the mezzanine, jogging up the stairs and commandeering the lifts. They were discreet; few other visitors even seemed to have noticed their presence. Barney turned and squeezed Kane's arm.

'I'm going now,' he said, quietly.

Kane stared back at him, unable to argue with the finality of his tone. He glanced at Freya, nodded and then turned away. He disappeared behind the Tower, headed for the back staircase.

Kane reached out for Freya and brought her around to face back over the barrier with him. 'Let's just stay here for a moment. Don't move,' he said.

With their backs to the floor behind them, Kane could not be sure whether Barney was followed. He felt a couple of Sentries swish past, the buckles of their trench coats jangling. From the other end of the mezzanine, he could just hear another pair of Sentries begin to address a stranger, the ping of their scanners. Kane flicked his eyes briefly in the direction of the activity.

'Now,' he said, nudging Freya sharply in the ribs. They walked in the opposite direction, his arm around her waist, and jogged down the staircase, faces to the floor as they slipped out through the doors into the air.

25

Barney stood on the doorstep of the Winstan home. He breathed deeply, summoning his energy as he rubbed at a mark on the brass step with his toe. The sun was shining brightly now and he squinted against it as it filtered through the azalea over his shoulder. He heard the latches and locks unfasten and Cherry opened the door enough to peek around, a pink dressing gown tied around her waist and a hastily applied smudge of hazel sheen across her lips. She smiled in immediate recognition.

'Mr North! What on earth brings you here?'

'A friendly hello and a more serious matter.'

'Well,' she paused uncertainly. 'You'd better come in. Take a seat and I'll put the kettle on for us.'

She ushered him into the lounge and disappeared. Barney looked around the room, wilting after years of being lived in and fought in. On one wall, school photos of Sal and his sister Tiane hung side by side, closer than they ever would have stood to each other in real life.

Cherry returned with two mugs of tea and took a cautious perch on the edge of the sofa next to Barney. She was now an elderly lady; her lips bore the lines of a lifetime's smoking and the lipstick was slowly seeping into the cracks like glaciers down a valley.

'Is your husband around, Mrs Winstan?'

As Barney's eye caught on a large, framed portrait of David sitting on the mantelpiece, he knew he had asked the wrong question and felt himself tense up for the response.

'Please, call me Cherry,' she said as she glanced over to the photograph. 'He passed on a few months ago, Mr North. It was a heart attack—sudden, y'know? Nothing they could do.'

'I'm ever so sorry, Cherry.'

'I think it was after everything with Sal, y'know?'

'Yes,' Barney said. 'I know he found it very difficult coping with the nature of Sal's character. It must have been a strain for you both.'

'No, no,' she shook her head forlornly. 'It was the losing of him I think, the death of his only son. And the circumstances. It tore him apart.'

Barney watched the tears well up in her eyes and thought to himself that those words alone might have been enough to save Sal from what happened. An ounce of affection might have been enough.

She took a deep breath and lowered her voice. 'Do you know what happened?' she asked. 'Only I've been told not to talk about it.'

'Yes, it's fine, I know.'

Cherry stood up and smoothed down her dress. 'The tea'll be brewed.'

Barney removed the brown envelope from his bag, placed it on the sofa beside him and on top of it laid a letter that he had written on the train journey here. While he waited, he gently ran his fingertip over the small wound on his neck. He wondered when he would become Barney again, when he and Leila would be safe again. He didn't have long here; he had to meet Msembe soon.

Cherry returned and placed a cup on the side table next to him. 'So what was it you wanted, love?'

'Cherry, I have some news about Sal. I've been involved with finding out some things about him that, as his former psychologist, I thought I should tell you about in person.' She was frowning but he continued with his practised speech. 'It has emerged that Sal was one of a small group of people who were part of an undisclosed experiment. In short, the diagnosis you received a week after his birth was, in some aspects, false. In particular, surrounding his criminality.'

'I don't understand. Are you saying that my son ...?' She trailed off, confused.

'Sal did not have a genetic predisposition towards violence, Cherry. This was a deliberate falsehood. Sal was part of a major experiment to test to what extent external factors other than genetics play in shaping a person.'

She stared back at him, her mouth slightly ajar.

'But ...'

'I'm sorry, it sounds technical, I know. I've written this all down here so that you can take it all in.' He tapped on the letter by his side and pushed it over to her. 'This must be a shock for you. In the envelope is the birth diagnosis you and your husband should have received. If you want to ask me anything else, my contact is at the bottom of the letter. Now, will you have company later?'

'Yes, Tiane is popping round after work.'

'Good, that's good.' Barney paused, trying to find the words he needed to seal this story shut. 'You know that I loved Sal, don't you?'

She nodded and reached out for Barney's hand, her eyes gazing at the framed portrait on the wall.

'I'm so sorry he's no longer with us,' he said. He felt his throat constrict with emotion but knew he had to say one thing more. 'I'm so sorry I couldn't help him.'

'You were the best,' Cherry said, squeezing his fingers tightly, her eyes glistening. Barney watched her closely for a while, seeking out signs of stability. As she took the cup to her lips and sipped, he rose to his feet.

'I'm sorry to have disturbed you this morning.' He reached down and placed a hand on her shoulder. 'It's a lot to take in, but I hope that you can come to terms with all of this. I'll let myself out.'

26

Kane perched on the arm of the sofa, uncomfortable but too distracted to move, the deadening tingle spreading up from his tailbone to the small of his back. He hoped they were safe here in Freya's flat for the moment. He was sure Msembe would be out there somewhere, standing guard. For some reason, Kane trusted Msembe and Angie. He tried to run through the events of the past few months in his head but quickly lost track. More than anything, what was happening now was about the future, it was no longer about the past or what had come before.

He found himself clasping his hands together, running his thumbs around each other and tracing the folds of his knuckles. He looked down at his hands and they seemed older than he remembered. Thick, dark hairs sprouted the length of his fingers and the skin around his nails was either rough or torn, depending on where he had nibbled between pulling pints and where the paintbrush had rubbed. They were a worker's hands. They were the hands of a man who had been busy trying to pass his life by, trying to move from one day to the next as quickly as possible.

He looked across at Freya and she looked back. The meaning behind her gaze was difficult to read; her eyes were narrowed and her face was tired. She sat silently on a chair across the room, her legs twisted beneath her. One arm was curled underneath her head so that she was all balled up like a cat. His eyes left hers and he dropped his gaze to the floor. He noticed a patch in the rug where it was worn away, the thick brown, criss-crossing yarns beneath the colour the only thing keeping his toes from touching the tiles. He found himself wondering why that particular patch was bare, what fate had befallen it, why he had not noticed it before. He stretched out his foot and rubbed his big toe over the hole. Straining, he could just about feel the cool ceramic through it and it chilled him right through.

'Kane?' Freya asked.

'Yeah?'

'Do you feel you know who you are?'

'Who I am? You know, I think I do. I think I always did. I wanted very little, just to paint—that was it. And to have a family; a few kids and a nice home.'

'In the conventional sense?'

'Yeah. When I was little, just a kid, I would think about having a wife and making a home with her. I remember I had these action figures ...' He laughed at the memory, seen now in a fresh light. 'I made one of them into a woman. I drew long hair onto her neck and gave her eyelashes.'

'And you wonder why your Background says you were gay!' Freya's frown popped and giggles bubbled out of her before she could stop herself.

'I know! But I was the male figure and she was my dream woman. What could be straighter?'

They smiled at each other. He ruffled his hair with his hand. Looking up, he noticed the glimmer had returned to Freya's eyes for a moment and he recognised the feeling in the pit of his stomach, a feeling lying dormant from many years before; frantic, passionate hope. He realised his fists were clenched upon themselves like a baby around a rattle. He tried to relax, spreading his fingers across his thighs.

'What about you?' he asked. 'Are you 'in touch' with yourself?' He sketched inverted commas in the air with his index fingers, grinning. The glimmer did not return. Instead, Freya turned and stared out of the window.

'No, I've never even thought about it. And I've never known what I wanted. I never felt that I was allowed to want things. Since my brother died, and with my health, I always knew that I'd have to work my life around other people. I thought it would be one day at a time forever.' She shuffled again and wrapped her arms around herself. 'And it has been.

Time has just trickled by.'

Kane came and stood behind her, awkwardly leaning down over her shoulder to hug her, his arms across her collarbone.

Through her sobs she whispered: 'Everything is happening so quickly. I should be happy, but I daren't be.'

As Kane squeezed her, rocking her gently from side to side, his right ear against her left, it was as if he could hear the sea.

It was dark in the flat by the time the envelopes were pushed under the door. Attuned to the silence that had settled between her and Kane, Freya heard the paper rubbing against the reed matting and jumped to her feet. She gathered the four envelopes into her arms and returned to the lounge. She felt sickly, nervous, yet Kane looked resplendent, his face glowing in the half-light cast from her dimmed lamp.

Tomorrow was the only word scrawled across the top envelope. The rest were blank, apart from their names written across the top. She placed them in a neat pile on the sofa.

Tomorrow? It was a source of constant astonishment to her how quickly the media cogs turned in these modern times when the State wanted them to. No sooner was something a rumour upon a person's lips than it was online, accompanied by amateur blurred photographs and gaudy opinions; no sooner were a few letters of electronic ink dispersed than they were broadcasted to the masses and narrow-casted in minute detail to the few. It was too late now, she and Kane had already supposed. The information was out; there was no taking it back. Just a couple of days ago, it had been a secret the State would have killed to protect, but now they would twist it as best they could, no doubt placing blame elsewhere if possible. Damage limitation.

They sat in silence for some time. Kane was the first to speak.

'I should go.' He stood up and tucked his hair behind his ears.

'No, stay,' said Freya, beckoning him to sit back down. 'We've been in this together, somehow, since the beginning, so we might as well do this bit together too.'

Like a child, she sat down cross-legged on the floor and turned up the lamp, feeling its heat across her back as she placed her envelope in front of her. He knelt on the floor next to her and they picked up the envelopes dumbly. Freya was slack-jawed at the sudden reality that confronted her, at the crystallised understanding that reading them would finally, permanently, change her concept of who she was, and who she had been, forever.

'I want to look at Marie's first,' Freya said, her fingers already slipping inside the envelope.

She could see immediately that the Anti-Genetics Movement woman, perhaps Barney, perhaps both, had already looked at this one in some detail; blue biro marks underlined and circled, cross-referencing between the falsified diagnosis given to her and the true one drawn straight from her blood, decades ago. She flicked through the pages, trying to follow the route that Barney had already marked out and murmuring aloud to Kane what she found.

'Wow! She was told she was a genius, with a high IQ ... but there was nothing in her genuine diagnosis to suggest she was anything other than intellectually average. Her genes weren't, just weren't extraordinary,' she said, looking at Kane.

Freya's mind skipped to the notebooks and the specialised, diagram- and algebra-filled Indexes that had been her bedtime reading for the past few weeks. At least the lies had given Marie something to aspire to. Marie had certainly tried her best to be the person she was supposed to become. Freya set the papers down to one side to look at in more detail later, when she was alone.

'And Sal?' she found herself asking, surprising herself by using his first name. She was curious but unable to touch the fourth envelope. It was still tainted.

Kane slipped his finger under the seal and drew out the contents, topped with a note, handwritten in capitals. Like Marie's, the pages below it were extensively scribbled upon, particular phrases highlighted and circled, question marks in margins. Kane read the top sheet of Barney's heavily slanted script aloud.

Sal's case, I should think, will become one of those most seriously discussed in the coming months. Sal was told he was something he was not, and I know that his father resented him to the level of hatred for it, his mother was scared of him, and he was schooled along with boys supposedly similar to him. Lacking in love from his family, he was easily led astray. I tried to help him of course, but he was a very angry young man; he made a few misjudged punches in the heat of the moment and that was that—his future was sealed. Indeed, he never had any future to speak of. In my early days as a psychologist, I didn't know the genetic background of my patients, but mark my words, it does not take a genetic predisposition to push someone in that situation towards crime and violence. Sal was not an innocent, but he was more innocent than we knew.

Freya and Kane read it without exchanging words, and then Freya slipped everything back inside the envelope. Perhaps Barney would try and take it to Sal's family after this all settled down. She hoped so.

'Okay. You first,' said Freya, gesturing at the envelope lying in Kane's lap.

'No, we'll do it at the same time,' he replied, not once lifting his gaze from the envelope.

She giggled nervously and pushed at his shoulder with the tips of her toes. She felt relieved at her own amusement and, as he smiled back at her, the atmosphere lightened. She nodded and they both pulled out the reams of white paper.

Freya wondered where A had managed to find a printer, imagining her at home in a little cubbyhole of an office, full of antiquated technology, books and photographs: the headquarters of a movement which might now change the world. The first document she saw was a brief summary of the main points raised within the diagnosis; behind that was the diagnosis itself, in full. She would need to set aside days to read through it properly.

So often in life, the most complex questions come down to a simple yes or no: the making of a decision, the categorising of something or someone, the forcing of a feeling into boxes. All you have to do is avoid the maybe, the possibly, the potentially. Freya stared at her name on the front of the paper, printed in bold capitals, and tried to imagine her own parents being handed something so very similar twenty-nine years before: a lifetime ago. She pictured her mother, cheeks glowing from breastfeeding, from the contentment of finally being blessed with the little girl she had so wanted. *You are my lucky girl,* she would whisper to Freya at bedtime, her soothing voice wavering in Freya's ear. Her father would have taken the diagnosis, would not have waited for the doctor to finish his or her summary but leafed through it for himself, irascibly confident in his own judgement of the situation. Her mother would have cried, Freya herself might have also cried as a result, curled in her arms, and her father would have stroked their heads and told them to ignore the doctor. He would have taken them home in the car, tucked Freya away in her cot with a kiss on the forehead and soothed her mother with a glass of wine, his velvety tones calming her into sleep. She thought back. He would throw her around the local park, push her so high on the swings that she felt she might fall. He never cared if she got dizzy, or if she tripped up. In his eyes, perhaps there had been nothing wrong with her. He had always believed what he chose to believe.

She glanced at Kane and started to read.

Kane watched her. He felt he could almost hear her purring with excitement. He turned to the document in front of him. Kane's eyes, so tightly attuned to the tiniest details of ink, scanned through the pages. While he had not expected a synthesis, the section he was looking for only housed two words and a single item of punctuation.

Sexuality: Heterosexual

The impact of that single, written word shocked him, each letter rippling out across his skin like a drawn-out static shock. And now the letters and their meaning had reached his toes and washed back, pooling in his chest and lapping over each other, cajoling him into tears.

He placed the pages on the floor in front of his crossed

legs and rested his head on his hands, the fists curled underneath his chin. The residual anger shook through him like a muted tornado. Faces flashed up before his eyes in quick succession. His mother's adoring gaze as she buttoned up his first suit; Dr Seymour and her divided expression of sympathy and impatience; Gemma's face bearing its obvious disgust; the many men he had met and their confused smiles; Freya's pursed lips, questioning him from the very beginning. As the fury whirled around his ears, already starting to burn out, his eyes worked their way wearily over the rest of the points but as Barney had said, he was no Veena: there were no malignant secrets. His body was not hiding anything from him anymore. Kane looked over to the easel in the corner of the room, covered in a cloth. His false profile, he knew, put him down as artistically creative; it was true that it was his passion, his meaning. But he found himself wondering, for the first time, whether the lies in his diagnosis extended further than his sexuality.

With a fond smile fluttering at his lips, he remembered his first trip to the art store with his grandfather, determined to at least make a true bohemian from his gay grandchild. He bought up half the shop; paints, charcoal, clay, guidance books and tools. Kane had loved the little wooden mannequin most of all, had spent hours on his bed switching him between contortions. It occurred to him that few other five-year-olds would have received the same gifts, the same expectation laid upon them, the same promise of success and talent. Even looking back upon his first sketches, Kane saw nothing of merit in them, nothing to distinguish them from any other child. *Oh no*, his mother would whisper in response, *no Kane, look at the detail you put into the hands—all five fingers! You always draw all five so well.* He felt his excitement shiver and cool as the possibility of his own genius, the lifelong belief in his own talent, melted from his mouth and slipped down into the pit of his stomach. He could not look at this section yet. Not yet.

Freya had found what she was looking for straight away. She had seen it before, in the library, but now it felt real. In her hands was everything which had been stolen from her. The medical section was the first one on the form and she had now read it three times. It listed things that were the same as the birth diagnosis she had grown up believing—little niggles, and parts of her that would need an eye kept on them—but there was a vacancy where there once was a life-filling burden. She finished reading it a fourth time and felt the thing that had been like a chunk of stone inside her crumble away and fade like dust through the pores of her skin. She felt weightless, dizzy.

All those times, she thought, *all those times I just had a headache.* Of all the emotions that she might have expected to feel, it was in fact a strange embarrassment that came over her as the information sank in. She thought of all the people she would have to tell; she imagined the confusion on their faces as they remembered the times she had cancelled work, or parties, or dates because she had been having a bad day. And she thought of her brother, unlike her, unable to escape the fate he had been dealt, dying with the hazy knowledge that he had not beaten his genetic destiny.

It was quite some time before they spoke. It was Freya who reached out first, her hand crawling like a bug towards Kane's and taking hold of his warm fingers, squeezing gently. There was really very little to say as they gazed at each other and nodded slowly in turn, wearily effervescent smiles emerging on their faces.

Kane suddenly pulled his Index from his pocket and unfurled it. Freya watched him as he read, and she could see the distress etch itself upon his face. It was surely bad news.

'It's anonymous,' Kane said, softly, turning the screen to face her. 'It's cheating some network to reach me.'

You will be safe, I promise. I'm sorry to tell you that Barney and Leila were killed, each separately, shortly after Barney left the library. It would have been over quickly, if that is a consolation. He was a wonderful man, but you must move on with your own lives now. You have everything you need. Thank you, A.

The message flickered once more and was gone forever.

27

Ten months later

The day was nearly through and the air was crystalline as the biting cold of the evening set in. Tomorrow there would be frost; Elin Nagayama felt the familiar ache in her wrists and knees. She tried to avoid the glare of the lenses pointed in her direction as she sought out the face she most wanted to see. Yet it was one that she would not recognise if she found it.

She had a picture in her head of the person who had exposed her, but how different it was from the reality she would never know—no one would. The stranger had somehow remained a ghost; its identity was not yet forfeit, but Elin sensed whoever it was would be here today to see it finished.

The crowd clustered outside the court were quieter than she had expected. Some of them called out her name, or thrust a camera in front of her face past her armed escort. She made it down the steps and to the police van's sliding door without making direct eye contact with a single one of them, her eyes narrowed, her gaze broad and her chin held up defiantly. The cuffs cut into her wrists as the policeman by her side pushed her inside. As she placed her foot on the step, she paused and looked around once, giving every camera-armed paparazzo the picture they wanted, as at that precise moment, her eyes locked with those of a woman that would remain forever in the shadows. That was the person she had been seeking. The woman was standing alone on the steps of the court, her head and shoulders elevated across the press mob. She was wrapped to the neck in a cream cape, and Elin thought her elegant, subdued, and younger than she

231

had expected; she had imagined them to be the same age.

In a three-second gaze that would have betrayed nothing to any outsider, with no nods, smiles or perceptible facial twinges that might signify an emotion, Elin and Angie shared a moment that neither of them would come to forget. They saw in each other the frustration of an ambitious woman, a woman that had set out to prove something, to convince the world of her beliefs, an incomplete mission that still hung, tattily, in the air between them, eternally unfinished. For not all things could be finished, they told each other, not all things were black and white, not all things could be drawn around neatly and placed inside a box.

Inspector Kim Cheung was one of the many in the crowd. She had slipped out of work and Ivan Msembe had watched her go wordlessly. They both knew where she was going. She had caught a rickshaw to the court and now she was amongst the other spectators, not as a police officer but as an onlooker, albeit less casual than the rest. So, the State had relented, had decided to incarcerate a former employee, taking the attention away from their own intimate involvement. It did not surprise her in the least.

And who was truly to blame for all those lost lives? Was it the controlling forces of the State and their lust for inequality, was it the man who was already dead, the woman who was being pushed into the police van, or was it the woman who had directed the whole operation? Kim was sure Angie Harper must be here somewhere, that she must be the kind of control freak who would need to see things finished.

As she gazed at Elin Nagayama's old, lined face, her eyes were drawn along the same line of sight to the steps of the courtroom. Kim, too, saw the woman who matched the furtive photographs in her Index, wrapped in cream cashmere. She bristled with frustration at the impotence of her situation, clenching her fists deep inside the pockets of her coat. Once, long before the Takeover, she would have been able to arrest her, to have seen her tried in a court of law as well. *But the word was out,* thought Kim, *with perhaps a little thanks to her bravery and determination. Times, just possibly, were changing. It was just a case of figuring out who was in the wrong.* She took a few deep breaths, then turned and walked away.

The same photograph of that moment, taken from different angles—the moment Elin and Angie exchanged glances, watched by the police inspector—would be the one all the press used. But no one would ever see the other two faces, only the face of the one who had been found guilty. Within minutes, several versions of the same photograph would be on news sites around the world, the expression of Dr Nagayama interpreted by body language experts and gossip-thirsty hacks alike. Her head hanging down slightly from her shoulders, the heavy-lidded frown, the slightly open lips and brows drawn together were unanimously voted to be an elderly lady's regret, apology, maybe even a final request for forgiveness. Each editor would sift it out from the pile and see in it what they wanted to see: the haunted face of that day's villain gazing upon her condemners, the guilt oozing from her drawn features. None of them would ever know that she was looking into the eyes of the woman who found her out, the woman who had more in common with her than anyone else in the world, the enemy who, obliquely, wanted the same thing she did: for people to no longer be judged by a few pieces of information. One of them was anonymous, one of them was going to prison, but perhaps they would both yet succeed in their task.

It was only afterwards, when each of them were alone— Angie in her office, unfolding the sofa bed that she slept on, Elin lying on her back in her cell—that they would consider how easily a person could be judged, how very natural it was for a multidimensional, constantly evolving person to capture someone else like they would a photograph. Their actions, they recognised, had shaped lives and ended lives. Paradoxically, in the name of life, in the name of freedom and the hope for a better future that might never come, they had both put people into boxes and thrown away the keys.

As the audience filed into their seats, Freya pulled her Index from her handbag and flattened it across her lap. She looked up at the stage but she could not yet see Kane. She imagined him sitting on the wings, sketching the faces of the audience from his hidden spot. While the crowd continued to murmur and the lights were still up, Freya leafed through the day's headlines on her Index. The story had made all but two of the lead stories and on one was a small photograph of Marie. In it, she looked much younger, a teenager, and her smile dazzled through the electronic ink. She was sitting on a patch of grass, the sun was out and she was squinting as she looked back over her shoulder at the photographer.

Freya put the Index back in her bag and drew out the journal that she had downloaded and printed out and bound at production quality as a memento. It was glossy and colourful with an artistically rendered image of a distant nebula on the front. It looked like a unicorn bursting out of a forest, purple at the edges and fading to a thousand colours of blue and white within.

She searched for the article in the contents page and flicked to it. She read the abstract and then lazily flipped to the end to see how long it was: Eight pages, eleven with references. The text and the algebra were alien to her and under her breath she whispered a sorry to Marie, wherever she was, for her lack of understanding, as if her spirit was in the actual pages somewhere, listening indignantly. A personal commentary followed the paper, filling the bottom two-thirds of space at the end of the references. It was written by the principal scientist to build upon Marie's ideas and Freya studied the small portrait of the woman first, noting her kind, grey eyes and smart bob. Freya sat up straight in her chair as the teenagers squeezed past her and made their way to their seats.

It was my great privilege to work with Marie Lane. Although we never met, and she never told me anything about herself, her questions and her obvious love for science renewed my own faith in my research at a crucial time when I was considering a change in the direction of my scientific career. I wish I had been able to tell her that. I must admit, however, that I am glad I did not know she was only seventeen when we first exchanged emails, otherwise I fear my prejudices would have stopped me taking her ideas at face-value. My thanks also go to Freya, who was able to send me the ideas on which this paper is founded long after Marie herself was unable to.

The theory outlined in this paper is the result of many years of shared ideas and calculations. As it stands, and it will be many years before the theory can be put to the full scrutiny of our peers, what our paper outlines is the potential for a step change in our understanding of physics and the universe. I feel the gaze of many great physicists who have been and gone heavy on my shoulders as I write this, and I am aware that many will feel this is an assault upon the many great advances in quantum physics over the past century. However, I feel we must look at this as a new beginning, an opportunity to push our understanding of the universe further, to a new level. The glass ceiling is smashed and lies in shards around our feet—the rain is falling in, but the skies are clearing, and I believe that now we have the ability to see further, and with more clarity, than ever before. This is a momentous occasion and one that should be filled with much excitement.

Although I am named as a joint author, I must make it known that it is only thanks to Ms Lane's bravery of thought that these mathematical models have been put forward. I was her mentor, but not her leader. I was her guide, but not her teacher. Let that be written in history.

For those of you that might think this a fairy story, let me remind you of the quintessential genius, the illustrious Albert Einstein. He did not speak until he was three years old. He failed his college entrance exams on the first attempt. And when his time for greatness came, with his Special Theory of Relativity, his landmark paper contained no citations, no footnotes and hardly any mathematics. C. P. Snow wrote that it seemed as though Einstein had reached his conclusions 'by pure thought, unaided, without listening to the opinions of others. To a surprisingly large extent, that is precisely what he had done.'

Sometimes, then, genius cannot be defined nor explained. It is too intangible, too inexplicable a concept to be pinned down. But seeing the world from a different angle, in a new and radical way, is something open to all of us if we go looking for it. Perhaps that 'eureka moment' is a kind of neurological magic, one that cannot be corroborated with magnetic resonance imaging or neuronal pathways. I, like many others, once believed that the ability to possess such talents was something one was born with, such as with a winning hand at poker. But in the wake of this discovery, I feel differently, and I take this opportunity to ask *others to take time to reconsider their own beliefs. Perhaps, in reality, our successes and our failures are built on the most unstable of foundations.*

Rest in peace, Marie.
Prof. Andrea Ziemberg

Freya sat back in her chair and allowed a single, heavy tear to drop down onto her cheekbone. She thought of Marie, that impulsive, crazy, tiny little woman, and imagined her unhurt, sitting cross-legged on her bed in a T-shirt at the age of seventeen, the door bearing the glittery M locked. In Freya's imagination, she gazes out of the window underneath that purple blind at the stars beyond, half-smiling in wonder and in thoughts only vaguely formed. Freya's mind wandered down the stairs that she herself once ran down and imagined walking in on Mr Lane at his kitchen table with a bottle of vodka and a glass at his side, reading the note she had slid under the door with the journal earlier that day. He is nodding to himself at the note and forgiving her for breaking into his house. He turns to the article, flicking through it as she has just done and going straight to Andrea Ziemberg's commentary. He reads these words, these world-altering sentences, about his own daughter, his own flesh and blood, and he starts to cry.

He is crying for his last memory of her lying in a hospital morgue, burnt black and white and disfigured. He is crying for not being there for her, for not being able to love her as much as she deserved. He is crying for all the things he never learnt to say, all the people he could have been and all the people she could have been, if he had only let her. Drunk, he is immensely sad, but in the coming months and years, he will feel the onset of a pride that he barely feels he deserves but just occasionally, at his happiest times, will let himself have. He will talk about her to his friends down at the pub and to his colleagues at work. He will write to Andrea, and they will marvel together in late-night phone calls and long emails at how she could have been so amazingly talented, and so secretive to never have told anyone. He will find her mother from somewhere and write an apology so that he can die knowing he has removed as much of the guilt on his shoulders that he possibly can. That is how Freya hoped it would be.

Freya found that much of her initial anger about her situation had evaporated, forced out through her pores by the happiness that had invaded her instead. There was only room inside her crowded head for one leading emotion for the time being. She did, however, find herself sympathising with Elin Nagayama, a recurring thought she had kept to herself. When she had read about the pregnancies Nagayama had been forced to have terminated, Freya could only see her as a fragile creature, trying to change her difficulties of her life as only she knew how. In short, although as a puppet of the State she was partly to blame, Freya felt Nagayama deserved more leniencies than she had received. In the photographs, she had looked so ravaged, so exhausted by her mistakes.

As Freya had repeated to her mother time and time again since everything came out, she was just lucky that she was not the girl with a malicious brain tumour, pitting her chances of survival on a mistaken belief in her health. The ghostly, unknown quantity of Veena always came to her mind, as did, of course, Marie. Sometimes, even, she found herself thinking of Sal, the man who had inadvertently brought everything together by blowing it apart. The Anti-Genetics Movement was still underground, deeper now than ever before, but with a network of shoots that were changing things faster than could be imagined. Soon, it seemed, birth diagnoses faced being phased out completely. Already in a temporary state of emergency, diagnoses were now optional, and parents were opting against them in their thousands.

As her thoughts came to a close, she realised the lights had fallen and a man was introducing Kane from the podium in the centre of the stage.

Kane took a last gulp of water and cleared his throat before he stood and walked up onto the podium. Blinking back tears, he sent a thought to Barney. He imagined him sitting at home eating dinner with his wife, sinking happily back into the quiet days of his retirement. *If only.* He thought of Marie and absent-mindedly rubbed his arm over the break line, remembering vaguely the roll of their bodies against the heat, a wheel of fortune.

Nerves he had not expected coursed through him and the adrenaline pulsed in his hands, making them shake. He lifted his eyes and allowed himself a slight nod to the well-dressed stranger standing at the back of the room, by the door. Kane saw the glint of a scanner in the man's palm, recording everything.

'Good afternoon, everyone. My name is Kane Ong. As some of you might know, I was one of the victims of the Black Notebook Scandal. I recently got married to a wonderful woman, but according to my birth diagnosis—which has since been proven to have been deliberately falsified—I am gay. Until my late twenties, I took this to be the case. I was never bullied for this or came across any discrimination, but I never felt truly content in a way that I couldn't explain to anyone else. I put it down to being part of a minority group. In hindsight, I spent far too much of my life trusting in other people's judgements, even those of my beloved family.

'But an experiment, authorised by the State, deliberately changed some key details of around three hundred birth diagnoses from a cohort of babies born in the UK between 2020 and 2022, including mine. Some cases were riskier than others. A girl called Veena Nealcross, for example, died of a brain tumour that was not on the falsified version of her birth diagnosis. Her family wanted to know why such a huge mistake had been made. In the end, they settled for an apology and a lump sum.

'Mine and Veena's executor, Professor Elin Nagayama, was jailed earlier today. She shared doubts about the birth diagnosis system with some health and social welfare officials within the State. She managed to gain enough influence to authorise this so-called experiment, this abuse of hundreds of people's lives, in order to start collecting evidence for any biases in the system. She believed—possibly correctly—that environmental factors, the way we live our lives, is equally as important as the genes we inherit, if not more so. She wanted to prove it. The State wanted to disprove it.

'People used to say the apple never falls too far from the tree.' He paused and looked around, as his notes instructed. As Freya had wisely advised him the night before, he made sure to try and capture the attention of each person in the room before continuing.

'They still say it. Everyone nods in agreement in response to this phrase, as if it is one of the few reliable truths in this world. Some of you are nodding now. It was always one of the first laws of families, of blood ties, before the molecular basis of inheritance that Watson, Crick and Franklin started to piece together a hundred years ago. In so many aspects of our characters, we have long been the prisoners of the relatives who have lived before us, inextricably linked from the moment we are conceived, both in our own minds and in those of the people around us, to our parents and our siblings and the network of individuals we call a family. 'She has her father's eyes,' they say, or 'she plays the piano like her grandmother.' In all types of society, this has been what we have been defined against. Those who have not known one or either of their parents have often spent their lives seeking what feels to be a lost quantity, looking to fill, perhaps, a misunderstanding of themselves. We deplore or embrace these traits given to us, these lingering characteristics that we will often, unwittingly, pass on to our own children.

'The apple never falls too far from the tree? Now, as they hum their approval, some people might think about the cover-up of what has become known as the Black Notebook Scandal. I think, actually, I coined that name for it, which is probably why many people find it confusing.' He stopped to allow the soft laughter to trickle across the crowd.

'For me and a few others, my wife included, the roots of the scandal stem from the night of a bombing in a London nightclub, not so far from here. The man that blew it up was also a victim of the scandal, although he never lived to find that out. He killed himself and one hundred and thirty-two others in a shockingly tragic way of raising the profile of the Anti-Genetics Movement, a terrorist society that you may have heard of. The bomber was informed in his birth diagnosis that he had violent tendencies—a falsehood that nonetheless turned out to be true. That same night, in one of those bizarre twists of fate, a fellow victim, both of the bombing and the scandal, gave me her notebook, a black leather notebook that eventually led me down the path that brought the cover-up to light. So for me, the story always starts with Marie's notebook.

'But all that is now history. What I am really here today to tell all of you is that no matter who you are, whether you are adopted or in care or somehow otherwise removed from your blood relatives, it doesn't matter. You have all been given another chance. You do not have to be anyone other than the person you want to be.

'Sal Winstan became a criminal of the worst degree not from his genetics but from being pigeonholed into a lifetime of resentment. My wife felt the symptoms of an invisible illness and her doctors saw the physical manifestations of it because they all believed in the authority of her profile. And conversely, Marie Lane, the owner of the black notebook, fought so hard to live up to the fictitious ideal that she would become a genius that she did, in many people's eyes, become one. As for me, I suppose that some things are too deeply ingrained in us to be denied. I think that even without everything that's happened, I would have ended up, sooner or later, living my life as a straight man despite the taboo that going against my Background would have meant. Some of you might have studied Shakespeare this term, and although he's a bit old-fashioned these days, some of what he said makes a lot of sense. In one of his plays, he wrote, 'To thine own self be true,' and I stand by that.

'I believe we have a battle on our hands. Is it right that we are told from birth the people we must become? How can we really know whether the information we have saved in our necks is the truth, and is there such a thing as the truth?'

Kane looked again at the Sentry standing at the back of the room, tightening his jaw and lifting his chin.

240

'My very words are being listened to now. I will be in trouble with the State for talking to you in this way. But no matter how advanced modern science becomes, no matter how deeply our genes and our brains can be probed, no one can ever discover the subtleties of your character, the element of your spirit that makes you *you*. My point is that it is for you to decide how to live your life and who to live it as. The power has, and always will be, in your hands.'

The crowd cheered and clapped and Kane smiled, relieved to have almost reached the end of his speech. He noticed a few of the older kids in the crowd, who were focussed quite intently upon him, and he saw the recognition of what he had said in their faces. This was why he did this: to make a difference. He looked at the empty back wall of the school hall and smiled, only to himself, sending a silent acknowledgement to Barney, to Marie, and, although he would never have consciously admitted it, to Sal.

'Although we are all fallen apples, and the distance we fall from the trees is our inheritance—that of genetics, and that of the way we have been raised—we all have it in us to choose our path for ourselves. In this increasingly connected, open world, the person you are is the one thing no one can take away from you. Never forget that.'

28

As Barney walked out into the hot morning sun, he found himself fighting for composure until he had walked quickly down the lane away from the ranch and was deep in the olive groves, crushing daisies underfoot. The news was good.

Breaking at first into a smile, the tears fought their way to the front and he had to breathe deeply to keep from choking. In his mind, Barney held the image of Kane and Freya as he would want to remember them should he never see them again: next to each other, their open-mouthed faces turned down upon the screen, its soft white glow lighting up their skin, cleansing it. He imagined each of them in turn as they read through their profiles, as though they had been conceived and born again, their DNA recombined in a different order, their newly formed heels pricked for the second time. He tried to picture their expressions as the truth appeared at last in words, attempted to see them smiling and hugging. He hoped they would find what they had so wanted to find.

The previous night, after they had waved off Angie's men into the distance, he and Leila had read through Sal's true diagnosis from cover to cover more than once. Barney had sobbed with anger for how Sal's childhood, his integrity, had been compromised so ruthlessly from the very start. Barney had lain in their makeshift bed under the Italian moon wishing he had not trusted the system so implicitly, slowly accepting, after hours of lying awake, that criminality was not something that can be spotted like a disease, not even by a professional such as himself. He concluded that it is, perhaps, helped along by a few genes, but can be sparked by anger so deep-rooted that it can infect even the softest of souls and those without a violent base pair in their DNA. Sal, although not blameless, had been infected by the hatred offered to him by his father, by the prejudgement heaped upon him by society and by using his intellect to clean the toilets of supposedly genetically superior office workers.

As he came closer to sleep, Barney had realised, in that drowsy, absolute clarity that sometimes comes before unconsciousness, why Sal had done what he had done. Barney knew that Sal had managed to deal with all of the setbacks and negative judgements upon his character with a subdued acceptance; he had seen it for himself. But in the final months of his life, what pushed him over the edge, to the full extent of immorality, was the intuitive suggestion (whether it came from himself or Angie or from both of them, Barney would never know) that the terrible lot given to him in life was in some way staggeringly incorrect, deliberately misplaced and shifted elsewhere, like his father's and the beautiful Ciara's love.

EPILOGUE

The following is a transcript of the final recorded interview with Professor Elin Nagayama three days prior to her suicide in jail in 2054. The State, for the security of the individuals concerned, has endorsed all censored text.

Tape begins. Coughing is heard and a chair scrapes along the ground.

INTERVIEWER: Why did you do it?

NAGAYAMA: [*laughter*] That's a good question to start on. Ease me in slowly, hey? Well … the word *why*, of course, is the very essence of science. I am a scientist, my colleagues were scientists, and we wanted to know why. That is what we do.

I: Let's address your failed pregnancies. Many of your most outspoken critics, Barney North included, suggest that these tragic events were your motivation. What is your response to that?
[*Extended silence.*]

N: That is my own business—I don't really wish to comment on that. So much of what has been published about me isn't true that I hardly know where to begin. But if I may, I would like to clarify the wording you have used there: They were not failed pregnancies, they were forced terminations. There is a huge difference between the two and I would expect you to be more careful to use the correct language.

I: My apologies. Despite the outcomes of your research, many people still consider what you and your team did to be completely immoral. What are your thoughts on that?

N: Yes, I am fully aware of that. It isn't always easy for me to see now, with hindsight, why we did what we did. But I do feel very much judged, very misunderstood.

[*Long pause. A heavy sigh is heard.*]

We were desperate, absolutely desperate for funding at the time—I was doing other research alongside it all, of course, work that has since saved lives. Doing this allowed that research to take place. And from a scientific point of view, our experiment worked. Of course, we couldn't have imagined where their stories would lead, and I do regret that we had to meddle with real people's lives. But I sit here before you a woman aged before her time, a sad old lady that has thought of nothing else for years, and I will admit to you that I was curious. As a result, I accept that we created confusion deep within these people, which resulted in some tragic outcomes.

I: But do you feel any good has come out of your research?

N: Yes, of course. After the initial idea was down on paper, there were people, funders, telling us it was the right thing to do, and a necessary thing. You hear all of those voices and your doubts start to become assertions, action. Misgivings are put to one side. And I'm glad they were, because it is plain to see that good did come out of it in the end—a greater good. Society seems to be learning that, as I've always believed, science doesn't have to be black and white. Like everything else in this world, it *can* be grey. I think that is a valuable lesson.

I: But surely, Professor Nagayama, the world has been

through enough already in order that unethical science in the name of progress is prevented ...?

N: Indeed. I'm sixty-nine years old; you don't need to tell me. But every new undertaking carries a new set of rules and the rulebook hadn't yet been defined for us. As I've told you, I maintain—and I think many now acknowledge—that good came out of our research, but perhaps the greatest lesson, learnt too late, was that too much knowledge can become quicksand. Before you know it, you are sinking without a trace. Certainly for Kane Ong, I think it was more of a valuable experience for him. Our project revealed that he was only trapped by his own prejudices.

I: And is it the same story for Marie Lane?

N: Why do you ask me such a question, when you can see clearly that it is not?
[*Long pause.*]

I: Professor Nagayama?

N: Then yes, I remember first reading her profile; she was born halfway through the project, and this might seem silly, but the ordinariness of her original birth diagnosis, the strong possibility that she would never be anything more than average, particularly caught my eye. It was a late night of shifting through data in my apartment and I had promised myself to try and find one more candidate before I went to bed; she was that candidate. The idea of genius, a concept I had struggled to understand for much of my life, and one that I doubted could be so genetically ingrained, is rarely found in birth diagnoses, but I wanted to appropriate this characteristic onto someone ...

I: To play God, to see if it would be a blessing or a curse?

N: I do not believe in God, indeed none of us are allowed to these days, but yes, if you must put it so crudely. With her and the others like her, I wanted to prove that genius—the ability for the brain to excel at a particular something so outstandingly—is not written into us from the moment we are conceived, but is hard-won, shaped by the events and the people that swarm over us in our lives. Marie showed us that was true. We shape our own successes, our own achievements in life.

[*Brief pause.*]

What I think is amazing is that she was one of the few whom so aggressively proved my hypothesis to be correct. A belief in herself, combined with something inside her, invisible and I believe impossible to quantify, made her the person she was. She had something special that science cannot yet define, and perhaps never will. I understand that she was the victim of a nightclub bombing and my sympathies go to her family—a sad event indeed, especially as I think she would have gone on to even greater things.

I: So, to sum everything up, do you admit that what you did was wrong? Are you ready to apologise?

N: I suppose that we all have things so far below the tips of our own personal icebergs, even we ourselves can choose to ignore them. I am still coming to terms with my actions, and although it has been many years since I talked to any of them properly, I'm sure my team feel the same. We told ourselves that we were advancing knowledge, and that it was worth it in the name of scientific progress and social change.

[*Tape cuts out briefly, suggests section has been removed during editing.*]

You have to remember, you really must remember … [*voice trails off*]

I: I'm afraid we have to leave you there—I'm being told our time is up. Professor Nagayama, thank you for taking the time to speak to us today.

A LITTLE NOTE & SOME ACKNOWLEDGEMENTS

The seeds of this novel were sown while I was working on the Science Museum's Who Am I? gallery, and I was in my mid-twenties, grappling with my own identity and place in the world.

As I researched and explored what science has to say about what makes us unique individuals, I came across some astonishing stories and some remarkable people.

It reaffirmed what I already knew: that human diversity is to be celebrated. We each have a universe within ourselves—completely unique—and shaped by our genes, the people around us, the substances that flow around us as we develop in the womb, and much, much more. Freedom to be the person we are—and to try to become the person we want to be—is a wonderful thing. So firstly, thank you to all the people who I worked with on this amazing project. And if you haven't seen the exhibition, go now!

I also need to give a big shout out to my brilliant editor. Thank goodness I found you, Sarah! Your insight and attention to detail gave me a different point of view that was much needed. Plus, we all need a bit of reassurance sometimes, right?

Thanks to Kit for lending me your design eye for the cover.

Thank you to my parents, my unerring supporters in this and in every endeavour I do. I'm very proud, and incredibly lucky, to be your daughter. I'm glad I didn't fall too far from the tree.

My gorgeous Tim. This hasn't just been my journey. I seem to remember this was one of your bright ideas. Either side of reading my manuscript for the first time at a roadside picnic table in New Zealand, you've helped keep my head above the water. We believe in each other and that's an awesome kind of love to have.

And lastly, to all my fellow indie authors. Thank you for all the help and support I've derived from your blog posts, videos, newsletters and lectures. I'm excited to be joining such an open and optimistic community. It's a jungle out there, but I've always been one for getting off the beaten track.

ABOUT THE AUTHOR

Holly Cave was born in Devon, UK, in 1983. She has a BSc in Biology and an MSc in Science Communication from Imperial College, London. She spent four years working at the Science Museum in London. After a career break to travel the world, Holly became a freelance writer and now writes about science for non-expert audiences alongside her fiction work. She lives in rural Buckinghamshire in a wisteria-draped pub (yes, pub) with her husband and dog, Cooper. *The Generation* is her debut novel (although she wrote a number of unpublished works with her father on his typewriter in the 1990s).

Learn more at www.hollycave.co.uk, where you'll find suggested book club questions and discussion points.

You can also find Holly on Facebook at facebook.com/hollycaveauthor, and you can follow her on Twitter at twitter.com/HollyACave

Other books: *Really, Really Big Questions About Science* (children's non-fiction)

Coming soon: *The Architecture of Heaven*

14365403R00154

Printed in Great Britain
by Amazon.co.uk, Ltd.,
Marston Gate.